SECRET LOVE

For there is nothing hidden, which shall not be manifested; neither was anything kept secret, but that it should come to light.

—*Mark 4:22*

BRENDA JACKSON
SECRET LOVE

ARABESQUE®

Recycling programs
for this product may
not exist in your area.

SECRET LOVE

An Arabesque novel published by Kimani Press/February 2009

First published by BET Books in 2000

ISBN-13: 978-0-373-83120-3
ISBN-10:   0-373-83120-X

www.kimanipress.com

Printed in U.S.A.

Acknowledgments

To my husband, Gerald Jackson, Sr. and my sons,
Gerald Jackson, Jr. and Brandon Jackson.
Thanks for your understanding and support.
You make writing my stories easier.

To my family and friends, who continue to
give their undying support.

To my avid readers, who believe in me and
the work that I do. This book is for all of you.

To my Heavenly Father, who makes all things possible.

THE MADARIS FAMILY AND FRIENDS SERIES

Dear Readers,

I love writing family sagas, and I am so happy that Kimani Press is reissuing my very first family series, the Madaris family. It's been twelve years and fifty books since I first introduced the Madaris family. During that time, this special family and their friends have won their way into readers' hearts. I am ecstatic to be able to share these award-winning stories with everyone all over again—especially those who have never met the Madaris clan up close and personal—in this special-edition collectors' series.

I never dreamed when I penned my first novel, *Tonight and Forever,* and introduced the Madaris family, that I was taking readers on a journey where heartfelt romance, sizzling passion and true love awaited them at every turn. I had no idea that the Madaris family and their friends would become characters that readers would come to know and care so much about. I invite you to relax, unwind and see what all the hoopla is about. Let Justin, Dex, Clayton, Uncle Jake and their many friends transport you with love stories that are so passionate and sizzling, they will take your breath away. There is nothing better than falling in love with one of these Madaris men and their many friends.

For a complete list of all the books in this series, as well as the dates they will be available in a bookstore near you, please visit my Web site at www.brendajackson.net.

If you would like to receive my monthly newsletter, please visit and sign up at www.brendajackson.net/page/newsletter.htm.

I also invite you to drop me an e-mail at WriterBJackson@aol.com. I love hearing from my readers.

All the best,

Brenda Jackson

THE MADARIS FAMILY

Milton Madaris, Sr. and Felicia Laverne Lee Madaris

Milton Jr. (Dora)

Lee (Pearl)

Nolan (Bessie)

Lucas (Carrie)

Robert (Diana)

Jonathan (Marilyn)

Jake (Diamond)⑧

Milton III (Fran)

Lee Jr. (Alfie)

Lee, Kane, Jarod

Nolan Jr. (Marie)

Lucas Jr. (Sarah)

Felicia (Trask)⑦

Justin (Lorren)①, Dex (Caitlin)②
Clayton (Syneda)④, Tracie (Daniel),
Kattie (Raymond), Christy (Alex)⑬

Blade and Slade (Skye)⑭,
Quantum, Jantzen

Nolan, Corbin,
Adam, Victoria,
Lindsay

Lucas, Reese,
Emerson, Chance

KEY:
( ) — denotes a spouse
○ and number — denotes title of book for that couple's story

① Tonight and Forever
② Whispered Promises
③ Cupid's Bow
④ Eternally Yours
⑤ One Special Moment
⑥ Fire and Desire
⑦ Truly Everlasting
⑧ Secret Love
⑨ True Love
⑩ Surrender
⑪ The Best Man
⑫ The Midnight Hour
⑬ Unfinished Business
⑭ Slow Burn

THE MADARIS FRIENDS

Maurice and Stella Grant

Trevor (Corinthians)⑥,
Regina (Mitch)⑪

Angelique Hamilton Chenault

Sterling Hamilton (Colby)⑤,
Nicholas Chenault (Shayla)⑨

Kyle Garwood (Kimara)③

Ashton Sinclair
(Netherland)⑩

Drake Warren
(Tori)⑫

Trent Jordache
(Brenna)⑨

Nedwyn Lansing
(Diana)⑭

KEY:
( ) — denotes a spouse
◯ and number — denotes title of book for that couple's story

① Tonight and Forever
② Whispered Promises
③ Cupid's Bow
④ Eternally Yours
⑤ One Special Moment
⑥ Fire and Desire
⑦ Truly Everlasting
⑧ Secret Love
⑨ True Love
⑩ Surrender
⑪ The Best Man
⑫ The Midnight Hour
⑬ Unfinished Business
⑭ Slow Burn

Prologue

The telephone rang—loudly, repeatedly.

After about the fifth ring, Jacob Madaris bolted upright in bed when the shrill sound finally infiltrated his sleep-entrenched mind. He took a deep breath, dragged a hand across his face then reached out to grab the phone before it reached its eighth ring.

"Yeah?" he said, glancing at the illuminated clock on the nightstand. It was three in the morning.

"Jake, it's Sterling."

There was a peculiar sound in his good friend, Sterling Hamilton's, voice that made Jake throw back the covers and move to sit on the side of the bed. He could think of only one reason why Sterling would be calling him at this hour and sounding so strange. Jake's heart suddenly began racing and knots began forming in his stomach.

"Diamond," he said raggedly, almost fearful. His mind suddenly clamored with images of what could be wrong. "What is it? What happened?"

Sterling, to Jake's way of thinking, didn't respond quick enough. "Answer me, Sterling!" He was on his feet now and his voice had escalated to a shout.

"Calm down, Jake. Diamond's fine, but—"

"But what!"

"She needs to come home."

More images, worse than the ones before, flashed through Jake's mind. "What happened? For Pete's sake, Sterling, what happened to Diamond?" The racing of Jake's heart increased.

"Someone broke into her home…and tried to attack her."

"What!" After that explosion several earthy expletives poured from Jake's lips.

"Jake, she's okay. Diamond's fine, Jake. Listen to me, she's fine."

But Jake Madaris was past listening. "Who was it? What happened?" One hand balled into a fist at his side, and the veins in his neck nearly popped.

"Some obsessed fan climbed over the wall and came in through a window, Diamond's bedroom window. Luckily she was able to get away from the intruder and call the police."

Jake closed his eyes and inhaled deeply. Thank God for that. "What about the security system? I thought that place was wired tight."

"The intruder managed to get past it."

More earthy expletives poured forth from Jake's lips.

"Your anger won't help Diamond, Jake. She needs you to be calm when you see her. She's pretty shaken up."

"I'm on my way."

"No need. She's on her way there. I'm sending her on my plane. In fact she should be arriving in less than an hour. Just be at the airstrip when the plane gets there."

Jake shook his head, angry with himself. He should have been with her tonight. He should have been there to protect her. Or better yet, she should have been here at his ranch, Whispering Pines, and not hundreds of miles away in California. He was her husband. The two of them should not be living apart.

His shoulders slumped when he remembered that their living arrangements weren't the tip of their problems. The real scorcher was the fact that very few people even knew they were married. His own mother didn't know, and only one of his brothers knew.

"I'll be at the airstrip, waiting."

"Call me after you get her settled in, and let me know how she's doing."

"All right and thanks." As soon as Jake hung up the phone, he quickly began getting dressed.

Slow down, calm down, he ordered himself, but it didn't work. He moved around his bedroom, putting on his clothes at a frantic pace.

When he and Diamond had married a little over year ago, he had gone along with her request that they keep their marriage a secret for a number of reasons. The main one had been for their privacy. If the tabloids knew that Hollywood's most sought-after African-American actress, Diamond Swain, was married to wealthy Texas rancher, Jacob Madaris, they would have a field day at their expense. Diamond had not wanted their special relationship, their extraordinary love, scrutinized, criticized or placed under the media's attention. She had been determined to protect the love they shared at any cost.

"Yeah, but not this cost," Jake muttered as he finished putting on his boots. He didn't care about the media. But Diamond, who was always in the spotlight, and constantly hounded by the press and paparazzi, had felt differently. She had wanted a secret place she could always come to when she needed to escape. He and his ranch had become her loving and safe haven.

Another reason for the secrecy was that there was no way he could ever give up his life as a rancher. Knowing that, he knew he could never ask her to give up her life as an actress. The decision to keep their marriage a secret had been a difficult one for him. The Madaris family was a close one. But he had gone along with her request, although he hadn't liked it, because at the time all the reasons for doing so had seemed for the best.

But now, none of that mattered. What mattered most was keeping her safe. As far as she was concerned, their secret had run its course.

As he rushed out of the house, he couldn't help but remember how it had begun. He couldn't help but call to mind another time, nearly eighteen months ago, when he had gone to the airstrip to await Diamond's arrival.

BOOK ONE

The Beginning

Chapter 1

He needed to have his head examined, Jake Madaris thought as he peered up into the sky. Dark clouds were forming, which meant there would probably be a torrential downpour later tonight. Evening was setting in, and with the possibility of bad weather, he had more things to do with his time that sit at the airstrip and wait on, of all things, a woman.

Maneuvering the vehicle's seat as far back as it could go, he stretched out his long legs and tilted his Stetson to cover his eyes. He frowned slightly and wondered how on earth he had let Sterling Hamilton talk him into this.

Sterling had known exactly what he was doing during his last visit to the ranch, when he'd suggested that they play what was supposed to be a friendly game of poker. The stakes had been whatever either of them wanted from the other...within reason. Sterling's desire had been a three-week stay at Jake's ranch, Whispering Pines.

Jake had simply shrugged upon hearing that, thinking Sterling's request was an easy one. After all, since the time he and the well-known movie actor had formed a friendship over fifteen years ago, Sterling had been a frequent guest at Whispering Pines, often staying for weeks at a time.

It was only after Sterling had won the poker game that he had dropped the bombshell that the three-week stay was not for him, but for a friend.

A serious frown encased itself in Jake's expression as he remembered that night two weeks ago. He had literally blown his stack when Sterling had announced just who that friend was. Jake shook his head, still ticked off when he thought about it. The last thing Whispering Pines needed was a visitor the likes of Diamond Swain.

Granted, some people would be honored to have the most sought-after African-American movie actress as a guest. But he wasn't one of them. Whispering Pines was not a celebrity resort or a dude ranch. It was a working ranch that encompassed hundreds and hundreds of acres of land for grazing cattle.

The Whispering Pines ranch was known worldwide to raise only the highest quality grass-fed Texas Longhorn cattle. And although the ranch house was a real piece of art, a massive hacienda-style villa that he himself had designed, it was not a hideaway for the rich and famous. He had told Sterling that in no uncertain terms.

But, as Sterling had pointed out, Whispering Pines was also like a fortress. No one got on its land unless

Jake Madaris wanted them there. That meant there was no chance of Diamond Swain being bothered by pestering reporters. The other thing Sterling had been quick to point out was the fact that the people who worked for Jake were fiercely loyal to him and could be trusted. That meant news of Diamond Swain's visit wouldn't get leaked to the press.

But Jake had not been appeased and had continued to put up a strong argument against her visit. Sterling had smoothly shot down every argument that he'd given, so here he was sitting and waiting patiently for the renowned Diamond Swain to arrive and not liking it one bit.

Jake shifted in his seat when he saw the first signs of Sterling's private plane as it jetted across the horizon. According to the media, Sterling and Diamond, who had appeared together in numerous movies, were an item and had been for years. Sterling had always flatly denied the rumor, claiming he and Diamond were nothing more than the best of friends. Her father, Jack Swain, was one of the few African-American movie directors to make his mark in Hollywood during the late sixties. Sterling's first starring role, at the age of twenty-four, had been in one of Jack Swain's films. That particular movie, made nearly ten years ago, had been the first ever to be directed by an African-American and nominated for Best Picture of the Year.

As Jake watched the plane land and then come to a stop on the runway, he wondered just what he was going to do with Diamond Swain for three weeks. He shrugged, deciding it would probably be best if he just ignored her. According to Sterling, her doctor claimed she was on the brink of physical exhaustion and needed a rest from the high pressures of her hectic life-style of moviemaking and public appearances. If that was the case, then hopefully she would closet herself in the cabin he had arranged for her to stay in, and keep out of his way. It was roundup time, and he and his men would be extremely busy. No one had the time to baby-sit some stressed-out movie actress who was probably used to getting attention.

When Diamond stepped off the plane and Jake took a really good look at her, he knew at that very moment that ignoring her would definitely be a problem. Oh, he'd known she was a beautiful woman. Like most people, he had seen many of her movies at one time or another. But what he hadn't counted on was her beauty being so vivid, so rich and so knock-him-dead brutal. And he sure hadn't counted on the sudden surge of desire that jolted his body.

He watched her graceful stride as she moved down the steps of the plane, thinking how elegantly her taut body moved—the lush curves of her hips in black denim jeans, not to mention the long legs. Her hair hung like a silk curtain around her shoulders.

Jake shifted in his seat, feeling sweat pop out on his forehead and perspiration form in his hands. A breath hissed forth from his closed teeth as he studied her almond-colored features that went above and beyond drop-dead gorgeous. Another ripple of desire tore through his body.

Jake clipped back a deep, gutted sigh. *What had Sterling gotten him into?*

Diamond Swain threw her black denim jacket over her shoulder and walked down the steps of the plane.

When her feet touched the earth, she gazed around at the beauty of the land that surrounded her. The aerial view had been gorgeous, simply magnificent. Even the clouded sky hadn't detracted from its loveliness. The mesquite-covered valleys had an unlimited area of canyons and mountains on one side, and miles and miles of lush green grassland on the other. Never had she seen a place so scenic. According to Sterling, the owner was someone by the name of Jacob Madaris. She wondered if anyone had ever approached him about filming a movie here.

She spotted a black Jeep Cherokee parked a short distance away. Sterling had said Mr. Madaris would be picking her up and that he was a good friend of his. As far as she was concerned, any friend of Sterling was definitely a friend of hers. Besides, she appreciated Mr. Madaris for extending an invitation to her to stay at his ranch for three weeks. That was very thoughtful of him, and she could definitely use the rest.

"I'll get your bags for you, Ms. Swain."

The sound of Sterling's pilot interrupted her thoughts. "Thanks, John. I think Mr. Madaris is parked over there," she said. She looked beyond him to the parked vehicle. She couldn't help wondering why Jacob Madaris had not gotten out and come to greet her.

No sooner had that question crossed her mind than the Jeep's door opened and what she saw nearly took her breath away. The man who straightened himself out of the vehicle had to be every bit of six feet seven inches tall. The Stetson on his head nearly covered his face, but even from a distance she could make out intense, dark eyes and skin the color of chestnut. Everything about him said diehard Texas cowboy. Dressed in western boots, jeans, shirt and his Stetson, he looked like the traditional cowboy. With the masculine swagger in his stride, he walked like the traditional cowboy.

"Welcome to Whispering Pines, Ms. Swain. I'm Jacob Madaris," he said, tipping the brim of his hat in greeting when he reached her.

Diamond smiled. With his slow, deep drawl he even sounded like the traditional cowboy. His voice was rough and sexy. And his smell, a musky male scent of outdoors, was enticingly cowboy. She looked into his face, and her smile vanished when he removed his hat. The man, who appeared to be in his early forties, was dangerously handsome. His curly hair, damp from sweat, was a succulent blend of black and gray. The premature strands of silver gray were in stark contrast to his hard muscled body and made him appear more mature, charismatic and sexy.

Her breath expelled and her pulse stopped. *He is gorgeous,* she thought to herself. He is as gorgeous as the land he owns.

"Ms. Swain?"

Suddenly feeling like she had a mouth full of cotton and unable to get any words out, Diamond swallowed quickly and took the hand he had offered her seconds ago. "Yes, and thanks for the invitation," she recovered her voice to say.

It was on the tip of Jake's tongue to tell her that he had not invited her, but decided not to. "I'll help John with your luggage."

Tilting her head to one side, Diamond watched him walk off, thinking that Jacob Madaris definitely knew how to wear a pair of jeans. The back view of him was incredible, fascinating. His entire body was physically potent. And his walk…he moved like someone aware of his surroundings and comfortable with them, as well.

She closed her eyes, swallowed sharply and pulled herself together. This was the first real vacation she had taken in years. Her agent, Shelton Penn, usually had her on an airtight schedule. There was no time in between filming to ever totally relax. That was one of the reasons her doctor had ordered that she find someplace to go and rest.

According to him, she couldn't keep up her vigorous pace without some sort of break. At first he had ordered six weeks of rest. But after she had given him every reason imaginable as to why she couldn't take off six weeks, he had then pushed for five, not less than four. She had countered with three, and seeing that she wouldn't budge any further, he had let it go at that. So here she was, in the heart of Texas on a ranch that was too beautiful for words, and whose owner could make her forget her vow not to get seriously involved with a man for a long time.

Her short and unbearable marriage to Samuel Tate had taught her a long-lasting lesson. When it came to the women they were married to, some men were possessive, overbearing and insanely jealous. Samuel had been all three. Never would she place herself in a position to live through something like that again. He had gone so far as to actually pay people to spy on her. He had even tried to destroy her long-standing friendship with Sterling. She knew for a fact that he was the one who started the rumor that had begun circulating after her divorce that she and Sterling were having an affair. She would never forgive Samuel for trying to cheapen her and Sterling's friendship. And then last, but clearly not least, she would never forgive him for his betrayal of the vows they had taken.

"I'm ready if you are."

Jacob Madaris's deep, husky voice broke into Diamond's thoughts. She turned quickly. Her gaze went straight to his face and once again she thought the premature graying of his hair gave him a abundance of raw sex appeal. More than any one man should have. Breathing deeply, she felt a strong attraction to him. Diamond's forehead wrinkled. Nothing like this—something this quick, spontaneous and gripping—had ever happened to her before. And more than anything, she didn't want it to happen. She was here to get some rest, nothing more.

"Is something wrong? You're frowning."

Relax, Diamond commanded herself. This man didn't miss much. He was sharp at picking up on things. "No, I'm fine. Just tired," she responded, forcing a weak smile. She almost lost it again when she gazed into his dark eyes.

He watched her for a few seconds before nodding. "That can be remedied. If you'll follow me, I'll see that you get settled in." He then turned and walked off.

Not even trying to keep up with his pace, Diamond followed him to the vehicle.

Jake's brow furrowed as he drove his Jeep toward the area where the cabin was located. He tried, against all odds, to ignore the woman sitting next to him. He couldn't remember a time any woman had caught his interest as seriously as Diamond had. And that was totally out of character for him.

"Now you're the one frowning, Mr. Madaris."

Jake couldn't help but smile at Diamond's observation. She must have been watching him pretty closely to notice. He took a glance over at her and his smile widened. "Yeah, I am, aren't I? And you can call me Jake."

Diamond nearly groaned out loud. His smile was deadly. "Thanks, and I'm Diamond. I've never cared for nicknames so if you don't mind, I prefer calling you Jacob."

Her voice was like silken oak. It stirred Jake's insides and sent his pulse spinning. It was on the tip of his tongue to tell her that she could call him anything she liked, but he decided it wouldn't be a good idea.

"Does your frown have anything to do with the fact that you really didn't invite me here, Jacob?"

Jake blinked in surprise at Diamond's question. He wondered how she had figured it out. "What makes you think that?"

"From the expression that crossed your face when I thanked you earlier." She then let out a chuckle. "I'm an actress, remember. I'm trained to display a number of expressions, as well as being able to read them on others. Although the expression crossed your face quickly, I was able to pick up on it."

When Jake still didn't admit one way or another whether she was right or not, Diamond glanced over at him. "What did Sterling do? Threaten you with bodily harm, or does he have some incriminating information on you?"

Jake couldn't hold back his laugh. "It was nothing as bad as either of those two," he finally answered, deciding to level with her. "I lost a poker game to him. I'm still wondering if he played fair. I'm usually a better poker player than Sterling."

Diamond smiled and her eyes lit up in a sparkle. "You're too trusting if you have to think about whether or not Sterling played fair. I doubt very seriously that he did. He knows how to cheat at cards when it suits him."

Jake considered her words. They were spoken like someone who evidently knew Sterling extremely well. Suddenly and expectedly, he felt a tinge of jealously at the thought of just how well that might be. He was tempted to ask, but decided it was none of his business. Sterling had told him on numerous occasions that he and Diamond Swain were friends and nothing more. He knew that although his friend might have a tendency to cheat at cards every once in a while, he was fairly honest otherwise. Besides, Sterling had no reason to lie to him.

Jake pulled the Jeep to a stop in front of the cabin. "Here we are."

Diamond took a good look at the structure they were parked in front of and became speechless. Before them was the most luxurious log cabin she had ever seen. A deck surrounded the house on three sides that provided a beautiful view of a half-acre lake.

She turned toward Jake. "Oh, Jacob, it's beautiful. I know that you really didn't invite me here, and a part of me feels I should do the noble thing and leave. But now, after seeing this, I don't want to leave. Please let me stay. I promise not to be a bother."

Jake didn't think it would be possible for her not to be a bother, when her very presence was bothering him already. But for some reason, the thought of her leaving bothered him as well.

"Of course you'll stay. Sterling may have cheated an invitation out of me, but I'd really like you to stay."

What Jake thought was Diamond's most heart-stopping smile appeared on her face. "Thank you, Jacob."

Jake felt his heart trip against his ribs with that smile and the sultry sound of his name from Diamond's lips. He stared at her mouth and his nostrils flared as he felt total awareness in the lower part of his stomach. He couldn't recall the last time a woman had gotten hold of his attention this much. He decided to get out of the vehicle before he did something really stupid like haul her into his arms and kiss her.

Chapter 2

Diamond leaned against the doorway with arms crossed as she surveyed the room. If you were looking for a nice private hideaway, you couldn't do any better than this, she thought. The cabin was located approximately four to five miles from the main house in a very secluded section of Whispering Pines. It featured a master bedroom with a king-size bed and a full bath and two other bedrooms. It also had a full kitchen, a mudroom with a washer and dryer, a spacious living room with a vaulted ceiling and a large stone fireplace.

While showing her around, Jacob had told her that he had built the house himself years ago but had not spent a night in it. She had found that surprising as well as intriguing but hadn't questioned him about it. And he hadn't felt compelled to share any explanations.

Diamond walked out on the deck. The sky was still clouded, and in the distance she could hear the distinct sound of thunder. After Jacob had brought in her bags, he had given her a quick tour of the cabin. He'd also given her instructions on how to reach the main house if she needed something. The phones, he had informed her, had direct lines to his ranch and in order to place a call somewhere off the ranch, she would have to come to the main house to do so. Then he had left.

She frowned. No doubt Sterling had known about the absence of an outside phone line at the cabin. He had made her promise that she would not be calling her agent or anyone else regarding work. He had wanted her to spend the next three weeks resting.

Diamond walked back inside. Jacob had told her that the kitchen had been stocked for her visit, but if she ever got tired of cooking to just pick up the phone and call the ranch, and he would have his cook prepare something and that he'd bring it out to her.

Although she knew he was doing certain things to assure her privacy, Diamond couldn't help but feel that he was also doing everything within his power to keep her at a distance. It appeared the ranch was his domain. He didn't mind sharing his land as long as she stayed in the space he had decided to give her.

Diamond tried to laugh at the thought of any man keeping her at a distance. She'd never had that sort of problem before and found the thought interesting. She had always become irritated with men who became obsessed with the way she looked. If her theory was true and Jacob was keeping her at a distance, it would be a first. But then, Jacob Madaris had started off being a first in a number of ways already. He was the first man, other than Sterling and her other childhood friend Kyle Garwood, who could elicit a genuine smile from her. And he'd been the first she had actually noticed as a man in a long time. A very long time. His masculinity was something any sane woman just couldn't miss…or ignore.

Opening the refrigerator door, she began pulling out the items needed to make a salad. The sound of thunder was getting closer. After dinner she would take a shower and curl up in bed with a good book. For the first time in years, she would spend her evening doing practically nothing.

"And you're sure she's okay?"

Jake stared out of his kitchen window. From the brightly lit patio he could see at least half a dozen roses already in full bloom. He could easily remember the day his ex-wife had planted a number of them in various places on his land.

"Jake, did you hear what I asked?"

Sterling's sharp words startled Jake out of his study of the flowering plants. Just as well, he thought. The last person he wanted to think about was his ex-wife, Jessie. He would have destroyed all of the rosebushes after she'd left if the darn things hadn't bloomed so beautifully that year and every year since.

"Yes, Sterling, I heard," he barked back into the telephone as he moved away from the window. "I've already told you at least twice that she's fine. A thunderstorm came up after dinner so chances are she's already retired for the night."

Jake's brow pulled tight over his forehead. "What's

with you and Diamond Swain anyway? I thought you told me there was nothing going on between you two."

"There's not. Diamond and I are just good friends. I'm worried about her, that's all. She's been pushing herself a lot lately and needs plenty of rest."

"Well, she has no reason not to get it here. I put her up in the cabin like you asked, so she has all the seclusion she'll ever need."

"If she'll stay secluded. You don't know Diamond. She actually likes being around people. Unfortunately in our line of business you can't afford to be too friendly. You never know whether or not the person you're befriending has a part-time job with the tabloids."

Sterling paused before continuing. "I have a feeling she'll love Whispering Pines so much that she'll eventually come out of her shell."

Jake frowned. "What shell?"

"The one she's been in since her divorce. Professionally she's doing fine, but personally I'm still worried about her. Her divorce last year was a nasty affair. I'm sure you probably remember reading about it."

Jake shook his head. "No, I'm not into reading that sort of stuff. I have enough to do around here without worrying about what goes on in someone else's life. I don't have time to concern myself with other people's problems."

"Hmm, I'll see how long that lasts."

Jake frowned. "What do you mean by that?"

"Nothing. Hey, look, I need to get off the phone and study my script. I'll check in again at the end of the week."

"Yeah, you do that."

Jake hung up the phone, wondering if Diamond had indeed retired for the night like he'd told Sterling. When the storm had hit earlier that afternoon, he couldn't help but think about her and wonder how she was making out. She hadn't called, so he could only assume she was doing okay. But maybe he should check on her anyway. Sterling seemed awfully antsy about her welfare.

Convincing himself that he was calling for Sterling's benefit and not his own, Jake dialed the number to the cabin. His forehead knotted into a frown when she didn't answer by the fifth ring. He was about to hang up when she finally picked up. He could tell by the quickened sound of her breathing that she had rushed to the phone.

"Where were you?" he demanded to know in a raised voice.

An intense frown covered Diamond's face, and her back stiffened. Jake's question brought back memories of when Samuel used to ask her that same question in a very accusing tone. "I was in the shower. Is something wrong?" she snapped defensively.

"No."

"Then why are you yelling?"

Jake scowled at the sudden realization that he had indeed raised his voice. "For no reason," he said, lowering it. "I'm sorry. I didn't mean to yell. Sterling called tonight and was concerned when he couldn't reach you earlier. So I thought I'd check on you to make sure you were okay. You had me worried when it took so long for you to answer the phone."

Diamond's anger deflated somewhat upon hearing

that he'd been worried about her. She wrapped a huge towel securely around her body. "I'm fine. I had planned to take my shower earlier, before the storm hit, but things didn't work out that way. I had to wait until now. I was just stepping out of the shower when I heard the phone. I barely had time to completely dry off."

Jake's heart began to thump erratically, and his hand holding the phone began to shake when a heated image of a half-naked Diamond rushing from the shower filled his mind. He hadn't had to look twice at the way she had filled a pair of jeans to know that her body was a real work of art, especially her perfectly rounded backside.

"Jacob, was there anything else you wanted?"

Her innocent question hung in the air. Yeah, there was something else he wanted but he wouldn't dare tell her what that something else was. He immediately squashed the thought. He and Diamond were as different as night and day. He was a rancher, and she was a Hollywood superstar, and that was far worse than her being just a sophisticated city woman. One sophisticated city woman had already taught him a lesson that he would never forget. Ranchers and sophisticates didn't mix. What he'd gone through with Jessie had helped to mold him into the man he was today, especially when it came to women. His strictest rule was to never get tangled up with another sophisticate again. Diamond was not only a sophisticate, she was a celebrity. That spelled double trouble.

"No, there's nothing else. Sorry I bothered you."

"You didn't bother me, Jacob."

Jake nodded, glad that he hadn't. He moved to the

window again and looked out at the roses. They were a constant reminder of what a fool he'd been at one time. He had no intention of repeating it.

"Do you think you'll need a car while you're here? If so, you can use mine. Maybe it's not a good idea for you to be so far out from the ranch without some sort of transportation," he said.

"A car won't be necessary. But what are my chances of getting a horse sometime later this week? I'd like to go riding. Would that be okay?"

"Sure, just as long as you don't mind the risk of running into one of my men. This is roundup time and although the location of the cabin is pretty secluded, they'll be out working all over the place if they ever have to look for strays."

Diamond nodded. "That's fine. I'll call you when I'm ready to go riding." There was a pause, then she said, "Sterling told me that the people who work for you can be trusted to keep my presence here a secret."

Jake leaned back against a kitchen counter. He couldn't help but smile when he remembered the meeting he'd held with his men yesterday morning to announce Diamond's visit to the ranch. At first all of them had simply stared at him, then one by one their mouths had dropped open. They had walked around the rest of the day tongue-tied. The thought of someone like Diamond Swain at Whispering Pines had some of them acting downright ridiculous. A few of them had even shown up for work this morning in what he considered as their Sunday best. He had sent them back home to change. No one in their right mind wore a suit to roundup and brand cows.

"Yes, they can be trusted. In fact, they've taken a

solemn oath to make sure your privacy is protected at all costs."

"That's very nice of them. I'd like to meet them while I'm here."

Jake lifted a brow. It surprised him that she would bother to take the time to do that. "I'm sure they'll get a kick out of it." He knew that was putting it mildly. His men would be overjoyed at the chance to meet her. Some of them were really big fans of hers.

After a somewhat lengthy pause, she asked, "How do you do that?"

Jake lifted his brow. "Do what?"

"Get your men to be so loyal to you."

Jake shrugged before answering. "Loyalty, like respect, is earned. A lot of the men have worked for me for years. I believe if you give people respect and loyalty, they'll give it back to you. There are three things my daddy always told me that have stuck over the years. The first thing is to watch older cowboys work; they know the simplest and least expensive ways to get things done, and they'll appreciate you for taking the time to show interest in what they do. The second thing is to always hire cowboys who are smarter and more skilled than you are. And lastly, never hire a cowboy who won't tell you when you're wrong. I have that kind of relationship with my men. I'm the boss, and they know it. But they also know their thoughts and ideas count. I didn't make Whispering Pines into what it is today by myself. I give my men just as much credit."

Silence fell, and Jake knew it was time to withdraw. He had shared more about himself with her than he had intended to. "Look, I know you're pretty tired, so I'll let you go."

"Thanks for calling, Jacob. Will I see you tomorrow?"

"Probably not, unless you need something. I'll be out on the range most of the day. Blaylock, my housekeeper and cook, will be here, and he'll be glad to help you anyway he can. Just pick up the phone."

"All right. Is there any particular day that you might be expecting visitors to the ranch?"

Jake knew the reason she was asking. That would be the day she would want to stay out of sight. "My veterinarian comes by every Thursday morning between ten and twelve to check on the cows. And then there's my family. They may drop by anytime. But most of them know that this time of year is a busy one for me here at the ranch and they usually limit their visits." Jake let out a deep chuckle. "Except for my mother. She thinks anytime is the right time for her visits. Usually one of my brothers will let me know in advance of her visits since one of them has to bring her. I'm her youngest son, and she won't let me forget it."

"Sounds like the Madaris family is a rather close one."

"We are." He couldn't help but grin when he thought about his brother and the nieces and nephews that he was close to. "It's been nice talking to you, Diamond. Good night."

"Good night, Jacob, and thanks again for calling."

After hanging up the phone, Jake closed his eyes to visualize Diamond's features, as he had last seen them that day. The darkness of her eyes, the full lushness of her lips and a mouth that had definitely been ripe for kissing had held him captive.

"Is there any reason you're standing in the middle

of my kitchen with your eyes closed and looking downright silly?"

Jake's eyes snapped open. Blaylock, the elderly man who had worked for him more years than he cared to count, stood in the doorway staring at him.

"Uhh, no reason. Well…I guess I'd better finish up with this," Jake said, holding up the book that contained the cows' breeding records.

Before Blaylock could ask him any more questions, he quickly moved out of the kitchen, went into his study and closed the door behind him.

Diamond placed the mystery novel she had been reading aside. The plot was a good one, and the characters were interesting, but the book could not hold her attention. No matter how hard she tried to get into the story, her mind and thoughts kept drifting.

She could not get Jacob Madaris out of her mind.

Standing, she walked across the room to look out of the window. The night was lonely and black, and the smell of the rich, wet earth filled the air. She turned her attention back to the room and looked around. Once again she marveled at how beautiful the cabin was. Jacob had built it, yet he had never stayed in it.

Returning to the overstuffed leather wing chair, she curled her legs beneath her. What was there about Jacob Madaris that she found so intriguing, so overpowering and so beguiling? Oh, he was a good-looking man, there was no doubt of that, but there was something else about him that pulled at her.

It would be absolutely, positively foolish to deny she was attracted to him, but then it would be just as equally foolish if she even considered doing anything about it. She thought about all the hell she'd gone through in her short one-year marriage to Samuel. There had been the arguments, the accusations, the bouts of jealous rages and then the betrayal. In the end, a man she had loved, and whom she thought had loved her in return, had shown his true colors. He had shown her just what he was capable of and had ended up being her worst enemy.

And that had hurt.

During the days and months following her divorce, she had worked herself into a frenzy, making one movie after another, allowing no rest in between and not allowing time for her pain to heal.

Sterling, being the good friend that he was, had detected her turmoil. He had known she wasn't as strong as she had pretended to be. And so, with her doctor's advice, he had decided to do something about it. He had thought that three weeks in a secluded cabin on the grounds of Whispering Pines would heal all. But what he probably had not counted on was her having such a gripping and profound attraction to his friend.

Diamond gave a quiet laugh. In his haste to help her, Sterling had unknowingly placed her right smack in the middle of the lion's den.

Chapter 3

As Jake rounded the corner of his barn, he came across a group of his men who were standing together talking.

"I'm telling you guys the truth. I did see Diamond Swain," Lowell Brown was saying to the men gathered around him. "I saw her from a distance. She was in the south pasture picking berries."

Jake stopped in his tracks and shook his head, frowning. It had been three days since Diamond had arrived and already there had been more Diamond Swain sightings on Whispering Pines than there were Elvis sightings around the country. At least half a dozen of his men claimed to have gotten a glimpse of her at one time or another. He couldn't help but wonder if any of them had actually seen Diamond or if it was just a figment of their overactive imaginations. He doubted she had even left the cabin since she didn't have any sort of transportation to do so. She was to call him when she wanted to use one of his horses to go riding. So far, he had not heard from her. Nor had he seen her since the day he had picked her up from the airstrip and taken her to the cabin. He had no idea what she'd been doing the last three days, and frankly, he didn't want to know. Just like he had originally planned, he was trying his best to ignore the fact that she was there.

Hearing his men talk about her wasn't helping matters.

"Don't you guys have work to do?"

Just as he'd known they would, the group of men disbanded immediately. Jake continued inside the barn to saddle his horse. The computerized range monitor had detected that a part of the fencing was down near the south pasture. If that was the case, it needed to be repaired as soon as possible. It wouldn't do for a bull from another breed to get on his land and mate with his pureblood Longhorns.

A brisk breeze ruffled the treetops as Jake rode away. One part of his mind was on the business he had to take care of with the fence. The other was on Diamond. He didn't want to think about her, but he did. And although he kept trying to convince himself that he really didn't want to know, he couldn't help wondering what she had been doing the last three days.

As he trotted his horse up the narrow slit of a trail that led to the south pastures, he knew that before he returned to the ranch he would stop by the cabin and find out.

A satisfied smile played at Diamond's lips as she stood back and gazed at the tray of cookies she had just taken out of the oven. She couldn't remember the last time she had taken the time to bake anything. But after finding that cookbook in one of the kitchen cabinets, she'd been tempted to do it. Baking had stirred up memories of how as a child, she used to work alongside her grandmother in the kitchen. Those had been happy times for her.

Diamond inhaled the aroma that filled the kitchen. She hoped the cookies tasted as good as they smelled. The recipe had been a fairly simple one to follow and upon discovering that the cabin's kitchen was stocked with all the ingredients she would need, she had gotten busy, enjoying herself immensely. Baking the cookies had kept her from thinking about Jacob. But now that she was finished, thoughts of him began to fill her mind again.

Sighing deeply, she removed her apron and placed it over the chair before opening the door and stepping out on the deck. Other than the mere bits and pieces she had gotten out of Sterling, she knew very little about Jacob Madaris, and a part of her knew she should leave it at that. But then another part of her couldn't. In their brief meeting, the man had stirred feelings inside of her that she had thought she would never feel again.

At thirty-one she no longer believed in love for ever after. If she had been smart, she would have stopped believing in love altogether at the age of twenty-two when her father had married for the fifth time. But somehow after meeting Samuel at a fund-raiser for AIDS Awareness, she had convinced herself that Samuel Tate, race-car driver extraordinaire, was the key to her happiness.

A year later, she had painstakingly discovered that no one was the key to her happiness. She had accepted the fact that just like her father, when it came to love, it wasn't for her. But unlike him, she didn't need five failed marriages to convince her of that.

Actually Jack Swain still wasn't convinced. After recently meeting the woman he was currently involved with, Diamond had a feeling that her father of seventy-one was about to tie the knot for the sixth time, with a woman young enough to be his daughter.

Some people never learned. But she was not one of them.

She squinted her eyes against the fading bright sunlight when she heard the sound of a horse and rider coming toward the cabin from across the high prairie. Her pulse quickened as she leaned against the post and watched their approach. Horse and man seemed attuned to each other.

The grounds surrounding the cabin were covered by a huge shadow as the sun began making its slow descent beyond the mountains. The setting was beautiful. But nothing, she thought, looked more beautiful than the man approaching on horseback. His movements were fluid and in full control of the huge animal beneath him. As she watched Jacob come closer, she became painfully aware of just how much she had wanted to see him again.

Unbeknownst to Diamond, Jake was thinking that very same thing about her, and that admission wasn't easy for him. In fact, it downright irritated him. He managed a tight smile when he reached her and sat up straighter in his saddle. His fingers gripped the reins tight as he tried to still his horse, not to mention the wild beating of his pulse.

Jake looked her over, suddenly realizing just how young she was. With him being forty-two, there had to be at least a ten- to twelve-year difference in their ages. He wondered why that fact seemed important to him now. He lifted his brow when he noticed something else about her. He couldn't help smiling a little when he asked, "Who won the fight? You or the flour?"

At first Diamond looked confused. Then a chuckle escaped her when she realized what he was talking about. She looked down at herself and chuckled again. Flour covered most of her clothing. She then raised her head and smiled up at him. "Would you believe I actually had on an apron?"

Jake shook his head. With a smile like the one she had just given him, he could believe just about anything. "I don't even want to think about how the kitchen looks."

She laughed. "I have to admit it's not the neat, clean place it was when I arrived three days ago. But I promise to get things back to normal." A huge grin covered her face. "I had so much fun baking."

Jake chuckled and nodded. There was even a dab of flour on her nose and cheek. "Yeah, I can tell."

Diamond looked up at him. Even sitting on a horse, he looked tall, lean and muscular. There were some qualities about him that reached out to her: strength and capability. "I was just about to sit down and enjoy some of the fruits of my labor. Would you like to join me for cookies and milk?" she found herself asking him.

Jake looked at her thoughtfully as he shifted in his saddle. Common sense told him to decline her offer. After all, it was pretty close to dinnertime and as usual Blaylock had probably prepared a feast. But the thought of sitting down at a table, eating cookies and drinking milk with Diamond was a whole lot nicer than sitting down to dinner with Blaylock and a few of the men who lived on the ranch. He glanced at the cabin before glancing back down at her. "Cookies and milk, huh?"

Diamond smiled. "Yes. Fresh-baked cookies and a tall, cold glass of milk. You can't go wrong with that, Jacob."

Jake nodded as he dismounted, thinking that in truth, he could easily go wrong with just about anything involving Diamond. He followed her inside the cabin, gritting his teeth and calling himself all kinds of names for having such a weak resistance to her.

The echo of his boots sounded on the hardwood floor when he stepped inside the kitchen and glanced around. Pots, pans and dishes were piled in the sink and a dust of flour covered the floor. For once the kitchen actually looked used. When he had built the cabin, he had added additional square footage in the kitchen on the assumption that it would get plenty of use. But Jessie had had other plans.

Diamond saw Jake glance around and mistook the meaning of his silence. "I'll clean up the mess," she said warily as she watched his expression.

Jake gave no sign of having heard her as he continued to look around the kitchen. He even noticed the cookbook lying on the counter. His six sisters-in-law had gone to great lengths to collect all those recipes for that cookbook and put it together. It had been a labor of love and just one of the many gifts his family had lovingly given; their contribution to the home he had built for his wife.

"Jacob, I said that I'd clean up my mess," Diamond repeated softly, slanting a glance at his rugged profile.

Jake turned and met her gaze. She was looking at him with intense concern, and he saw an apology shimmering in her eyes. "There's nothing wrong with how this place looks. In fact, as far as I'm concerned, it looks just like a kitchen should."

He smiled down at her. "I'm dying to try out those cookies to see if they were worth the fight. Now, if you'll excuse me, I'll go wash up." He held her gaze for another quick second before abruptly moving toward the mudroom.

"You know," Jake commented to Diamond a short time later, "you may want to consider a career in baking if you ever decide to give up acting. These cookies are delicious." They were seated across from each other at a table in the kitchen by the window.

Diamond smiled, appreciating his compliment. She had tried baking for Samuel once or twice. He had laughed at her effort. "It was really nothing. I simply followed the recipe." She motioned to the leather-bound cookbook lying on the counter. "Whoever put that book together did a fantastic job."

Unable to help himself, Jake reached for another cookie. It seemed he had eaten a couple of dozen of them already. "My sisters-in-law will appreciate hearing that. It was a joint effort between the six of them and was intended to be a gift to the woman who was my wife at the time."

Diamond nodded, hearing the slight bitterness in his voice. Sterling had told her that he was a divorcé. "Did she forget to take it with her when she left?"

"Nope." Jake's eyes narrowed. "She didn't want it. She didn't want anything to remind her of this place."

Diamond knew it was probably none of her business, but she couldn't help asking. "Why? It's beautiful here."

Coolly, Jake's eyes met Diamond's inquisitive ones. "She didn't think so. She hated this place. She was a city girl from Boston, and married me hoping she could one day convince me that ranching wasn't what I was good at, and that I'd eventually move with her back to Boston. On the other hand, I believed that one day I'd be able to convince her that ranching was what I was good at, and that she would be happy here. In the end, we both lost out. She went back to Boston and I remained here. End of story."

Diamond's eyes grew thoughtful as she watched Jake take another bite of his cookie. She doubted in all actuality that that was the end of the story. It was all he cared to share with her at the moment.

"So tell me. What brought you by? Did Sterling ask you to check up on me again?"

Drawn as if by magnet, his gaze locked with hers. "No. Coming out here was my idea. I was wondering how you were getting along."

Diamond smiled. "Other than my fight with the flour today, I've been fine. On my first day I mostly slept in, and yesterday I decided to explore the great outdoors. I even went berry picking. I collected two pailfuls."

Jake nodded. So Lowell had actually seen her near the south pastures picking berries after all. "What do you plan to do with all those berries?"

Diamond lifted a brow as if the answer to that question should have been obvious to him. Since it wasn't, she decided to respond. "I'm going to make pies."

"Pies?"

She nodded. "I came across a pretty good recipe in that book. I believe I picked enough berries for at least ten pies. They will be my gift to your men. That's the very least I can do for their willingness to be discreet about me being here."

Jake fell silent as he studied her. He was astounded that she was again thinking about the men who worked for him. He shook his head. He wasn't sure if any of them would be able to handle receiving a piece of pie made by Diamond Swain's very own hands.

He downed the last of his milk, knowing it was time for him to leave. The last thing he wanted to do was to get any ideas that Diamond was different from most sophisticates that he knew.

Jake stood. "Thanks for the cookies and milk."

"You're welcome, and if you're out this way again, Jacob, do stop by. I enjoyed your company."

Jake looked at her and felt that same sizzle he always felt around her. He was attracted to her, way too attracted. Suddenly he jerked his attraction back like a whiplash, refusing to go there. It had been years since he'd had woman troubles and he intended to keep it that way. His love affair was with Whispering Pines. She was the only lady in his life right now. He felt content in knowing she would always accept him for what he was and not try making him into something he was not.

"I doubt I'll have time to drop by again. There's plenty of work to do around here. I can't very well expect my men to pull their share of the load if I'm not pulling mine," he said curtly.

Because he had presented his blunt statement like he had expected some sort of response, Diamond said, "Of course you can't. And I apologize if I've kept you from your work, Jacob."

Jake didn't like the idea that she thought she had kept him from his work. Then again, he thought maybe it was for the best for her to think that way. He couldn't afford to share another quaint and cozy meal with her again, even one of cookies and milk. It was best if he went back to his original plan to keep his distance. Especially since each time he saw her he couldn't help but wonder how her mouth would taste under his.

"The next time I talk to Sterling, I'll let him know you're doing okay. I'm sure he'll want to know." He then turned and walked out of the house.

Diamond followed him out to the deck and watched as he mounted his horse. Just before he was about to ride away, he glanced over at her. After making what appeared to be a quick but unwilling decision about something, he said, "You didn't keep me from my work, Diamond. I was where I wanted to be."

Without saying anything else, he rode off at a gallop and not once looked back.

Chapter 4

Smiling to herself, Diamond backed into the cabin and closed the door. Her eyes sparkled at the thought that Jacob had grudgingly admitted, in so many words, that he had wanted to spend some time with her. She was glad to know that he was fighting his attraction for her as much as she was fighting hers for him.

Diamond sighed as her mind began operating on some sort of adrenaline high. The very thought of Jacob was assaulting her senses and giving her a heated rush. For some reason, her attraction to him seemed instinctive, natural and sensible. He was handsome, rugged and downright appealing. What woman in her right mind would not be captivated by those attributes?

She remembered how at the table while they were eating cookies and drinking milk, Jacob had smiled at something she'd said. For one precious second, she had become mesmerized by that slow, seductive smile. It had taken all the willpower she possessed to maintain her composure.

Diamond shook her head, trying to fight off this unusual state she found herself in. She immediately reached the conclusion that she must be going through some type of hormone crisis. She was in total awe of the emotions Jake aroused in her. She struggled to clear her head, reminding herself that she'd come to the ranch for peace, quiet and relaxation.

She slumped down in a nearby chair, too weary and too confused to start tackling the cleanup of the kitchen just yet. She blew out a breath of frustration. Whispering Pines might be just what the doctor ordered, but Jacob Madaris was not. She wanted to convince herself that he was just another man, and in her line of business, she'd been around plenty. She drew her brows together. What was there about Jacob that wanted to make her forget the fiasco of a marriage she'd had with Samuel? It was a marriage that should have taught her a lesson. But one look at Jacob and she forgot everything, even the hard, cold fact that when it came to the affairs of the heart, she was a complete failure.

Diamond stood on her feet. She would put Jacob Madaris and how she intended to deal with him out of her mind for a while. She had a kitchen to clean and ten pies to bake.

Jake cursed himself for having admitted what he had to Diamond. The last thing he wanted was for her to start getting ideas that he was interested in her. She was used to men falling at their feet over her, both on and off the screen, and he had no intention of being one of them. Women who thought too much of themselves irritated him to no end. Usually they were women who lived in a world where money, looks and social status mattered a lot more than a person's character. Over the years, he had dated a number of those types. He'd even been married to one nearly twenty years ago.

Jessie Wellington, of the Boston Wellingtons, had had this farfetched opinion of what a real man should be. Besides being good-looking, of course, he needed a wealthy family background, a big home and plenty of money. Although he hadn't had any of those things at the time he'd met her, in him she had seen potential, and therefore she'd had no doubts about marrying him. After all, he had graduated at the top of his class from Harvard with a master's degree in finance, and he was good friends with the newly elected senator from Texas, Nedwyn Lansing. And everyone knew Senator Lansing was going places.

Jake shook his head. Jessie had gotten angry, frustrated and put-out with him because she could not bend him the way she wanted. She hadn't appreciated a man who valued honesty and hard work. She had wanted a man who would spoil her and give in to her childish tantrums like her father had always done. It had taken a little less than a year for her to discover that he was not that man. Her leaving had hurt because he had truly loved her. But she had shown him that there was no such thing as true love.

Looking back, he knew he and Jessie had been a bad match from the start. They had been as different as night and day, and she had thought she could mould him into something he was not. She had also thought that she could destroy his love for this land.

He had been born on this land in a small house that still stood on the other side of the north pastures. The Madaris family had settled on the land six generations ago, back in the eighteen hundreds after acquiring a ten-thousand acre Mexican land grant. At a time when most newly freed Blacks were still waiting for their forty acres and a mule from the United States government, Carlos Antonio Madaris, half Mexican and half African-American, along with his wife, Christina Marie, were shaping their heritage on the land they used to raise cattle. A parcel of land they named Whispering Pines.

Jake thought about his six brothers. All of them were alive and well except one. Robert had gotten killed in the Vietnam War. Jake was the youngest of the Madaris brothers. His mother had been in her late thirties when she gave birth to him and his father pretty close to fifty. All of his brothers, except for him and Robert, had chosen the profession of educator instead of rancher. There had never been any doubt in Jake's mind that he would run Whispering Pines one day. It was as much a part of him now as it had been then. He had spent six long years away from the land he loved while attending Harvard. The day he returned, he had vowed never to leave it again. He had also vowed to build it into everything his ancestors would be proud of, and where future Madarises could take pride in their heritage. Believing that he would fulfill his dream, his brothers had signed their shares of the ranch over to him, keeping only an investment interest. That act of faith and show of confidence from his brothers had made him that much more determined to succeed.

And he had.

With the things he had learned from working closely by his father's side while growing up, and by putting to use the vast education he had received from Harvard in the financial sector, the Whispering Pines ranch had tripled in size and now employed thirty men on a full-time basis. All of them had been hand-picked by him, and all of them were men he knew he could trust.

"There you go again, staring into space. At least this time you have your eyes open."

Jake muttered something about not being able to go anywhere to find peace, before turning around to Blaylock. Blaylock Jennings, who was in his late sixties, had once been a rodeo star during a time when very few African-Americans competed on the national circuit. He had been doing pretty good for himself until a mean and nasty bull decided to plow into him one night. In the end, Blaylock's battered body had been rushed to the emergency room with internal bleeding, a bruised kidney and a deep, long slash on the side of his face when the horn of the bull had tried ripping him apart. That slash was now a horrendous-looking scar that got a lot of attention when people saw him for the first time. Jake didn't know of any one person who had a heart of gold like Blaylock nor a man who could be trusted more. His job around the ranch was to keep him and the ranch hands fed and to keep the ranch house clean. Blaylock did both effortlessly. His only fault, as far as Jake was concerned, was thinking that anything that went on around Whispering Pines was his business. He thought of Jake as a son, and Jake had to admit that he looked up to Blaylock as a father figure, as did most of the younger men who worked on the ranch.

"Don't you have the dinner dishes to wash or something?" Jake asked. His question was gruff but he knew the teasing in it came through.

"They're all done. You barely touched your meal tonight. You're not coming down with something, are you, boy?"

Jake wanted to laugh. He was a long way from being a boy. "No, I'm not coming down with anything." He saw no need to tell Blaylock he had ruined his appetite for dinner when he'd eaten about two dozen cookies and drank nearly a gallon of milk earlier that afternoon.

"So, Jake, how's your little actress doing?"

Jake frowned. "I guess she's doing fine, and she's not my little actress."

Blaylock shook his head. "Now that's where you're wrong. Anything that sets foot on Whispering Pines is yours, and that includes Miss Hollywood."

Jake laughed unexpectedly. "I'm sure Diamond will be glad to know that."

"You and Miss Hollywood are on a first-name basis, are you?"

Jake frowned. "Why wouldn't we be?"

Blaylock laughed. "Yeah, why wouldn't you be indeed?"

Without answering the man's question, Jake walked off the porch toward the barn where he knew a lot of the men were finishing up their chores and getting ready to retire for the night.

The night was dark, and Jake thought it was lonely. A shaft of moonlight spilled across the yard and the branches of a few trees stirred with the night's gentle breeze. Jake stopped walking and inhaled the scent of magnolias and bluebonnets. Another scent was also entrenched in his mind. It was the scent of the perfume Diamond had been wearing when he'd seen her that day. It was a lush scent, an appealing fragrance.

Silently Jake stood in the shadows and tried to recall the moments he had spent in her company that day. Their conversations over cookies and milk had been light and impersonal, until he had begun talking about his ex-wife. He had told her more about himself than he had intended.

Jake stared long and hard into the night sky as Blaylock's words came back to him: *"Anything that sets foot on Whispering Pines land is yours...."* The thought of Diamond being his made his heart pound and caused a tightening in his gut.

Jake sighed as he moved out of the shadows and began walking back toward the house. He doubted he would get much sleep tonight.

Diamond's foot tapped to the sound of the Temptations as they bellowed out a song about their girl. Whoever had used the cabin before her had graciously left behind the CD *The Temptations Greatest Hits.* She had found herself dancing around the kitchen all afternoon while tidying it up and then later while baking her pies.

Now, five hours later, she had ten blueberry pies baked to her credit and was feeling pretty pleased with herself. The music had stimulated her and the baking had given her immense pride and fulfillment. She hoped Jacob's men would be pleased with the finished product.

She looked around the kitchen, knowing she would have to clean it up again before retiring for the night. But that thought didn't bother her. When she was through she would take a long, relaxing bath.

As she tapped her foot to another Temptations' tune about somebody's father being a rolling stone, she couldn't help but wonder what Jake was doing. Was he still up? Had he gone to bed for the night? Had he been thinking about the time he had spent with her that day, the way she had been thinking about it?

Darned if she had been able to think about much else the rest of that day. And the funny thing was she kept telling herself that the thought of getting mixed up with him during her three-week stay on the ranch would serve no purpose. Although the media claimed otherwise, she was not one to engage in casual affairs. Her father had done that enough over the years for both of them. Being discreet had never been one of Jack Swain's strong points.

Diamond shook her head and let out a deep breath as she tried convincing herself that an involvement with Jacob Madaris was the last thing she wanted.

Chapter 5

Jake stopped his horse at the end of the path and looked down at the cabin below. He raised his eyes toward the heavens and saw that the dark clouds he'd awakened to that morning were now moving away. He was grateful for that since his steers would need to graze in the pastures the majority of the day.

He fixed his gaze again on the cabin. He was tempted to go down and pay Diamond a surprise visit like he had done yesterday but talked himself out of it. He was too old to go sniffing behind a woman like a stallion in heat. Besides, it was too early. Chances were she was still asleep.

Jake frowned. He hadn't been able to get a good night's sleep. Visions of black hair, dark eyes and kissable lips had kept him awake. He turned slightly, about to lead his horse away, back up the path, when a

movement caught his eyes. The door to the cabin
opened and Diamond stepped out on the porch. Even
from a distance, he could see that she was holding a
mug of steaming hot coffee in her hands. She was
dressed in a denim work shirt and faded jeans. Her feet
were braced apart with her free hand tucked into the
front pocket of her jeans. Her stand emphasized the soft
curves of her body.

Jake sat in the saddle, transfixed. Even dressed like
a cowgirl, everything about Diamond spelled feminine. "Oh, for heaven's sake!" he muttered in annoyance to himself. "You have more things to do, Jake
Madaris, than to sit here and spy on a woman."

He released a deep, heavy sigh. He had always
prided himself on being able to handle any female re-
lationships. Caught in the thought that he was deviat-
ing from the norm bothered him. His dreams had
always centered around Whispering Pines and not
some woman's warm arms and soft body—like they
had last night.

Jake spared one last glance at Diamond before
turning his horse back toward the pastures. There was
work to do.

When Diamond heard the sound of the vehicle's
engine, she took a deep breath. Jacob had arrived. She
had called for him earlier and had spoken on the phone
to Blaylock. He was such a nice man. He had told her
that Jacob had ridden out early that morning and wasn't
expected back until midmorning. He said he would
give him the message when he returned that she wanted
to see him, and to come via way of his Jeep and not
horseback.

She felt the knot in her stomach clench. Never before had she allowed any man to get next to her like Jacob Madaris was doing. She frowned. He was just a regular man. But that thought didn't stop her from taking another deep breath when she heard the sound of his knock on the door. She walked over to the door and opened it.

Diamond's breath caught in her throat. There was nothing regular about Jacob Madaris, she thought as she studied his features. They were the same features that had invaded her dreams every night since she'd come to Whispering Pines. But for some reason, today those features appeared more manly and prominent. Today he looked like the quintessential cowboy/rancher. If anyone could combine the two successfully, it would be the handsome man standing before her.

"Hello, Jacob."

"Diamond." Jake breathed in her scent. It was warm, sweet, seductive. She was still wearing the cowgirl outfit he had seen her in that morning when he'd watched her from high on the mountain while she'd stood on the porch drinking a cup of coffee.

He cleared his throat when it suddenly became apparent that neither had said anything else to each other for a full minute after their initial greeting. "Blaylock said you wanted me."

Diamond blinked. She wanted him all right, she thought, willing her pulse to stop beating so rapidly. "Pardon me?"

"Blaylock said you wanted to see me and to bring the Jeep."

"Yeah, right," she said, getting her mind back on

track. *Relax,* she commanded herself, or Jacob will think you're one ditzy woman. "Please come in. I need help with the pies."

"Pies?"

"Yes. Remember I told you that I would bake them for your men; ten of them from the blueberries I picked."

Jake frowned as he walked into the cabin. "You actually did bake them?"

Diamond chuckled. "I told you I would."

Jake glanced around. A huge vase of roses sat on a nearby coffee table. He frowned when seeing the roses brought back memories.

Diamond saw his frown and didn't understand the reason for it. "I picked them yesterday," she said, explaining. "I would have gotten your permission first had I known that picking them would upset you. There were so many of them, and they were so beautiful. It was strange seeing them growing all around. I first noticed them when I went out picking berries a few days ago."

Jake nodded. "I don't have a problem with you picking them. Sorry if I gave you that impression. My ex-wife took a notion to plant over a thousand rose-bushes on this land right after we got married. She was used to seeing roses where she came from and said Whispering Pines looked dreary without them."

Now it was Diamond's time to frown. As far as she was concerned, there was nothing dreary about Whispering Pines. "I happen to disagree with her. This land of yours of beautiful, Jacob," she said, leading him to the kitchen. She then motioned to the clean and spotless kitchen. "No mess this time. No fight with flour."

Jake smiled. "I'm impressed." In all actuality, he was. It seemed everything about Diamond was beginning to impress him, especially when she had defended the beauty of his land. All Jessie had ever done was to put Whispering Pines down. She had hated it here. And she sure as heck would never have given thought to doing anything nice for his men. She had told him on more than one occasion how she detested them. She saw them as a group of men who barely had a high school education. She thought they were irresponsible men without any goals in life other than to play cowboys without the benefit of Indians. Jessie never had a word, kind or otherwise, to say to any of them. She had placed herself on a higher level than they were. But Diamond was a well-known movie star, who was known worldwide, and whose film credits were remarkably impressive. Yet she had taken the time not to bake just one pie, but ten of them for his men.

"I talked to Blaylock to be sure it would be okay since I didn't know what type of menu he had planned for them today. I didn't want to overstep my boundaries since he's their cook."

Jake nodded. That was another thoughtful gesture on her part. He was beginning to realize that Diamond Swain was a very unique woman.

"He's really a nice man."

Jake frowned. "Who?"

"Blaylock. I talked to him on the phone for over an hour. He gave me a recipe for vegetable soup. I'm going to make some tonight."

Diamond felt a fluttering in her heart when Jake smiled. "Well, once you get the pies in your Jeep,

we'll be ready to go," she said, as she began placing
the pies inside a huge cardboard box.

"You're coming?" Jake asked her in surprise.

She glanced up at him. "Sure. Remember I told
you that I wanted to meet them." She studied his
features closely. "That won't be a problem, will it?"

Jake saw the worried look on her face. Her expression indicated she wasn't sure if she would be doing
something wrong or against his wishes.

"No, that won't be a problem, and I'm sure they'll
get a kick out of it." *And I won't be able to get a lick
of work out of them for the rest of the day after they
meet you,* he thought further to himself.

He watched her features soften into a relaxed
smile. "Good."

"Do you know anything about cows?"

Diamond glanced over at Jake, wondering about the
question he had asked out of the clear blue sky. They
had been riding in his Jeep for the last few minutes or
so without much conversation. She tried not to concentrate on the large work-hardened hands that gripped
the steering wheel and wondered how those same
hands would feel on her.

Her brows furrowed. The middle part of her body
reacted to that particular thought. "I guess I know the
same thing about them as everyone else," she replied,
deliberately turning to look straight ahead.

"Which is?"

"They give milk," she said, looking back at him,
meeting his gaze.

Jake smiled warmly. Another thing he liked about
Diamond was the fact that she had a sense of humor.

"Yes, they do give milk but I'm not running a dairy, although all the milk served on the ranch is fresh."

"Even the milk we drank the other day with the cookies?"

"Yes."

Diamond nodded, smiling. "No wonder it tasted so good. I thought it was delicious."

Her compliment pleased Jake. "Thanks. My father used to run a small dairy and make door-to-door deliveries to the neighbors."

"Have you ever considered going back into the dairy business?"

"Nope. We have enough to do just to make sure we get the steers to the market on time. That alone keeps us pretty busy."

"I'm fascinated by all the things that you do around here. I'd like to learn more about it."

"Why?"

Diamond shrugged. "I don't know, I just do." She didn't want to tell him that for some reason, she wanted to know all she could about Jacob Madaris. She had a feeling that to know and understand Jacob Madaris, the man, she would first need to know and understand Jacob Madaris, the rancher. From the little bit Sterling had told her about him and what she had observed since arriving, Whispering Pines was his life.

"Just what are you interested in?"

She wanted to say *you*, but didn't. "I'm interested in everything about this place. From fixing fences, driving the herd, doing the roundup to this very chic system I understand you use to guarantee you're delivering the very best beef to the consumer that money can buy."

"I thought you came here to rest."

"I will be resting, Jacob. I haven't enjoyed myself this much in years. There's something about Whispering Pines that's so exciting and refreshing. Everything here is so clean, pure and unique. I love it here."

Jake didn't say anything as he kept driving. Jessie had also been excited when he had first brought her here. So excited that she had been adamant about planting those rosebushes everywhere, even in the least likely places where they would survive. But soon, like it usually happens with city slickers and sophisticates, the novelty wore off and instead of finding the ranch exciting, she had found it dreary and boring. One day Diamond would feel the same way. She was too well-traveled not to. Whispering Pines was just a hole in the wall compared to the other exotic places she had visited. The only saving grace for the ranch was that it didn't come with reporters and provided her a lot more privacy than she was used to.

When Jake turned the Jeep onto the road that would take them to the ranch house, he glanced over at Diamond and said, "We're almost there."

Chapter 6

Diamond fell in love with the sprawling hacienda-style ranch house the moment she saw it. The sight of it simply took her breath away. It was truly magnificent, and the closer she got to it, another word immediately came into her mind.

Gorgeous.

It was as gorgeous as the land and the man. The scenic setting gave a breathtaking view of the ranch, the pine tree–filled valley and the big blue Texas sky. When Jake brought the Jeep to a stop, she just sat there mesmerized. A deep breath filled her lungs. It seemed as if the structure was beckoning her. She closed her eyes momentarily, not understanding this strange feeling that surrounded her, absorbing her. To her surprise, she began wondering what it would feel like to wake up each and every morning here in this house. What would it be like to wake up to the fragrance of pine, mountain laurels and bluebonnets, and be surrounded by such natural beauty?

"Diamond, are you okay?"

Diamond opened her eyes and turned her gaze in Jake's direction, then tipped her head back and smiled. "I was just thinking of how beautiful your home is. I don't think there are enough words in the English dictionary to describe it."

Jake didn't want to place much stock in her opinion of his home. It was a home he had designed and built after his divorce from Jessie.

"I had no idea," Diamond went on as she continued to explain, "that a home could be made to look so inviting and welcoming."

Jake couldn't help but smile. No one had ever said such things about his ranch house before. The cabin had been a surprise gift for Jessie, one he had painstakingly worked day and night to complete. But she had refused to live in it, even for one night. Then when she had left him a week or so later, he had been determined to one day build another house, one that did not have memories of her. The only lingering memento of her short presence at Whispering Pines was the roses. Unfortunately she had planted several bushes on the site he had later chosen for his home to be built. As beautiful as they were, the roses served as a constant reminder of what could happen if you gave your heart completely to someone else.

Jake took his time watching Diamond, not knowing what was truly real and not just an overwhelming impression that would eventually wear off. "Are you ready to go inside?" he asked, deciding not to dwell on what she thought of his ranch house any longer.

"Yes."

Jake tried to appear casual as he got out of the Jeep and walked around the vehicle to open Diamond's door. He even pretended indifference when extending his hand to help her out of the Jeep. But he couldn't mask the look in his eyes when they met hers, their gazes holding a bit longer than necessary.

"Thanks." Diamond finally said in a soft, shaky voice. She would have backed up, but couldn't. She was already pressed close to the Jeep's door.

"Don't mention it." Jake took a step back to give her space. It was space he hadn't wanted to give her. He took a long, deep breath and glanced around. Luckily for him, the yard was empty, which meant the men were inside the huge bunkhouse eating lunch. He was glad no one had witnessed his moment of standing spellbound before Diamond.

"This way," he called over his shoulder as he turned and began walking away. There was no way he could walk next to Diamond. It took some excellent skill of mind over body control to make it not so obvious just how much she had aroused him. That was the last thing his men needed to notice.

As he knew it would be, the eating room of the bunkhouse was noisy. The clatter of dishes and the clamor of voices going at the same time met Jake and Diamond the moment they entered the building, unnoticed.

"Maybe this isn't a good time to interrupt them," Diamond whispered to Jake, trying to keep her voice low. "They seem rather hungry."

Jake shrugged. "Cowboys are always hungry. It won't take but a second to get their attention."

Jake walked a little ways into the room. "Afternoon, guys. We have company."

All the men looked up at Jake. Then they followed his gaze to Diamond, who was still standing in the doorway. Suddenly all movement at the table froze and total silence filled the room. Diamond took a deep breath as thirty-plus pairs of eyes stared at her without blinking. She hoped they weren't upset that their lunch had been interrupted. She was sure to these men that after putting in so much time in the saddle, lunch was probably a very important part of their day. Ready to brave the storm that could erupt from the hungry men seated at the long table, she took a deep breath and walked into the room and stood next to Jake.

"Hi," she said to the men, who had gone speechless. "I didn't want to interrupt anything, but I wanted to meet all of you. I know this might not be a good time but I brought you something."

When none of the men said anything but just continued to stare at her, she glanced quickly at Jake. His lean features that lighted into a smile gave her encouragement, so she continued. "I baked pies for all of you. Blueberry pies. Ten of them. I checked with Blaylock, and he said it would be all right for me to serve you a piece as lunch dessert."

The men still didn't respond.

Diamond gave another quick glance in Jake's direction. He was smiling. In fact, if she didn't know better she would think he was downright amused. She shrugged and decided to add, "I think I did a pretty good job on the pies, but I'll let you be the final judge. Would anyone like to help me get them out of the Jeep?"

Jake saw, before Diamond did, all thirty-plus men jump out of their seats at the same time, nearly knocking over their chairs in the process. "Hold it right there," he commanded in a loud voice before any one of the men could get within five feet of Diamond. "Sit back down. I'll get the pies. Blaylock, maintain order until I get back."

It was only after he had made the request of Blaylock did Jake remember most people's reaction to the man upon first seeing him. Jake took in a deep breath as he watched Blaylock hesitate a second before coming forward. He knew that as usual, Blaylock was bracing himself for another person's cruel response to seeing the scar on his face.

Jake saw Diamond glance around to take note of the man he'd spoken to. He then watched in astonishment as she flashed the older man a pure, radiant smile. Jake's eyes then widened when she left his side and walked over to Blaylock and gave him a huge hug like they were old friends.

"Blaylock, I'm so glad to meet you. Thanks for walking me through the dough part of that recipe. You were right, kneading the dough that way made the cookies taste lighter. You're going to have to share more of your cooking secrets with me while I'm here."

Jake knew that Blaylock was just as taken aback as he was. He looked at Jake with questioning eyes. Jake simply shrugged. Diamond hadn't even blinked at the sight of Blaylock's scar. It was as if she hadn't noticed it, which Jake knew was not the case because it ran the full length of the man's face.

Jake shook his head. The woman was something else. That simple act of human kindness she had bestowed upon the elderly man touched him in a way he couldn't describe. He also knew it had earned her a special place in Blaylock's heart for life.

"I'm glad it worked for you, Miss Diamond," Blaylock finally found his voice to say.

"Just Diamond. After helping me out with that new batch of cookies, I feel like we've moved to the rank of buddies."

She glanced over at the men, who were still staring openmouthed at her before letting her gaze come to rest on Jake. "The pies, Jacob. You forgot to go get the pies."

Silence broke among the men when one of them coughed to cover a chuckle and whispered to another. "She called the boss *Jacob*. Nobody calls him Jacob around here and gets away with it."

Jake's gaze fell on Simon Bellamy, giving the man a hard stare. "She does," he said before he spun around and walked out of the bunkhouse to fetch the pies.

"Today was a very interesting day," Diamond said as she got out of the Jeep when Jake opened the door for her.

That's an understatement, Jake thought. It was pretty close to midnight, and he was just returning Diamond back to the cabin. It should not have surprised him when she had served each man a piece of pie herself, even ordering him and Blaylock to sit down and be served.

No joke, the pie had been delicious, but he doubted many of the men remembered much about the taste of it. They had sat in awe, totally dazed, that movie actress Diamond Swain was there in the same room with them, and of all things she had cooked pies for them. After making sure all the men had been served, she had sat down and eaten a piece with all of them, joking with them about the cookies she had baked and her fight with the flour.

Jake had forced all the men back to work. But not before Diamond had thanked each and every one of them for keeping her secret about being at Whispering Pines. Jake had shaken his head at the look of adoration in their eyes, and knew that no matter what, her secret was safe. He doubted that after today, any of them would betray her trust.

Jake couldn't help but remember how Blaylock had invited her to stay for dinner and how quickly she had accepted, pleasing the older man immensely. Knowing that like his men he had work to do, he had left her with Blaylock. When he had returned hours later for dinner, he had found that she had made herself comfortable in his study and had curled up in a chair asleep with a book in her hand. Her sleeping form curled in the overstuffed chair next to his desk had taken his breath away. He couldn't help but stand there in the doorway and look at her. He had heard the sound of a dog barking in the background and the whining sound of the engine from the milking machine out back in the storage house. But Diamond had slept through it all.

"Don't wake her, boy. Let her sleep," Blaylock had said to him over his shoulder. He had nodded, then turned and left the room to go upstairs to take a shower. By the time he had come back downstairs an hour or so later, he knew she had awakened when he had heard voices coming from the kitchen. He had stopped short when he walked into the kitchen and had seen twelve extra faces crowded at his dinner table. He had frowned. They were men who usually ate elsewhere in the afternoons. Other than the few who had permanent residences on Whispering Pines, he couldn't recall any of the others ever joining him for dinner before. He wasn't stupid. He knew why they were there.

"Is there any reason the masses of you aren't giving your business to Pearl's Diner tonight?" he had asked them.

The men, he had noted, had the decency to blush. However, it was his foreman, Percy Davis, who had laughed before audaciously saying, "Jake, didn't you know that we enjoy being around you so much, it's just natural for us to be eager for your company."

"Yeah, right," he had snorted before taking a place at the head of the table. Blaylock had seated Diamond at the other end, facing him. It was a spot that should have been reserved for the lady of the house. Since there was not one, that seat had normally remained vacant during meals. It had seemed strange to see someone sitting there, especially since that someone had been Diamond.

"Do you really think the men enjoyed the pies?"

Diamond's question intruded on Jake's thoughts, and brought him back to the present, reminding him they were now back at the cabin. "Sure they did, couldn't you tell?"

Diamond smiled. "Yeah, I guess so. What about you, Jacob. Did you enjoy it?"

They had reached the door and stood facing each other. Diamond looked up at him for an instant, and a part of her wished she hadn't. His eyes held hers, and she couldn't do anything but stare back at him. She took in a quick perusal of his features under the moonlight. His handsomeness dazed her.

Blinking, she forced herself to turn her gaze away from his. Her cheeks flushed with sudden heat when she felt the pit of her stomach go hot. "Did you enjoy your pie?" she asked him again to get conversation going. She needed something—anything—to break the deep attraction she was feeling for him. She licked her lips.

That single gesture pushed Jake over the edge. It had been an edge he had been dangerously close to falling off of all day. "Yeah, I liked the pie," he said. "And I think I'm going to like this here even better."

His mouth was halfway to hers when the meaning of what he said hit Diamond. She was more than ready for his kiss and tilted her mouth up to meet him as he leaned toward her.

First he softly kissed the corner of her mouth before closing his full mouth over hers, gently inserting his tongue for the sweet taste he knew awaited him. His desire for her suddenly became overwhelming. He intensified the kiss when he heard a soft moan escape her throat, then wondered if the sound had really come from her and not him.

Their lips continued to fuse together hotly for a long, delicious moment. Neither was in a hurry for this time to end as rampant, hot and heavy emotions tore into them. Jake deepened the kiss even more, and his fingertip lightly traced patterns on the back of Diamond's shirt.

Her hands were busy, too, as they encircled his neck. Her fingers caressed the side of his face underneath his ear. Both of them were drowning in the smoldering depths of the devouring kiss, their need spinning, raging.

With a deep tormented moan, Jake broke off the kiss to breathe. Heavily. Forcefully. Getting air past his lungs was a struggle not only for him, he noticed, but for Diamond as well.

When the impact of what had transpired between them hit him, he took a step back. He'd always been able to hold back and control his desire. But not this time. In the instant that he had touched his tongue to hers, his masculine urges had become dominant.

And he didn't like it.

Diamond Swain, he thought further, was not the type of woman he wanted to get involved with on any level. Now or ever. She was more than just a sophisticate, she was totally dangerous to his peace of mind. Jessie had literally destroyed his belief that ranching and city women mixed. For a brief time, he had forgotten how he had learned the hard way not to become involved with a woman who could never accept him for what he was—a man born of the land. There was no way there could ever be a future for him and Diamond. She was who she was and he was who he was. Nothing would ever change that, so why go through the hassle. He knew that having a no-strings affair with her was out of the question when there was a chance he could lose his heart completely.

"Sorry, I shouldn't have done that," he said apologetically, knowing it sounded lame and out of place when deep down he wasn't sorry at all.

Diamond reached up and touched his lips with her fingertips. "Well, I'm glad you did it. Good night, Jacob."

Speechless, Jake watched her go into the cabin and close the door.

* * *

Later that night while in bed, Diamond thought about her afternoon at Jake's house. At first he hadn't seemed pleased when Blaylock had invited her to stay for dinner, but had been a gracious host nonetheless. To avoid getting in anyone's way, she had found solitude in his huge study.

In addition to being a place where he managed the business side of the ranch, the room had also been filled with a large collection of various books, several antiques and photographs of his family. From studying the numerous framed pictures that decorated one huge wall in his study, it was evident that he was a man who truly treasured his family. And if the photographs were any indication, the Madaris family was a rather large one. It was one he was truly proud of.

Diamond thought about her own family. Up until her fourth birthday, her mother had tried using her as a pawn to milk money out of her father. He had ended her cruel game by fighting for custody of her and winning. Her young mother, who had lived a wild and reckless life filled with parties and shifting from one man to another, had died less than a year later when her lover, a depressed stuntman, had shot and killed her in a jealous rage and then had turned the gun on himself, ending his own life.

Diamond had spent a lot of her early years with her paternal grandmother in North Carolina since Jack Swain traveled most of the time. Jennie Swain had been everything a grandmother should be. She was a warm, loving person, sensitive and considerate of others' needs; a lady who was adored by anyone who knew her. One of the things her grandmother enjoyed doing was giving plenty of hugs. She always said that a hug a day would keep whatever ails you away.

Diamond smiled. Sterling claimed she had inherited her grandmother's trait of being a huggy person, and she knew he was right. She would instinctively hug most people she met. It was something that sometimes got misread as a come-on to some men in Hollywood who saw a hug as an invitation to something else. Over the years, she'd had to limit her hugs to those she felt comfortable in hugging.

Diamond released a huge sigh. With the passing of her grandmother four years ago, that left only her and her father, and they were a long way from being a family. Deep down she believed he loved her, he just had a strange way of showing it at times. Over the years, she had gotten used to his ways. However, that didn't stop her from wishing things were different between them. She couldn't help but envy the relationship Jacob had with his family. It must be a wonderful feeling to be a part of such a close group of people.

Diamond touched her lips with her fingertip when she thought about his kiss. She had tried hard not to think about it and to forget it ever happened, but she couldn't.

And she doubted that she ever would.

Unlike him, she had not regretted the kiss and had been honest with him and herself when she had told him so. She could tell he hadn't been pleased with that bit of information from her, either.

When Diamond finally dozed off to sleep a short while later, her mind was still filled with thoughts of Jacob and his kiss.

Chapter 7

Jake Madaris was in a bad mood. A very bad mood. He knew it. Blaylock knew it. And his men knew it.

But what Blaylock and the men couldn't figure out was why. Of all the men who had been around Diamond at lunch two days ago, Jake had spent more time with her than anyone. So everyone couldn't help but wonder what had him in a tiff. If anything, to their way of thinking, he should have been a man on top of the world. What man wouldn't be in his shoes?

All of them would have been surprised to know that Jake didn't want to be in those shoes. He didn't want to be the man Diamond had spent most of her time with that day. It was for that very reason that he had deliberately avoided her since then. The night he'd taken her back to the cabin was one he was trying hard to forget, but the memory of her taste wouldn't let him.

And that was the reason for his bad mood.

The men were still talking about her visit and the pies she'd baked for them. There was nowhere he could go on the ranch without hearing her name or someone singing her praises. He knew she had baked another batch of cookies, this time for his men. It had been Blaylock whom she had called to pick up the delivery, not him. A part of him should have been overjoyed at the thought that he hadn't had to see her again, but he wasn't.

It had been two days and two nights, and instead of feeling relieved, he was feeling annoyed. Which was one of the reasons he had deliberately not gone back to the ranch at midmorning like he normally did. Blaylock had casually mentioned at breakfast that he would be going to the cabin to fetch Diamond to the ranch for a cooking lesson in chili making.

Jake shook his head. Although everyone knew that Blaylock made the best chili this side of the Mexican border, he couldn't figure out why on earth Diamond would want to know how to do it. She had enough money to hire the most expensive cooks that money could buy. Why would she want to learn anything about cooking chili?

Just for the novelty of it, an inner voice told him. *It's something new and different to her. It'll wear off soon enough, and she'll be just like the other sophisticates, bored as sin. Who knows. She may even become bored enough to shorten her three-week stay at Whispering Pines.*

Jake's jaw tightened and the muscle there began to twitch at the thought of her leaving before she was supposed to. He suddenly became irritated with himself yet again for even caring what she did. Totally frustrated, like he had been for the past two days, he stomped out of the barn and walked toward the house.

Opening the door, he paused in the doorway when he heard the sound of voices. More specifically he heard Blaylock's chuckles and a woman's laughter. No one had to tell him that laugh had come from Diamond.

Jake frowned. Blaylock had assured him Diamond would be gone when he returned to the ranch later that afternoon, so what was she still doing here? He decided not to even find out. He was about to ease out of the door and go back to the barn before anyone realized he'd come in, when Diamond and Blaylock walked out of the kitchen into the hallway. They looked over in his direction and saw him.

Jake swore beneath his breath as his gaze met Diamond's. He suddenly felt the walls crashing in on him, tumbling his world as he knew it. His breath got lodged in his throat. Heat gripped his entire body. Waves of awareness washed over him. All these things were happening, it seemed, all at once. And it didn't help matters that she looked so darn beautiful.

Taking a deep breath, he forced himself to breathe normally and to get control of himself. He tried not to notice how totally feminine she looked in a floral print sundress. And he sure as heck tried not to notice that she was wearing her hair differently. It was combed back in, of all things, a ponytail. And to make matters worse, it didn't help any for her to look at him with such a warm smile on her lips. Especially when they were lips he now knew the taste of. If only he didn't remember that.

"Hello, Jacob. It's good seeing you again. How have you been?"

Infuriated with himself for letting her get next to him again, he folded his arms across his chest. "If you must know, ma'am," he drawled with agitated politeness, "I haven't been doing so hot. But thanks for asking."

Diamond lifted her brow, and Jake saw a flash of comprehension form in her eyes. "Really, Jacob? Now isn't that a coincidence. I haven't been doing so hot myself."

"Getting bored already?"

She smiled at him again—darn it. "I could never get bored here."

Jake shook his head. He had heard that one before. "Well, don't let me stop whatever the two of you were about to do. I'll just run upstairs and take my shower."

"I was about to take Diamond back to the cabin, Jake, but now that you're here, maybe you could take her back. I need to get dinner started," Blaylock said, reminding them of his presence.

Jake stared at Diamond for a second before making a decision. "Sure, why not. Are you ready to leave now, or can you wait until after I've showered?"

"I can wait."

Nodding, Jake turned toward the stairs. "I'll be back down in a half hour."

"I didn't mean to be a bother, Jacob."

Jake had brought the Jeep to a stop in front of the cabin and instead of getting out, he had turned in his seat. He was staring at her, Diamond thought, and had even pushed his Stetson farther back on his head, away

from his eyes as if to get a better view. He had not said
one word since leaving the ranch house. But he didn't
have to, she concluded. What she saw in his expression spoke volumes. Desire, hot desire, flared in his
dark eyes, and the sparks from it flamed her all over
and took her breath away.

Diamond tore her gaze away from his. The heat
penetrating from his eyes had become unbearable. The
woman in her recognized his need. It was surrounding her, entrenching her. The woman in her also recognized his resistance. He didn't want to have anything
to do with her. She understood. Deep down she didn't
want to have anything to do with him, either, but the
attraction was too strong, too overwhelming for either
of them. She had realized that fact two nights ago
when he had kissed her. She had realized it again today
when she had seen him for the first time since that
night. Even with Blaylock in the room with them, they
hadn't been able to mask the heat, the wanting, the
desire. When he had mentioned that he hadn't been
doing so hot, she had wanted to go to him, stroke away
the hardness that had formed in his cheeks and then
soften his grim mouth with her own.

Diamond sucked in air as she fought her senses
from leaping someplace they should not.

Jake took a long, deep breath. He recognized his
needs, too. Normally he took care of them. After
Jessie, he had learned to keep his business interests,
his personal life and physical needs separate. And
Rhonda Henry made it easy for him to do just that.
Rhonda wasn't a city woman, but she wasn't a country
gal, either, although her father owned one of the largest
horse ranches in Wyoming. Rhonda fitted nicely some-

where in between. She could be as classy and sophisticated as she wanted to be one minute, then break in
a horse or rope a steer better than any man the next.
She was a woman on the move, a mover and a shaker
who took her job as public relations administrator for
her father's prosperous horse-breeding business seriously.

She was a divorcée and was only four years younger
than he. They had met a few years ago at a political
fund-raiser in Washington for his friend, Senator
Nedwyn Lansing. Like him, Rhonda wanted the sep-
aration of business, personal and physical. She didn't
want any strings attached and didn't like men interfer-
ing with her affairs and knew not to interfere with
theirs. Their relationship was one of physical needs
only. Whenever they came together for their inter-
ludes, they met on what they considered neutral
ground, keeping any place near their ranches out of the
loop. When they got together, it was strictly for play,
not work. There was no time or room for emotions.
That's the way she wanted it, and that's the way he
wanted it. And either could walk away at any given
time. No hard feelings. No regrets.

If he were to get mixed up with Diamond, Jake ad-
monished himself silently, there would be hard feelings and regrets. And there would be emotions to deal
with. There was no way he could take anything lightly
with this woman. Nor would there be any way he could
keep things separate. He had a gut feeling that with
Diamond it would be all or nothing. And that was
something he did not want with any woman.

"It's not going to work, Diamond," he finally said.

Diamond knew exactly what Jake was referring to

and didn't pretend otherwise. He was stating the obvious—the strong sexual attraction between them. She shook her head sadly. "I know." She hesitated for a moment before saying, "But I don't know how to stop it. You are quite a challenge, Jacob Madaris. I've never been faced with anything like this in my life."

Jake nodded. Neither had he. He hadn't been this hot for a woman in years, if ever.

"There has never been anyone I've felt such an attraction to, Jacob," Diamond continued. "I know it won't work. I know it's even crazy to think otherwise. I didn't come here for this. I came here for three weeks of rest and relaxation. Not three weeks of being in heat like one of your cows."

Jake couldn't help but smile at what she'd just said. He, in turn, had been just as bad. He'd been like a lusty bull who'd gotten the scent of that heat and wanted to mate.

Diamond saw his smile and frowned. "This isn't funny, Jacob. Since we know it won't work, what are we going to do?"

Jake's smile widened as he studied her for a long spell. The woman was too open and too straightforward with her feelings. She wasn't acting coy about anything or trying to place the blame at his feet. She was acknowledging that whatever was going on between them was mutual.

"I could say it's just an overabundance of lust in our system, and one surefire way to get it out of there is one quick roll in the hay," Jake finally said, his gaze still locked on hers. "But a part of me, Diamond, the part that's aching right now, refuses to let me believe that anything I do with you can be quick." He let his gaze travel over her slowly. He saw her watching his eyes, knowing she saw the heat and the desire in them. Then he saw hers darken likewise. In addition to his ache, he suddenly felt this horrendous pull in his gut. That need he'd recognized earlier became fierce and took his senses away.

"I want you," he said, following her lead by being open and straightforward. "I want you, too much to be quick. I'd want to savor the moment, to feed on it and prolong it. I doubt very seriously if I'd be able to stop with having you just once. I'd want you again and again and again."

Jake's voice had the honesty and sensuous warmth Diamond wasn't ready for. The texture of his words, as well as the words themselves, seeped through to the very core of her. Her body became electrified, sensitive and achy to his words. In her mind, she saw them rolling in the hay. And like him she didn't see them being quick about it. She saw him taking his time and making slow, hot, unadulterated love to her. She saw his body mating with hers over and over again, taking no time out in between to rest, using all his strength, all his physical exertions, his keen focus and abundance of energy to pleasure her.

"Jacob, I—"

Diamond didn't finish what she was about to say. Jake didn't let her. He leaned over and captured her mouth with the heat of his. Effortlessly lifting her from her seat into his lap, he continued to kiss her. His tongue entered her mouth, mating with hers, generating more heat. The kiss grew hotter, urgent.

Jake knew he should pull back, but when his hand touched her breasts, all thoughts of ending the kiss left him. Even through the material of her dress, her breasts were a perfect fit in the palm of his hand. It was as if they were made for him. He heard her groan in his mouth when his fingertips touched them. He deepened the kiss, wanting and needing to feed off her groans and her moans.

Aching for more torture, he reached down to the hem of her dress and lifted it up partway. He needed to touch her thighs, he wanted to feel the heat and the need in her. But first, he had to breathe. He was dying a suffocating death of mind-killing arousal. He suddenly broke off the kiss, his breathing forced, labored, exerted.

Jake knew he had to do something to regain control of his mind and his senses. If he stayed around her any longer, there would be no choice in the matter. He would be tasting her everywhere, he would be making love to her each and every day she remained on the ranch. He wouldn't give any thoughts to Whispering Pines. His only thoughts would be to stay inside her body, mating with her, seeing her features flushed with his heat, knowing that the skin covering her body was entrenched in his scent.

He knew that getting involved with Diamond would demand all that he had, and he couldn't let that happen. He couldn't let his lust for a woman be this strong, this addictive. Even with Rhonda it wasn't like this. It didn't even come close. He hadn't seen Rhonda in over eight months, and he hadn't felt a potent urge to call her. He hadn't experienced such raw longing until Diamond's arrival on Whispering Pines. Somehow he had to fight this pull, this overwhelming urge.

Taking another deep breath, Jake pulled Diamond's

dress down and gently lifted her out of his lap and placed her back in her seat. Without saying another word, he opened his side of the vehicle, got out and walked around to hers. Opening her door, he picked her up in his arms and carried her to the door and placed her on her feet.

The light on the porch created an intimacy neither of them needed right now. He stepped back, knowing he couldn't dare touch her again. He kept his gaze steady with hers, trying not to notice her lips, swollen and moist from his kiss, and the longing and wanting that were still in her eyes.

"Do you want me to leave Whispering Pines?"

Her whispered question broke the quiet stillness of the night. "No," he whispered, when deep down he knew he should be saying yes. "No, I don't want you to leave. What I want is for us to know that it will never work."

"And you're sure of that, Jacob?"

"Yes, so accept that as I have. In the meantime, we'll have to be mature enough to deal with it. We're not two animals whose only urge is to mate. We're two intelligent human beings who can recognize when a situation won't work. This is one of them. I don't want to hurt you and I refuse to let you hurt me."

"And you think I will hurt you?"

"Yes. I discovered long ago that nothing is usually as it should be, not the way you'd like it to be." He took a step back. "I'll be by early in the morning to get you for the cattle drive, since you're determined to go on our first day out. Good night, Diamond."

She watched him walk back to his Jeep and leave.

Chapter 8

Jake wasn't surprised the next morning to find Diamond dressed and enjoying a mug of coffee when he arrived at the cabin during the predawn hours.

To make matters simple, he had saddled up a horse at the ranch, a mare he'd felt would be easy enough for her to handle, and had hitched the animal to his horse and brought it along. Diamond had been standing on the deck, waiting for him when he'd ridden up. She had immediately put down her mug and smiled, evidently pleased with his choice of a horse for her.

"She's beautiful, Jacob," she said, as she took a good look at the horse she would be riding that day. She reached up to touch the animal's muzzle. Diamond's smile widened when the horse nickered and playfully tossed her head.

You're beautiful, too, Jake thought as he watched Diamond interact with the huge palomino. Even now he doubted she was wearing makeup, but the smooth freshness of her dark skin, her eyes the color of whisky and the fullness of her lips made her a delectable sight early in the morning.

"I'm glad you like her. She belongs to one of my nieces, but I'm sure she won't mind your riding her. Christy's a real big fan of yours."

Diamond glanced up at Jake and smiled again, the same smile she gave him whenever she saw him, the one with the ability to stir his insides.

"Are you ready to ride?"

Diamond nodded. "Yes, I'm all set."

Jake watched as she mounted the mare, not surprised with the ease with which she did so. According to what she'd told Blaylock yesterday, which the older man had been most eager to share with him and the men over breakfast, was the fact that Diamond was not a greenhorn when it came to riding a horse. Although she had not been raised on a ranch, as a child her father had made sure she had gotten numerous riding lessons.

"Then let's go," Jake said, turning his horse toward the north pastures. He decided to set out at a slow pace. It would be a long workday and he didn't want to tire out the horses too soon.

They rode in silence. Jake tried not to think about what had transpired between them the night before and knew that nothing had truly been resolved. If the truth were known, he wanted her now more than ever. His suggestion that they behave like two intelligent human beings and not like two animals with a strong urge to mate wasn't working. At least it wasn't working for him. All he had to do was to glance over at her, sitting comfortably astride the horse, looking every bit as tempting as she had yesterday, and his body was reacting. He was aware of the blood flowing hot and thick through his veins and the quiver surging through his loins.

There was something sexy as hell about a woman in jeans, he thought, especially tight jeans. His mind suddenly began imagining all sorts of things. For instance, the pleasure he would feel in peeling those tight jeans off her body.

Jake cursed under his breath. He definitely didn't need those kinds of thoughts. He needed all his strength and focus to be concentrated on today's activities, which were to move the herd to the high pastures without any problems.

He shook his head. The only problem he could think of was riding on a horse next to him. "Watch yourself today, Diamond," he decided to say, breaking into the silence by making the first attempt at conversation since leaving the cabin. "I'll be too busy to keep an eye on you."

"I'll be careful, Jacob."

"And another thing."

She glanced over at him. "Yes?"

"The men, they'll be branding the cows. I don't want them to get careless and start branding each other. They need to stay focused on what they'll be doing, and you'll be a distraction."

When he saw Diamond raising a questioning brow, he continued, "You have the ability to make a man lose focus, Diamond. The men are in awe of who you are. I don't want any careless accidents to happen."

For some reason, Jake got the impression she was caught off guard by what he had just said to her. He wondered why she would be. Surely the woman knew how beautiful she was and that there were a number of men fascinated by that beauty both on and off the screen. He had even seen a huge poster of her in one of his teenage nephew's bedrooms a few months ago.

"Do you think I shouldn't come?" she asked quietly.

"To be quite honest with you," he said slowly, "right now I'm questioning my decision to let you come along. I can't afford any on-the-job accidents."

Diamond brought her horse to a stop. "I'll go back then, Jacob. The last thing I want is for my presence to cause problems for anyone."

Jake looked at her, studied her. She wasn't acting sulky or pouty. He saw genuine concern in her features. He wondered how often she'd felt that because of who she was, she would have to act or behave a certain way not to cause problems either to herself or others. He knew from being good friends with Sterling that most Hollywood types fell in two categories: those who gave a damn and those who didn't. Sterling was one who didn't, but he believed Diamond was one who did. Sterling was right when he'd said the other night that Diamond enjoyed being around people, but in her line of business, she couldn't get too friendly with anyone.

But she had.

She felt comfortable being on friendly terms with everyone on the ranch. No one had been excluded from her friendliness or acts of kindness, not even him. Being kind and friendly seemed to make her happy and relaxed, and he wasn't about to take that away from her.

Jake shook his head. "You won't cause any problems. The only problem you'll cause is by not showing up. The men know you're coming, and they're looking forward to your spending a day out there on the range with them. They really like you, Diamond."

He saw her face light up in a smile. He knew his words had meant a lot to her. "I like them, too. You have a special group of men working for you, Jacob. They are good men. I can feel it."

Jake looked at her consideringly. After a long moment he asked, "What else can you feel, Diamond?"

Fierce, hungry desire was obvious in the dark eyes staring at her. Instinctively Diamond felt the core of her body quivering with renewed need. She flushed and looked away. Moments later she looked at him again. "I thought we had decided to try and stop this thing from developing between us, Jacob."

He moved his horse close up beside hers. He wondered how he was going to make it through the day with her around. They stared at each other for a long, silent moment. Neither of them blinked. Then finally, after he had gained a semblance of control, Jake said, "Yeah, we did, didn't we? Sorry." He then urged his horse on and without saying a word, Diamond and her horse followed.

Jake had two choices. He could ignore Diamond or he could not ignore her. And he was finding that he could not ignore her. It seemed the men were handling her presence better than he was. Once they had gotten used to her being there, they had gone about doing their normal chores, and she had stayed out of everyone's way by volunteering her services in the meal wagon. Willie Beads, the range cook, had been more than grateful for another pair of hands, even those belonging to Diamond Swain. And she had been a big help. She had assisted Willie in unpacking the cooking utensils and had been most eager to help serve the men lunch and dinner. Then later she had helped Willie get everything cleaned up and put away.

Nearing the afternoon, Jake sat on his horse frowning as he watched her, thinking of just how well she was able to fit in out here on the range. She was such a natural outdoors. And that's what bothered him. Diamond Swain was not acting in any of the ways he had expected a sophisticate to act. She wasn't afraid of breaking a fingernail by doing a little hard work, and she didn't seem to be getting bored yet.

It takes longer for some, his inner mind told him. *She'll come around and find that this place is cramping the style she's used to. She'll begin missing the excitement and glamour of the life she left in California. It will be just a matter of time before Whispering Pines loses the allure and charm it now holds for her.*

He knew this. It was expected. But the thought still bothered him. To be more precise, it bugged the hell out of him. And that, he thought, was dumb. He could not figure out why he was letting her get next to him. He set his lips in a firm line as he stared at her. He was way too smart to get tangled up with a sophisticated lady again. She was here for another two weeks, even less when the boredom finally settles in. So why was he feeling so agitated, so annoyed; and why had he gone back to feeling like a lusty bull again?

To tell the truth, the feeling had never left him.

He raised his chin, took off his hat and looked over at her. For once she was standing alone, looking out over his herd. She had taken off the wide-brim hat she had brought along and was using her hands as a shield as she squinted the sun out of her eyes. Her shoulder-length hair fell loosely around her shoulders. Even from a good fifty yards away, he could almost feel its softness. It would be the kind of hair a man would want to twirl his fingers around while he made love to her. It was the kind a man would want to bury his nose in at the same time the heat of him spilled deep within her body.

At that moment, as if she felt his gaze on her, she dropped her hand from shielding her eyes and turned and met him across the distance, eye to eye. For what seemed like an eternity, neither of them blinked. She slowly smiled with wide moist lips, which was not intended to tease, but did so anyway. The attraction that he had tried fighting suddenly intensified to a roaring blaze, a towering inferno.

Jake stared at her for a little while longer before finally making a decision. He slowly moved his horse toward her. When he reached her, he watched as she nervously ran her fingers through her hair and licked her lips, biting the bottom one softly.

"Diamond," he said quietly.

She raised her face and looked up at him questioningly. "Yes?"

They looked at each other, tension shimmering

between them, surrounding them, engulfing them. "It's getting late," he finally said. "I thought this would be a good time for me to show you some more of Whispering Pines. Are you interested enough to want to come with me?"

Diamond knew she should turn down his invitation and stay put. Being alone with Jacob was the last thing she needed, but unfortunately it was everything she wanted. She would be returning to the cabin at the end of the day while he and his men continued to drive the herd to the high pastures, a process that could take three to four days to do. The thought of not seeing him for that length of time bothered her. She wanted to spend every chance she got with him.

"I'd love to go with you, Jacob. It'll only take a minute for me to get my horse."

"We can both ride mine."

She frowned, not sure that was such a good idea, but when he reached his hand down to her, without hesitation she placed hers in his. She took a deep steadying breath when he leaned over, reached down with big strong arms and pulled her up into the saddle behind him. She placed her arms around his waist to hold on.

He glanced back over his shoulder. "All set?"

"Yes."

"Okay then, let's go." Setting off at a steady clip, he trotted his horse toward the mountains.

Jake was losing what little control he had. Diamond was holding firmly on to him. With each and every powerful movement his horse made as it galloped up the path, her body rubbed against his. He could feel the softness of her breasts brushing against his back, and the feel of her soft feminine thighs cradling his own as she held on to him around the waist. Neither of them said anything as they rode farther and farther away from camp and deeper and deeper away from the ranch.

When Jake finally brought his horse to a stop sometime later, Diamond glanced around. It was a very secluded place. A little creek ran the length of an area covered by a thicket of pine trees. They had stopped under a huge canopy of thick branches. There were wildflowers and an abundance of bluebonnets everywhere. The place, she could tell, was a private one, some sort of secret hideaway.

"I discovered this place as a kid and still come here whenever I have a lot on my mind and want to think about something," he said as if reading her thoughts, as he slid off the horse. "It's still my own special private place."

When he stood on the ground, he reached his hands up to her. She braced her hands on his shoulders and slid down into his arms. Midway they faced each other before he slowly and carefully lowered her to the ground. When her feet touched the hard earth, she dropped her hands from his shoulders. But he made no effort to remove his hands from her waist.

"You can let me go now, Jacob," she said in a velvety voice.

A hard sheen of wanting and desire glittered in Jake's eyes. "No, I don't think so, Diamond. I really don't believe that I can," he murmured softly as he leaned closer to her. "At least not now," he breathed thickly against her mouth before his lips covered hers.

Diamond wanted this kiss as much as Jake did and didn't pretend otherwise. She forgot about the decision they had made just last night. She couldn't think of anything but the taste of his tongue as it probed her mouth, filling it, torturing it, loving it. He deepened his embrace, crushing her until the feel of her breasts against his chest fueled the desire that tore at them and drove them to partake in this intoxicating moment. She was only mildly aware of him sweeping her into his arms.

She was too conscious of the way he was still kissing her to notice or to care where he was taking her. All she could think about was the feel of his mouth on hers and the feel of his strong, muscled arms holding her. For reasons she could not understand, she was experiencing more emotions with this man than she had with any other man, including Samuel. No other person had ever made her feel this way, wanton and unresisting.

She felt the warm clovers beneath her back when Jake laid her down on a soft bed of green grass. Lowering his body next to hers, his mouth slid down her skin, tasting her soft flesh. Her breath caught at the feel of his warm tongue touching the tender skin underneath her ear.

"Jacob."

As far as Diamond was concerned, there was no reality for the moment. She didn't want to think about the fact she had met Jacob Madaris only a week ago. She didn't want to remember that in two weeks she would be leaving this place and a continued relationship with him was not possible. She didn't want to dwell on the fact that she was not a person who made a practice of engaging in casual affairs. Regardless of how the media painted her, she had never been a woman with loose morals. But right now the only thing she wanted to think about was the fact that Jacob Madaris was seducing her in a way she had never been seduced before.

Right now was all that mattered because deep down in her heart, as strange as it seemed, and as much as she didn't want it to be true, she had fallen head over heels in love with Jacob Madaris.

Diamond's responses to his caresses were everything Jake hoped for. He had tried ignoring her, avoiding her and not wanting her. But each and every time he had looked at her, he had felt that hard quickening in his loins. Although he knew there could be no future for them, he had failed to get his mind to communicate that conclusion to his body. He had felt a pull at him that wanted to join his body to hers, to mate with her. With a groan he broke off the kiss and buried his face in her hair, twirling the soft strands around his fingers.

"I want you. I don't understand why it's like this between us. I can't figure it out. I won't figure it out. Tell me to stop, and I'll walk away."

Diamond looked at him, seeing the same flame of fire in his eyes that was in hers. "I can't tell you to stop, Jacob, because I want this to happen as much as you do. I want you, too." She wouldn't say she didn't understand it because she did. For her this was love.

Jake leaned down and his mouth devoured hers, hungrily, heatedly. Without breaking the kiss, with trembling hands he began removing her shirt. She let out a sensuous moan when his hands cupped her breasts and he leaned down and kissed them.

A delicious daze transcended her body when he began removing her jeans, his strong arms pulling them down past her hips. And when he had her fully unclothed before him, he proceeded to remove his own clothing.

She heard the sound of him ripping open a condom packet. Then a few moments later, with a deep, guttural moan of anticipation he kissed her again as his body covered hers.

With a soft growl of need and one smooth motion, he entered her at the same time that he intensified their kiss. The sweetest of passion, the hottest of desire tore between them as they became wrapped up in the torrid, fiery mating of their bodies. He established a rhythm for them, slow, fast, then slow again. He wanted to savor each and every moment inside her.

Diamond released a small cry of pleasure as every stroke of Jake's body into hers fed a fierce hunger she'd developed only since meeting him. It flamed a resplendent fire that blazed to life only whenever he touched her. Her body was intoxicated with the pleasure he was giving her as he took his time and made love to her in a way she had never been made love to before, outdoors under the shafts of fading sunlight.

Jake broke off the kiss and looked down at her. Her eyes were half-closed, drowsy with desire as he made love to her, moving in and out of her body, making her his in this elemental and primitive way, and on a parcel of land he considered as his private domain. He wanted to please her in a way that he had never before pleased another woman. He was making love to her under the big blue Texas sky on the land he loved. Wanting more of her, he slipped his hands under her hips to lift her to him, locking their bodies even closer together. "Look at me," he whispered hotly. And she did, meeting his gaze while he made love to her.

When he felt her body spiraling to gratification beneath his, he felt that same sense of pending ecstatic culmination as raw, pulsating pleasure overtook him. He kissed her more deeply as they both became victims of the greatest pleasure of all, one of mind-shattering, uncontrolled passion. Their cries of pleasure became the only sounds that could be heard as their needs exploded into complete and total fulfillment.

Moments later Diamond drifted hazily back down to earth, fully aware of Jake's hands still touching her as he held her in his arms. "Please don't say you're sorry," she whispered silkily, burrowing her head against his shoulder.

Jake lifted her chin and met her gaze. Still half-dazed by what they had done, how they had done it and where they had done it, he looked at her. He had wanted her from the moment he had first laid eyes on her, when she had walked off Sterling's plane onto his land. Every curve of her body had made him want to get inside her, and her smile had made him want to kiss her hard, long and deep. She was able to bring out a side of him that was uncontrolled, intense, consuming. No woman had ever done that before.

For some reason that he couldn't explain to himself, never before had anything felt so right when it should have been all wrong. He should not be feeling such a sense of being overwhelmed, such a sense of captivation for this woman. But he did. She was the first woman he had ever made love to in his special private place.

He leaned up and looked down at her. "The only thing I'm sorry about is the fact that we have only two weeks left to be together," he said before devouring her mouth again.

Chapter 9

Jake and Diamond returned to the cabin just before dark. Their bodies were tired but totally satiated. They had remained in Jake's private place, making love over and over again, and each time they had wanted each other that much more. But making love had not been all they had done. They had talked.

She had told him of her strained relationship with her father, her less than amiable parting of the ways with her ex-husband and her special friendship with Sterling. She had explained how she and Sterling had decided to take advantage of the rumor Samuel had started and feed the media's frenzy that they were having an affair. That way men wouldn't try coming on to her, and women—the less than brazen ones—would assume Sterling was spoken for. That worked out fine since neither of them wanted a serious relationship with anyone.

Jake in turn told her about his childhood growing up on Whispering Pines, and about the five older brothers he loved and respected. He talked to her about the brother who had gotten killed in Vietnam over thirty years ago, leaving a wife and two-year-old daughter behind. He had spoken of his love and affection for his nieces and nephews and that three of his nephews, Justin, Dex and Clayton, were so close to him in age that oftentimes people assumed the four of them were brothers.

As they stepped into the cabin and closed the door behind them, Jake pulled Diamond into his arms. He had to leave and return to camp. The men would be spending the next three to four nights on the range to continue moving the herd and as was customary, he would be with them. But now, the only thing he wanted was to take a hot shower and go to bed—with Diamond.

He didn't want to think of the mistake he was making, knowing there could never be anything between them but these stolen moments. Their worlds were as different as day and night, but while she was here in his world he wanted to be with her.

He refused to compare her with his ex-wife any longer. Jessie had been spoiled, selfish and self-centered. Diamond was different. She was thoughtful, kind and considerate. She was everything that was good and decent. And she didn't hate ranching and cowboys like Jessie had. She respected both, and he appreciated her for it. But he knew he could not even think about them sharing anything beyond two more weeks.

"I have to leave, Diamond, to go back."

"Yes, I know and I understand," she said, unwrapping her arms from around his waist.

Jake thought for a moment. Yes, she would understand. She was that type of woman. "What are your plans while I'm gone?" he asked her, wondering if she would be doing any more baking to pass the time away.

Diamond didn't say anything for a long while as she looked up at him. Finally she said, "I'll keep busy until you come back and make love to me again."

Her words combined with the warmth of her smile nearly made him lose control all over again. He gently pulled her back into his arms. "Are you trying to make it hard for me to leave you?" he asked, placing a kiss on her temple.

Her smile widened against his shoulder. "You asked me what I'd be doing, didn't you?"

Yes, he thought, he had asked her, and one thing he had discovered about Diamond was that she was straightforward and open with her answers.

He leaned down and kissed her lips. "Come walk me out."

She walked him out onto the porch and watched as he mounted his horse. After he'd gotten settled, he sat with his hands folded on his saddle horn and looked down at her.

"Good night, Diamond. Pleasant dreams."

She smiled saucily. "And they will be, Jacob, since they'll be all about you."

He grinned before urging his horse on. He told himself to keep riding and not look back, and he'd almost done just that until he had gotten to the top of the valley. Then he couldn't help himself and glanced back anyway. Diamond was still standing there, looking at him. Jake stopped his horse. He turned around and began galloping back down the path at a swift speed.

Diamond saw him coming back and wondered why he was returning. She stepped off the porch into the yard, not afraid that his horse would trample her. One thing she knew for certain was the fact that he was an expert horseman. Coming alongside of her, he reached down and captured her in his arms and swung her up in the saddle in front of him.

Jake captured the startled surprise off her lips, kissing her long, deep and hard. Then he quickly released her and placed her back down on her feet before turning and galloping off again. This time he didn't look back.

"Wow!" was the only word Diamond could say at the moment. She just stood there until horse and rider were no longer in sight. It was another minute longer before she turned and went into the cabin.

Once inside she released a deep sigh as she replayed in her mind the scene that had just taken place. She touched her lips and felt heat surge through her body. She also felt something else…aches.

She couldn't remember the last time her body had ached so much. Her thighs and backside were killing her. But these aches were special aches. She had never been happier to have aches that resulted from making love to the man she loved.

Sighing again, her thoughts slid back to all the activities she had been a part of that day. The time spent on the range and with Jacob. She shivered at the memory of how he had made love to her with such tenderness. The physical pleasure they had shared took her breath away just thinking about it. She would have those memories until he returned.

She refused to face reality just yet. She didn't want to think about the fact that her days at Whispering Pines were numbered. Even if he did want to continue seeing her after she left, she would go against it. He was a private person, and Whispering Pines was his private haven. Right now he had the freedom of coming and going whenever he felt like it without the worry of being photographed constantly or having a microphone shoved in his face. If the media got wind that he was her new love interest they would never leave him or Whispering Pines alone. His every move would be watched, chronicled and reported. Pesky reporters would camp outside the borders of his land, the snooping paparazzi would fly helicopters overhead and the tabloids would offer money to anyone willing to divulge any kind of scoop on Jacob and his family, as well. They wouldn't stop with the present, they would also dig into his past. And even worse, if they couldn't find anything they thought would be interesting to print, they would go to the extreme and make up something. Their goal was to sell magazines and newspapers. In doing so, Jacob's life would become an open book, and she refused to let that happen to him. She loved him too much for that.

Knowing what would happen, she knew what she had to do. She would cherish the time she would spend with him on the land he loved and when she left to return to her other life, she would have her memories and there would be no regrets.

With a determined and made-up mind, she headed for the bathroom to take the long, hot bath she so desperately needed.

"Blaylock to Diamond. Blaylock to Diamond. Are you with me?"

Diamond's attention was pulled back to the older man sitting across from her as they peeled a huge basket of apples for the jars of fruit preserves he planned to make. "I am now," she said, smiling over at him. She wouldn't tell him that her thoughts had been on Jacob, but she had a feeling he probably knew it already.

It had been five days since he and his men had left. What had started out as a three- to four-night trip had turned into six due to a heavy downpour of rain the day before. Blaylock had explained that when the rains came, an alternative route to the high pastures had to be taken, which would cost them another day or so. That had been the last thing she had wanted to hear. She was missing him something fierce.

Blaylock had been kind enough to pick her up from the cabin each morning to bring her to the ranch. He claimed with everyone gone, he was dying of loneliness. The time she had spent with him had been special. She had enjoyed listening to him as he recounted his former days on the rodeo circuit.

She smiled when she remembered the day that one of Jacob's neighbors had unexpectedly dropped by. She'd had to hide out inside the ranch house a full three hours until he had left. But hiding out in the ranch house had been fun. Jacob had a beautiful home, and she had given herself a complete tour of the place. All the rooms she had found to be enormous as well as immaculate.

When she had reached the second floor, she had known the moment she entered Jacob's room. It was everything she had expected it to be. A fireplace covered one wall, and his bed was bigger than king-size. The huge room was tastefully decorated and looked quite comfortable. Maybe that was the reason she had decided to get in his bed and take a nap that day. She had been totally embarrassed when Blaylock found her there sometime later. The older man had been dropping hints of something going on between her and Jacob ever since. She had neither admitted nor denied anything.

"What were you asking me, Blaylock, before I became distracted?"

He smiled at her like he had known just where her thoughts had been. "I asked how do you like the cabin?"

"I like it. I can't believe Jacob built it, but he's never spent a night there."

Blaylock frowned as he stood and walked over to the stove. "He has his reasons. That cabin holds some painful memories for the boy."

Diamond looked a little puzzled. "In what way?"

Blaylock turned from the pot on the stove. "That house was a present for his wife. When they married they had moved into the old house with Jake's mama. It was supposed to be a temporary arrangement. It's my understanding Jake's wife thought living on the ranch was going to be a temporary thing altogether. She thought once they were married she could convince Jake to give up ranching and move back to Boston and work at her father's bank."

A picture of Jacob in a business suit and carrying a briefcase formed in Diamond's mind. She slowly shook her head. "I can't imagine Jacob being anything but a rancher."

"Anyone who really knows the boy wouldn't be able to see it either. Don't get me wrong now, Jake's got brains. He's smart when it comes to that financial stuff and has made a bunch of money over the years with investments. He knows how to play the stock market like nobody's business. If anything, that's his second passion. He even got the men around here investing their money, and it pays off real nicelike for them. Why, I even got me some hefty stock in several profitable corportations thanks to Jake. And he acts as a financial advisor for others including his family and your friends Sterling Hamilton and Kyle Garwood."

Blaylock poured a cup of coffee as he continued. "But ranching is Jake's first love. Yep. That's the way it is for him, and that's the way it'll stay. He can wine and dine with the best of them city folks if he has to, but he prefers a bunkhouse to an opera house any day."

Diamond nodded. Of all the things she and Jacob had talked about that afternoon they had spent alone at his private place, his ex-wife had not been one of them. "Did you know her? His ex-wife?"

Blaylock shook his head as he came back over to the table and sat down. "No, she was before my time. But I heard from his ma that she gave the boy a hard time of it, though. That was a pure shame since he truly did love her and all. She hated it here and didn't care who knew it. Jake went out of his way to make things nice for her here, but she didn't care. She was a real city gal who enjoyed going to parties, the opera, sleek restaurants, those sorts of things. Jake's just the opposite. He feels if it's not here on Whispering Pines, he doesn't need it."

Diamond thought about all the things that Blaylock was saying. A woman who truly loved a man would not ask him to give up any of the things he loved for her. Knowing what he had gone through made her even more determined that there could never be anything more between them than what they would share before she left. Her life was filled with movie premiers, jetting all over the country and the latest fashions—none of the things he would ever be interested in. In a little over a week, she would be gone and that would be the end of it. She would never pressure him to disrupt his calm lifestyle for her chaotic one.

Diamond got up and walked over to the sink. She glanced out of the window. "Do you think the men will be returning tonight?"

Blaylock nodded. "If not tonight, it'll be early morning." He turned around in his chair and gazed thoughtfully at her before asking, "Do you want to hang around here tonight and wait for Jake?"

She couldn't help but smile. She hadn't fooled the old-timer one bit. "No, that's okay. I'm sure he'll be too tired when he gets in for company. I'll go back to the cabin."

Blaylock chuckled. "I bet no matter how tired the boy is when he gets here, he'll be glad to see you. Jake Madaris ain't no fool."

* * *

It was near sunset when Blaylock returned Diamond to the cabin. Her earlier conversations with the man were still clearly in her mind. During the ride back, so many things were being debated inside of her all at once. First of all, she reminded herself, she was probably jumping the gun to think Jake had feelings for her. Just because they had made love didn't necessarily mean anything. She was old enough to know that people slept together all the time with no special meaning other than the pleasure they would get out of it. Jake had not told her that he had any special feelings for her, so all her worry about leaving could be for nothing. The time they were spending together could very well be a casual affair to him and nothing more. If that was the case, she didn't have to stress herself out about him not wanting whatever they were sharing now to end. There was a possibility he would expect it to.

By the time Diamond had finished her shower and curled up in a chair to try and read at least a chapter from a book she'd borrowed from Jake's study, she knew she loved Jake no matter how he felt about her. And no matter what, she would never ask him to choose between a life with her or the ranch. The ranch would always come first. She would see to it.

Chapter 10

Jake had been back at the ranch less than five minutes and already he was in his room, preparing to take a hot shower. The five days spent on the range had been hard ones, and the torrential downpour that hit a few days ago hadn't helped matters.

As usual, he was proud of his men and the fine work they'd done. They had gone above and beyond in displaying their skills as cowhands. Working together, they had successfully moved the entire herd of cattle to the high pastures. There had been no injuries and no flare-up of tempers.

His days had been busy from sunup to sunset. It was only at night after he settled into his sleeping bag that his mind became filled with thoughts of Diamond. There was nothing about her that he didn't think about or remember. Whether it was the way she held her head whenever she smiled, or the way she had stood so tall and so beautiful on the porch that afternoon, which had made him turn his horse around to give her that last parting kiss.

Thoughts of them making love had heated his body during the cool nights, and the fiery flame of the campfire had reminded him of the one afternoon their passions had blazed out of control. Every thought of her had been personal and intimate and had helped him through the exhausting days of the cattle drive.

He wanted to see her and didn't want to wait until tomorrow to do so. The need to hold her in his arms had driven him in a mad race for home. As soon as he could take a shower and get back into some clothes again, he would go to her. He didn't want to question this obsession with seeing her tonight. He would chalk it up to the fact that she was a lover unlike any he'd ever known.

He was about to unbutton his shirt when a knock sounded at his bedroom door. "Come in."

Blaylock walked in and handed him a large tube of liniment. "I thought you could use this."

The right side of Jake's mouth curled into a smile. "Thanks, old man," he said, taking the tube and placing it on his dresser. "I knew I was keeping you around for something." He went back to unbuttoning his shirt.

"Her scent is still in here," Blaylock said casually.

Without bothering to look up from what he was doing, Jake asked, "Whose?"

"Diamond's."

Jake's head snapped up sharply. He frowned, then took a raspy breath. "Diamond? She was here? In this room?"

"Yep," the older man replied, smiling. "Reed Duncan dropped by unexpectedly. Diamond was here that day and went upstairs to wait out his visit. Reed ended up staying a spell, and the next thing you know three hours had passed. After he left I came upstairs looking for Diamond and found her there sound asleep."

"In my bed?" Jake asked. When he had first entered his bedroom, he'd thought he had picked up Diamond's scent but assumed he'd imagined it.

Blaylock leaned against the wall and crossed his arms over his chest. "Yep, imagine that." He stared long and hard at Jake. "And she was sleeping in it like it was a natural place for her to be. If I didn't know better, I'd swear she'd been in that bed before, but I know that can't be the case. But the way she was curled under those covers with so much familiarity, one would think that she had."

Blaylock paused a second before asking, "Now isn't that odd?"

Jake swallowed as he glanced from the older man to the bed. The picture of Diamond in his bed started a fire burning deep within him. He would've given anything to have been in that bed with her. He drew a long ragged breath. "Yeah, I guess so."

"And you know what they say about a woman finding her way to a man's bed."

Jake raised his head slightly. He lifted his chin. "No, what do they say?"

"Some claim that once a woman finds her way to a man's bed, it's hard as heck to get her out of there. The problem is that they go straight from the bed and into his head. And once a woman finds her way into a man's head, he can't seem to think of anything else but her." Blaylock straightened his form. "You planning on going out tonight?"

Jake frowned as he looked at the older man. "Yeah, I thought about it. Why?"

"No reason. Just asking." Blaylock crossed his arms over his ample belly. "I tried to get Diamond to wait here for you this evening, but she figured you'd be too tired for company. Would you have been too tired to see Diamond, Jake?"

Jake really didn't like where this conversation was headed but he answered truthfully anyway. "No, not in this lifetime."

"I didn't think so," Blaylock said simply before turning and walking back out of the room.

Jake was in such a hurry to finish undressing that he didn't notice Blaylock's smug smile.

The Jeep's tires rumbled over a dip in the graveled road, making Jake tighten his grip on the steering wheel to retain control of the vehicle. "Whoa, slow down before you kill yourself," he mumbled to himself. He was a half mile from the cabin when he eased his foot off the gas pedal and slowed down.

He took a deep breath, wondering why he was driving so recklessly in his mad rush to get to the cabin. He knew the answer without really thinking about it. Ever since Blaylock had told him that Diamond had taken a nap in his bed, he hadn't been able to think of anything else. In his mind, he could see her under the covers but she wasn't asleep and she wasn't curled up either. He could see her awake with her body stretched out and ready to receive his.

Jake swore under his breath. If he didn't get himself together, he would lose control of his mind as well as his vehicle. This thing with Diamond was going to be the death of him if he didn't put it in perspective. He rubbed his chin with his fingers, feeling the stubble there. For Pete's sake! He hadn't even taken the time to shave. Blaylock was right. Once a woman got into a man's head, he couldn't think of anything else.

His heartbeat increased when he saw the cabin in the distance, and the first thing he noticed was that the lights were on, which meant Diamond hadn't gone to bed yet. He could feel his pulse race, and a sweet-hot ache of desire coiled deep within the pit of his stomach. His fingers that clutched the steering wheel tightened and felt damp.

Jake couldn't help but wonder why he was going through these changes with a woman. After all, the only thing the two of them had shared that afternoon six days ago was hot, delicious sex, nothing else. He knew not to even think of anything more. Years ago another woman had made it very clear that when it came to ranch life, highbred sophisticated ladies couldn't hang for the long haul.

After he brought the Jeep to a stop in front of the cabin and got out, he stood around for a few minutes before walking up to the door. Despite the old bitter memories that were trying to resurface tonight, Jake had a feeling that once he crossed over that threshold and came back out later he would not be the same. For once he had to be honest with himself and admit that despite everything, he was hopelessly in danger of falling hard for a woman. But he was just as determined not to let that happen.

* * *

At first Diamond thought she was hearing things but then realized that wasn't the case when another knock sounded at the door. Her heartbeat accelerated at the thought that her late-night visitor could only be Jacob. She took a deep breath and let it out slowly as she walked over to the door.

"Who is it?"

"Jake."

It seemed that her entire body suddenly became ultrasensitive to the sound of his voice. Diamond's hands trembled, and whispers of nervousness vibrated through every part of her body as she undid the latch and opened the door.

She could barely catch her breath when she saw him standing silhouetted under the dim light on the porch. For a long time, she stayed perfectly still and just looked at him, realizing how much she had missed him during the last five days.

Diamond wasn't the only one mesmerized. Jake suddenly was hit with a strange disoriented feeling when he saw Diamond, thinking she was even more beautiful than he last remembered. He tried not to notice how perfect her body looked dressed in a short silk nightshirt, or the look of her glossy hair that was spread sensuously around her shoulders. He tried to ignore the scent of her that was like an aphrodisiac. The fragrance gave him one huge galloping high as blood rushed fiercely to his brain, destroying any sane thoughts he may have had when he'd first arrived.

He smiled, and her responsive smile was automatic. She still had that smile, he thought. It was the one that made him want to kiss it right off her lips. His pulse began escalating from the way his thoughts were going.

"So, how have you been?" he asked in an attempt to break the awkward silence surrounding them. He didn't know about hers, but his heart was beating in overdrive. The part of him that was trying hard to dominate was instinctively male.

"Fine. What about you?" Diamond asked, noting her voice was a little shaky. As far as she was concerned the man standing before her represented the essence of everything male, starting with the Stetson covering his head, down past the whiskered roughness of his chin to the boots he wore on his feet and the snug-fitting jeans in between. He was the epitome of man.

Jake crossed his arms over his chest and casually leaned against the door's opening, nearly taking up the entire space. "If you must know, ma'am," he drawled, still watching her closely, "I haven't been doing so hot. But thanks for asking."

Diamond's smile widened as she remembered another time he had said those very words to her. "Would you like to come in, Jacob?"

He looked at her. "That would be nice."

It would be more than nice, Diamond thought as she stepped aside to let him enter. It would be downright pleasurable.

As soon as he was inside the cabin he turned to her. "I missed you," he said slowly, dispensing with small talk. He reached out and captured her face in the palm of his hand. "And I want you. There's this chemistry between us, this heat. It's been there from the first. Feel it?"

Diamond nodded, acknowledging his words to be true.

"It makes me want to taste you every chance I get and want to be inside of you every chance I can."

Diamond was unprepared for the shiver of pure pleasure that ran through her with his words. Looking up into his face, her fingers shook as she reached up and took the Stetson from his head and placed it on hers. Removing the hat exposed his eyes, dark, intense and filled with red-hot desire.

Jake glanced up at his Stetson on Diamond's head. His hat had always been his private and personal possession. It was something he didn't share. It was a part of who he was and what he represented. From the time he was a kid he'd been told that a cowboy's boots and hat were an ingrained part of his being, his inner person. They were the very core of what a cowboy represented—ruggedness, able-bodiedness and strength. In earlier days, it was an honor for a cowboy to die with his boots and hat on. For the first time, he not only felt those same things about his hat, but also shared those same feelings with a woman. This woman. What he was sharing with Diamond was private and personal. And tonight for a little while, she would be his to possess and not to be shared.

He leaned down and covered her mouth with his, claiming her, possessing her. As expected, the desire that sparkled between them blazed into a flame with the intimacy of their kiss.

Diamond tasted all the things on Jake's tongue that she felt—hunger, longing, heat. Her arms around his waist tightened. She never wanted to let him go and wondered how she would when the time came.

The kiss deepened. Who initiated that move, neither Jake nor Diamond was sure, they just rolled with it, fueling a hungry greed within them. Jake picked her up in his arms and carried her down the hall into the bedroom. It was a room he had built but had given one of his sisters-in-law the chore of furnishing. He placed Diamond in the center of the bed, following her down and reclaiming her lips.

The same heat and fire that had blazed out of control and had driven them to a mad, fast and satisfying mating once before took over, as Jake quickly removed all of their clothing.

Jake moved fast, placing her body under his, then gripping her hips in his hands as he entered her, catching the moans escaping her throat with his mouth. As before they were one, meshed in heart, body and soul. Their blissful sighs were the only sounds in the room before exquisite ecstasy tore through them, exploding upon them, making them scream out their fulfillment. Then they drifted through all the wondrous sensations that followed.

Later, as Diamond lay wrapped in Jake's arms, sighing in contentment, their bodies still connected, she silently asked herself: When the time came, how was she going to walk away from him without looking back?

Chapter 11

The ringing of the telephone jolted Jake awake. He didn't move for a moment, and then sighing heavily he reached for the phone on the table next to the bed. Diamond shifted in sleep and moved closer into his arms.

"Yeah?"

"Jake? Sorry, man. My mistake. Thought I was calling the cabin and not the ranch house. Catch you later."

Jake was about to tell Sterling that he had not made a mistake when a click sounded in his ear. Knowing Sterling would be calling right back, he depressed the hook and continued to hold the phone in his hand. When it rang he answered immediately, not wanting the intrusive noise to wake Diamond.

"Yeah, Sterling."

"Jake? How the devil did I get you again? I was trying to reach Diamond at the cabin. Are the lines crossed up or something?"

"No, the lines aren't crossed," Jake responded as he rubbed his whiskered chin, thinking he definitely needed a shave, and hoping that his unshaven skin had not left any marks on Diamond's body when he'd kissed it all over.

"You're at the cabin?"

Jake sank back into the pillows. "Yeah." He stared up at the ceiling, knowing more questions were coming.

"Isn't it kind of late, Jake?"

Jake yawned, fighting off sleep. "I would think so, Sterling."

"Then what are you doing at the cabin?"

Jake frowned. "I *was* asleep until you woke me up."

There was a pause. "You're sleeping at the cabin?"

"I *was.*"

"Where the hell is Diamond?"

Jake glanced down at the woman in his arms, who was snuggled tight against him. He smiled, recalling their night spent together making love. Just like the last time, the experience had been explosive. Her responses to him had been passionate, wild, tempestuous. Holding the phone securely in his hand, he leaned slightly toward her and placed a kiss on her closed eyelids. She looked even more beautiful asleep. He straightened up his form and leaned back against the pillows again.

"She's asleep."

"Asleep? Damn it, Jake. What's going on there?

Why are you at the cabin with Diamond this time of night? And why aren't you sleeping in your own bed back at the ranch house?"

Jake rolled his eyes upward. "Hamilton, I suggest that you think through those questions real good, then call me back later when you come up with your own answers." He felt Diamond stir in his arms. "But make it much later, will ya?"

Jake dropped the phone back in place, thought better of it then took it off the receiver. He relaxed and settled back into a comfortable position in the bed and pulled Diamond closer into his arms. The pleasant memories of making love to her lulled him back into a deep sleep.

Diamond opened her eyes and blinked several times upon realizing that it was morning. A ray of sunshine streaked across the room and hit her dead center in the eyes, almost blinding her. To escape the bothersome beam of light, she rolled over and fitted her face into the V of Jake's neck. She felt his arm around her tighten and forced herself to raise her head. "Good morning, Jacob."

Instead of responding, he leaned down and kissed her. His kiss brought back memories of the night before when he had made love to her with such an intensity, she'd been sure she would die from it. But she had lived. She had somehow survived every thrilling and fulfilling moment. The heat of Jacob's passion had seared through her, sending her over the edge more than once, more than twice and driving her crazy with a need only he could satisfy.

And satisfy her he did.

Even kissing her the way he was doing now was making her body ache. His tongue was stroking hers, intimately, greedily and possessively. This was definitely one form of nonverbal communication she enjoyed sharing with him. She kissed him back hungrily, fervently.

Jake finally broke the kiss to draw in a deep, ragged breath. He held her tight, enjoying the way she felt in his arms.

"Jacob?" she whispered finally, with barely enough breath to get his name out.

"Hmm?" he responded, nuzzling her neck.

"What about the ranch?"

Lifting his head, he looked down at her, his gaze holding hers in place. Lines of confusion shadowed his forehead. "What about the ranch?"

"Don't you have chores to do? It's morning time." Blaylock had told her this past week how Jacob got up each morning around four to began his full day of work on the ranch. "Blaylock said you get up before dawn every day to take care of the ranch."

He nodded, understanding. "Normally I do, but after a cattle drive I give both my men and myself a few days off to relax." He smiled. "You're not trying to get rid of me, are you?"

"No, I just didn't want to keep you from taking care of the ranch."

She went silent on him after saying that. Her eyes were cast down so he couldn't read her thoughts. But he definitely knew what his own were. For whatever reason, she was letting him know that she would not try to compete with his duties at the ranch, which was something his ex-wife had done constantly. Somehow

Diamond knew, understood and accepted that his ranch was important to him. He drew her to him and put his index finger beneath her chin.

"At the risk of sounding slightly arrogant, and maybe a little cocky, I think I can do a pretty decent job of taking care of both you and the ranch. Besides, when it comes to taking care of you, you make the job easy. You're in a class by yourself. A very beautiful and desirable class."

Diamond smiled. "You're quite a charmer, Jacob Madaris."

He grinned. "I'm also pretty good at making breakfast. Hungry?"

She nodded her head and laughed. "Very."

"So," Jake said as he poured more coffee into Diamond's mug. "What do you think of my cooking abilities?" He leaned back in his chair and took a sip of his own coffee.

Diamond set her elbows on the kitchen table, cupped her face in her hands and smiled at him. "I think your cooking skills rank right up there with your lovemaking skills. Both are superb."

The images of her words elicited sensuous memories in Jake's mind. Before he had left the bed to fix breakfast, they had made love again. Afterward, it had been a determined effort to get out of bed and not make love to her yet again. He could feel his blood pressure rising from just thinking about it.

"I do have a few things to take care of at the ranch, but then afterward I'll be free for the rest of the day. How would you like to spend the day with me?"

Diamond arched an eyebrow. "Is that a sneaky way of getting me to help you with your chores, Jacob?"

Jake chuckled as he pushed his chair out from the table. "You're too smart. I didn't think you'd figure that part out until much later."

"Oh, Jacob, he's such a beauty," Diamond said as she gently stroked the four-day-old calf's smooth hide. After breakfast she had returned to the ranch with Jake and upon entering the barn she had immediately seen the animal. It was standing in the same stall as its mother, trying to retain its equilibrium while glancing around the barn as if trying to sort out everything in its newborn mind.

Jake, who was busy spreading hay around the stall, stopped what he was doing and looked at the calf thoughtfully. "Yeah, he's a beauty all right. In a couple of years, he'll be a real nice piece of T-bone on someone's dinner plate."

Diamond gasped. "Jacob!"

Jake shook his head, grinning at the shocked look on Diamond's face. "You look surprised. I run this ranch for the sole purpose of raising the highest-quality Texas Longhorn cattle for the buying public. I'm sure you've appreciated a good steak every now and then."

Diamond stared down at the calf, then back up at Jacob. "But he's so precious, Jacob. He's just a baby. How can you even think of him being a part of anyone's menu?" She looked back down at the calf.

The smile vanished from Jake's face when he became fully aware that the knowledge of what would eventually become the calf's fate bothered Diamond. He dared not tell her that sometime next week his men would take a hot iron to the critter and place Whispering Pines's brand on the animal's rump. She would probably see it as unnecessary torture to the poor beast.

He placed the pitchfork aside and walked over to her. Catching her chin, he urged her to meet his gaze. "I'm a rancher, sweetheart. I run a business here at Whispering Pines," he said, trying to get her to understand. "The day I begin feeling sentimental about my breeding stock is the day I stop being a rancher and become a pet shop owner."

"I know you're right, Jacob. I guess I'm making a big deal out of things."

"Only because you're a caring person." A sense of admiration flowed through Jake for her. Although sentimentality was the last thing needed on a cattle ranch, he understood. He'd had to deal with those same feelings from one of his nieces. When Christy had turned ten, she had adopted one of the calves for a pet and named him Shadow. She had carried on something awful when she'd discovered the animal's fate some years later. To keep his niece from going into early cardiac arrest, he'd let her keep the blasted animal. Now Christy was in her third year of college, and Shadow was still alive and enjoying life. Even today, as far as Christy was concerned, Shadow belonged to her.

He pulled Diamond closer. "It's past lunchtime. How about going on a picnic? It shouldn't take Blaylock long to throw something together in a basket for us. How does that sound?"

Diamond's smile returned. "Wonderful."

"Are you sure?" Diamond asked as she gave a searching glance around the creek. Although the creek was surrounded by heavily wooded green lands, she wasn't sure it would be safe for her and Jacob to go swimming. At least not the way he wanted them to.

Jake laughed. "I'm positive. This area is just as private as my secret hideaway." He saw her flushed face at the mention of his hideaway. He knew the memories were just as vivid for her as they were for him.

"Okay, let's plan to go swimming another day. How about if we just continue to relax here on the blanket and talk off lunch. I think Blaylock outdid himself, don't you?"

Diamond bit her lower lip to hide her grin as she lay back down on the blanket next to Jake. Blaylock had packed fried chicken, rolls, a container of potato salad, coleslaw and a couple of large red apples in the basket. And they had consumed all of it.

"Yes. I'm going to have to go on some sort of weight-loss program when I get back to California," Diamond said, rubbing her stomach.

Jake turned his head and looked at her. Thankfully she had closed her eyes. He was grateful she hadn't seen the sudden jolt that passed through his body at the reminder that in a week, she would be leaving. For some reason, that was the last thing he wanted to think about.

"Tell me about your life as a movie actress," he said calmly, forcing his feelings of regret aside. He watched her eyes open as she stared up at the sky. She lifted the corners of her mouth, but for some reason the movement did not come across to him as a smile.

"Acting is one of the things I can truly say I'm pretty good at. Having Jack Swain as a father made it so. I had no choice in the matter."

Jake watched as she took a deep breath and began chewing on her lower lip. He stared at her for a moment before asking, "Why do you feel that way?"

Diamond angled her head to look over at him. "Because I was his daughter, his only child. That made the expectations high," she said softly. "Early on, everything I did was done to please my father. Carrying the Swain name wasn't an easy task. It still isn't. I try not to worry about pleasing my father since it seems I never can. There's never a performance where I'm good enough for him. As far as he's concerned, my acting can always be improved."

Diamond sighed. "It used to really bother me that he felt that way. Now I try not to think about it. Over the years, I've tried focusing on pleasing me and believing that I'm good at what I do. Hollywood is finally recognizing and respecting me not because I'm Jack Swain's daughter but because I'm a really good actress. But it's taken me a long time to reach that point."

She turned and looked back up at the sky. "So I guess my life as a movie actress has been a lot of hard work, but it's enjoyable work that I love doing. It's going through script after script after script trying to find the one that you feel is right for you, the one that will earn you an Oscar."

Jake remained silent for a few minutes before asking, "Is that what drives you? Your quest for an Oscar?"

Diamond shook her head. "I guess in a way it does, but that's no different from an athlete working sunup to sundown to one day go to the Olympics and win the gold. In every line of business there's this goal we're working hard to achieve, and a prize we'll get when we get there."

Diamond pulled herself up and sat cross-legged on the blanket. "Don't you agree, Jacob? Aren't you working each day from sunup to sundown to make your ranch the best it can be while seeking some material form of satisfaction and recognition for doing so?"

Jake looked at her solemnly, knowing she was right. For years he had worked hard to make Whispering Pines a success, and he had done so. He would be the first to admit he had enjoyed all the kudos, accolades and recognition he had garnered each year from the Texas Cattlemen Association for his hard work. Last year he had been selected nationally as Rancher of the Year. It was the highest honor he could have ever received in his profession.

"So winning the Oscar means everything to you?" he asked. For some reason, a part of him just had to ask.

Diamond nodded, not trusting herself to speak. She feared she would admit to him that until she had met him, she could answer that question with complete certainty. Until she had met him, making it to the top was the only thing she cared about it. But now...

"Then one day you will," Jake said, sitting up and lightly squeezing her shoulder. "I have all the faith in the world that you can and that you will do it."

Diamond fought back the tears that threatened to cloud her eyes. She swallowed, feeling at odds and not knowing what she really wanted anymore. "Thanks, Jacob," she whispered. He'd known her for only two weeks and he had more confidence in her abilities than her own father, who had known her all her life. Jack Swain was a perfectionist and he had expected no less of her.

She smoothed her hair back and glanced around, not wanting to think of her father any longer. "This is such a beautiful place. I don't think I've seen anyplace on Whispering Pines that doesn't leave me completely breathless. I'm really going to miss it here, Jacob."

He gazed at her. "Are you?" he asked, wanting desperately to believe that she would, and that she did care something for the land he loved.

"Yes," she replied. *And most assuredly I'm definitely going to miss you,* she wanted to say.

Jake reached out and traced a finger alongside her face. He felt her body tremble beneath his touch. He didn't want to think about her leaving. He refused to do that. For now, he wanted to think about kissing her, loving her and being an intimate part of her. He didn't want to think about why he was feeling that way, but the truth of the matter was that he was. He shook his head as if to clear it, but it didn't work. Leaning toward her, he captured her lips with his, searching for some way to exorcise her from his mind before she wiggled her way into his heart.

Jake and Diamond spent the next couple of days together at the cabin or riding the range of Whispering Pines land. The more she saw of it, the more she fell in love with it. Whenever he had to leave to take care of things at the ranch, she would go with him. With all the men gone, the ranch looked deserted. Blaylock had taken advantage of the men's short vacation to go and visit his sister, who lived in Waco.

The more time Jake and Diamond spent together and the more they got to know each other, the more their protective layers began peeling away. Both had

had what seemed like a lifetime of protecting themselves against hurt and pain.

Spending time with Jake also had its drawbacks for Diamond. The more times they were together, the more she was challenged to care more deeply for him and not to concern herself with making it to the top of her career. For the first time in a long time, she thought about having children and watching them grow under her and their father's watchful eyes. In her thoughts, that man, the father of her children, would always be Jacob.

Each and every time those thoughts surfaced, she would push them away. She knew she had to be realistic. Both of them had endured former marriages that had left a bad taste in their mouths. They had suffered pain that they were both still trying to get over and deal with.

And then there would be the prying eyes of the world that would be fed by the gossip-hungry tabloids. They would never have a normal marriage. Diamond knew the only thing they could do was enjoy the time they had together and treasure the memories. And they were both content to do just that.

One afternoon Jake and Diamond had returned to the ranch after riding the range. They sat in his kitchen, sharing cups of tea that he had made. Dusk began covering the earth and silence surrounded the ranch. Blaylock and the men were still away.

"Jacob, this tea is delicious. What's in it?"

Jake smiled. "I can't tell you. It's a secret."

"A secret?"

"Yes," Jake said, pouring more tea into their cups.

"It's an old family secret that can be shared only with the men in the Madaris family, and only after they've reached the mature age of thirty-five."

Diamond became intrigued as she always did whenever he spoke of his family. There was always warmth and love in his voice whenever he discussed them. "And just whose idea was it to exclude the women from this secret?"

"My great-great-grandfather. He made that decision after finding out his money-hungry wife had plans to sell the family secret to some major tea company and run off with the proceeds and with one of his cow-hands."

The aroma of the succulent brew of herbs and spices filled the room. Diamond lifted a brow as she took another sip of her tea. "And from then on it was felt that the women in the Madaris family couldn't be trusted," Diamond concluded.

Jake smiled. "I won't go that far, but the men in the family figured why dangle a carrot in front of them when they knew they were better at keeping secrets than the women."

Diamond met Jake's gaze over the rim of her cup. "You know what they say about keeping secrets, don't you?"

"No. What do they say?"

"Nothing is safe as a secret forever," she said softly. She remembered how her ex-husband had found that out the hard way. His secret affair with the young daughter of one of his financial backers had come to light when the eighteen-year-old had gotten pregnant.

Jake stared at Diamond for a long time. "You sound like you know what you're talking about."

Her gaze met his. "Trust me, I do." Diamond suddenly felt the need to switch subjects. Remembering Samuel's betrayal only brought pain. She stood. "It's getting late, Jacob. I guess it's time for me to get back to the cabin."

A part of Jake wasn't ready for her to go back. He wanted her to stay here with him and spend the…

He sucked in a deep breath to rid his mind of that thought before it fully formed. He refused to break the "house rule" that he had established for himself. He had made a decision over twenty years ago that no woman would ever share his bed at Whispering Pines in this house that he had built. Any affairs he got involved in would not take place under this roof. This house was his sanctuary, his haven against the wiles of any woman, their demands, their greed, their betrayals. He never wanted the complications that getting serious with a woman caused a man. His bedroom, like his boots and hat, was private. He didn't want the memory of any woman left there to haunt him.

But the truth of the matter was that Diamond's memory was already there in his bedroom, and had been ever since Blaylock had informed him that she had taken a nap in his bed.

Jake took another deep breath, deciding to take her back to the cabin and away from the ranch. He had to put a stop to this madness once and for all. Diamond was getting to him. Thoughts of her were consuming his every waking moment. And even while he was asleep, she invaded his dreams. He had thought that making love to her would help rid his body of wanting her, but it had only increased his desire.

"Jacob?"

He looked up at Diamond when she called his name. "Yes?"

"Are you ready to take me back to the cabin?"

Jake opened his mouth to say yes, but instead he said, "No."

He saw her eyes draw together quizzically. "No?"

"No."

He slowly stood and walked around the table to stand in front of her. Lifting his hand, he fingered the side of her face, the smooth skin there. As always he was stunned speechless by her beauty. She was everything he should be avoiding—sleek and sophisticated. But then again, she was everything he wanted, and admitted defeatedly that he would willingly break every rule for her.

He leaned down and let his lips hover close over hers. "Stay with me tonight, Diamond," he whispered huskily. "Stay here. In my home. I want to make love to you in my bed. I want to wake up beside you in the morning, here. Say you'll stay."

Chapter 12

Diamond could not respond.

Although she didn't fully understand what was happening between them, she was intuitive enough to know Jake was asking for more than her to spend the night with him. The relationship they shared had escalated beyond a mere physical attraction. She had acknowledged that for herself in accepting she loved him, but now looking into his dark eyes she saw more than desire there, and what she saw took her breath away. She knew he was inwardly acknowledging some feelings for her, too, although it was obvious that he was fighting them.

She had a gut feeling that spending the night with him would mean more than the two of them satisfying some basic urges. During all the times they had made love, it had always been more than that to her.

Oh, there had been the satisfying of wants and needs, but she had always felt there had been more. There were those unspoken and unaffirmed feelings lurking deep down that neither of them had wanted to surface or explore. Whenever they had made love, there had been the tenderness, the sensitivity and the passion. He had made love to her with all the things she had been missing in her life from a man. They were feelings she hadn't hidden, although a part of her had known revealing them would lead nowhere. Considering everything, there was still no way they could ever have a future together. She knew it and accepted it. But she wanted her memories. She would need them. It would be the memories of her time with him that would sustain her for the rest of her life.

She met his gaze and said, "Yes, I'll stay here with you tonight."

Diamond knew in reality that she was offering a lot more and added, "I may be a little late in telling you this, but I feel I need to say it now, to set things straight between us. No matter what you may have ever read about me, Jacob, and no matter what we've done together since I've been here, I want you to know that I don't sleep around. I've slept with only two men in my lifetime, my ex-husband and you."

Jake was stunned speechless. Somehow this beautiful woman had retained her traditional values while in an arena of people who were reputed as not having any. He knew that more times than not, the lives of the rich and famous were exploited and degraded unfairly. The majority of the stuff people read in the tabloids wasn't true. He had been friends with Sterling long enough to figure that out. Half the time when Sterling was reported as being somewhere in seclusion with some beautiful woman, he'd been here at Whispering Pines. And the only thing he'd been romancing was a rod, a reel and his favorite fishing hole.

Jake reached out and traced the tender skin of Diamond's upper arm, skimming his fingertips and palms over its softness. "So you're a nice girl," he whispered teasingly against her cheek. His lips brushed her temple then moved down to capture her earlobe.

"I believe that I am," Diamond said, trying to disguise the tremble in her voice and the flood of emotions going through her. He knew all the right buttons to push to make her body shift smoothly into overdrive. Sensuous sensations were oozing through her veins. The warmth of his lips against her neck made her breathing thicken. This was first-class seduction, Jacob Madaris's style.

"I believe that you are, too," Jake whispered against her ear. "I believe you are a woman of the highest quality and standards. I believe that you are a woman with a heart of gold. Everything about you is goodness, richness and right."

He wanted to also say that despite her ex-husband's stupidity, there was a man out there who would appreciate her and who would be worthy of her, but he couldn't. The thought of any other man being intimate with her bothered him. For some reason that he was too emotional at the moment to think about, he wanted to brand her his. Tonight he wanted to make her Jake Madaris's woman.

Jake refused to think about what doing that would mean. Not only would he be breaking his "house rule," he would also be breaking his "heart rule," which was to never let another woman get under his skin and into his heart.

Too late, he thought as he stared into Diamond's eyes. Diamonds are forever, and the one standing before him, shining brilliantly with a smile that sparkled so radiantly was undoubtedly so. She would be forever. At that exact moment, he knew he had to face the final truth. He loved her. And when Jake Madaris loved, he loved hard.

He reached out and slid a hand around her waist and brought her body close to his. He needed to hold her in his arms now that he had come to terms with what he had been fighting for the past few weeks. As crazy as it seemed, he had fallen in love with a woman he had met less than three weeks ago. A woman who in less than a week would be walking out of his life.

Jake shook his head. Maybe falling in love with her wasn't so crazy after all. His nephew Dex had fallen in love with Caitlin less than three weeks after meeting her. And like him, a woman had been the last thing on Dex's mind at the time. Of all his nephews, the family claimed he and Dex were more alike. He would even admit they usually thought alike. And now it seemed they fell in love alike as well.

"Diamond..." He said her name huskily, tenderly, before slanting his mouth over hers, hungry for whatever she offered, and for the love he had for her. Memories of past hurt, pain and mistrust had no place here. He kissed her like a man dying for the next breath of love, a man hungry for the mere taste of it. When he finally released her mouth to take a soul-cleansing breath, he heard her whisper his name, breathlessly, sensuously.

He took his lips and smoothed the side of her throat, warming her skin, drowning in the taste of it. Making love to her tonight would be different. After tonight she would wear his brand. There would be no mistake that she was his woman. And by golly if she didn't love him now, she soon would. He would see to it. Jake knew with every breath in his body that there was no way he would let her walk out of his life. He would fight for her with every bit of his strength. Love was a lifetime commitment, one he intended to share with this woman, no matter how the odds stacked up against them.

He picked her up in his arms and took her up the stairs, holding her close to his heart, where she belonged and where he intended for her to stay.

Jake placed Diamond in the middle of his bed. Drawing away, he stepped back to look at her. As incredible as it was, this woman had completely captured his heart. And now because of her, he could allow himself to have hopes and dreams. For the first time in years, more than he cared to count, he was filled with a deep sense of inner peace. It was an emotion he thought he would never experience again.

For a long minute he continued to stare at her, inhaling her scent, analyzing her striking features. He watched her take a sharp intake of breath when his hand went to his belt buckle and begin tugging it through the loops. He saw the heat darken her eyes when he pulled his shirt free and began unbuttoning it. And he saw the slight trembling of her hands when he removed it.

The bedroom lamp's soft incandescent glow danced

shadows across her clothed body. She looked right in his bed. But, he thought, as he reached for the snap to his jeans, she would look even better with no clothes on.

Diamond sank into the soft covering on Jake's bed as she watched him take off his clothes, piece by piece. She drew a steadying breath, thinking no man had a right to look so masculine. She watched the pulse in his throat, thinking that it matched the irregular beating of her heart.

She continued to watch him, captivated by his broad shoulders, hairy chest and the dark line leading down into his jeans. When he removed his pants, her gaze ran down the full length of his nude body. The startling evidence of his physical need for her caused her bones to tremble within her flesh. For a moment, she was rooted to the spot on his bed and held immobile by the hungry look in his eyes. Diamond barely breathed a sound when Jake began walking back toward her.

When he got to the bed, he reached out his hand to her. When she placed hers in the palm of his, he gently tugged her upright and brought her smoothly against the solid wall of his chest. Then he wrapped his strong arms around her and lightly, ever so lightly, his lips unerringly found hers.

Driven by a desire greater than any of the other times they had made love, Diamond kissed him back as a heat, hotter than any she had known, spread through her. He feasted on her mouth; he devoured it. She tried to wiggle closer and found her clothing restrictive. She wanted to be skin-to-skin with him.

As if reading her thoughts, Jake's hand moved

lower to her jeans, searching for the snap. She gasped when he found it and undid it. She cried out when he touched her, letting his fingers come in contact with her belly. Drawing in a deep stuttering breath, she expelled it. With a hungry growl, he broke off the kiss and immediately reached for her shirt. His impatient fingers popped the buttons free.

From there he didn't waste any time undressing her. He tossed her clothes in a careless heap on the floor atop his. When he turned back to her, he knew that tonight would be a critical turning point for the both of them. Their silence was strangely comfortable, wordlessly soothing. But now, he had to break the silence that encased them. He could no longer fight the flood of emotions consuming him.

When he moved in place over her and kissed her again, he lifted his head and met her gaze and whispered, "I love you," before smoothly entering her body in a single stroke. He then began making love to her slow and easy.

His body devoured her and all of her emotions. His mouth took possession of hers, fueling a need within her. He made love to her as he tried to ignore the demands of his own body, knowing what he had to do before that time came and hoping he would have the control to do so.

Jake gritted his teeth when Diamond curved her body more fully around him. He sucked in a deep groan when she locked her legs around him.

Pull back, his mind commanded, but instead he instinctively drove farther into her when the rhythm of their motions became one. He felt the heat inside him build low in his belly, and flood all the way to his toes.

Pull out, his mind screamed. *Now!* Jake had every intention to withdraw before he lost control.

And he would have if Diamond had not chosen that exact moment to whisper, "And I love you, too, Jacob," when the power of passion overtook her body.

Too late. He lost it then—control, focus, all rational thought.

He also lost himself in her as ripples of intense passion tore through him, and he closed his eyes as his body shattered in a long scalding release that jetted into her. He tightened his arms around her as their bodies trembled together, both accepting the love they had never acknowledged to each other, until now, until tonight.

"Marry me, Diamond."

Jake was amazed at what he had just asked her. It was something he had promised himself he would never ask a woman ever again. At first he thought that he would push only for an affair, but his heart couldn't let him do that. He needed permanence. He wanted a forever commitment. He craved something with her that he thought he would never want again with a woman.

Diamond lay there, counting the seconds and hoping she had not heard Jacob correctly. She loved him but there was no way she could marry him. Them getting married would lead only to pain and regret.

Jake felt her tense, and a sudden tightness gripped his chest. He refused to let her just walk out of his life and at her silence decided to take another approach. "You might be pregnant. I didn't protect you this time," he said. "It wasn't intentional and in truth it was downright irresponsible, but I don't regret anything I've done with you tonight. If we've made a baby, I'll be happy about it."

He shifted their bodies to a more comfortable position before continuing. "When I love someone it means a lifetime commitment. I'm not asking you to give up anything to become my wife, Diamond. You have your career, and I understand and respect that. All I'm asking is for you to be my partner in love by marrying me."

Diamond forced herself to swallow past the lump in her throat. Slowly, carefully, she eased out of Jake's arms, knowing what she had to say would require distance. She wouldn't be able to say the words while he was holding her in his arms. She never realized giving up the person you love could hurt so much. She sat up in bed and looked at him.

"I can't marry you, Jacob. We've shared some wonderful and special moments together, but when I leave here next week, I'll walk away without looking back. I can't look back, and I won't."

Her words hit his heart. They tore into the very soul of him. He remembered a time when another woman's words had done that very same thing, and his body was about to re-erect that shield that had always protected his heart. But when he looked deeply into Diamond's eyes, he saw the raw pain there. Her lips might be saying one thing, but her heart was feeling another.

"Tell me, Diamond," he said huskily, determined. "Tell me that you lied and you really don't love me, that you really don't care, and I'll leave you alone."

Tears stung her eyes, but she didn't even bother to fight them back. She had a good cause to cry. She was giving up the best thing to ever come into her life, but she knew what she had to do for both their sakes.

"I don't love—" She couldn't say it. She couldn't get the lie she was about to say past her throat. She covered her face with her hands. After a few agonizing moments, she took her hands away and looked at him, seeing how concentrated his gaze was on her. Waiting.

"I can't say it because I *do* love you, Jacob," she whispered raggedly, against the lump in her throat. "If possible, I love you more than any woman has a right to love any man. You and Whispering Pines are the best things to ever happen to me. Being here has meant more to me than you'll ever know. It has given my life so much meaning. Every day I've spent here I've felt safe, protected and special. You made me feel all those things, Jacob."

She paused to wipe away the tears welling in her eyes before continuing. "You represent all that's good. You are everything a man should be—honorable, respected, admired and loved. And you take your responsibilities seriously. The same would hold true with your responsibilities as a husband. And doing that can destroy you, and I refuse to let that happen. I love you, too much."

Her gaze became more intense. "My life is everyday news, Jacob, and if you married me yours will be, too. I can't let that happen to you. I won't let that happen. I won't let the media rip apart your world. Whispering Pines is your world, it's who you are. If we were to marry, this place would become a circus. Life as you know it wouldn't be the same. There would be reporters constantly trying to get on your land to filter out a story, there would be helicopters flying around overhead to get pictures, any word you say might end up being misquoted in some tabloid or another. Your life, Jacob, would become a living hell. I love you, too much to let that happen."

Jake looked at her, feeling more love for her at that very moment than he thought was possible. "Fine. I hear what you're saying, but I still want to marry you," he said softly. "You don't have to protect me, Diamond. I can handle all those things you've mentioned. With you by my side, I'll be able to handle just about anything."

"But that's just it, Jacob, I won't be here by your side most of the time. I'll have to travel, and at times I'll be gone for long periods of time while filming."

"I know that, and I can handle that. But no matter where you go, you'll know Whispering Pines is your home and that I'll be here waiting for you. Waiting for the day you will return so that I can take care of you, ease your stress and give you the loving care you deserve and need from the rat race of your career."

Diamond shook her head. "The price you'd pay isn't worth loving me, Jacob."

"Any price I pay for loving you, Diamond, would be worth it."

Diamond began to cry, and Jake reached for her and pulled her down into his arms. He held her. He knew her fears and even understood them. He'd been friends with Sterling long enough to know how relentless and cruel the media could be sometimes.

She cried harder, and he held her tighter, comforting her and whispering words that things would be all right because they had love on their side, and their love would be enough.

Diamond struggled out of Jake's arms and looked up at him. Her gaze was pleading. "But our love *won't* be enough."

Jake looked at her, caught by her distress and determination to sacrifice their love to protect him. "So there is no way you'll agree to marry me?" he asked, his voice tight. No matter what, he refused to give up.

Maybe it was the way he asked the question, with deep and intense emotions, or the heart-wrenching thought that once she left Whispering Pines she would never see him again that made Diamond finally say in a subdued voice, "Yes, there is a way. And it's the only way I will agree to," she said, her voice raw from emotions.

"And what way is that?"

"If we marry secretly, at least for a short while. Then the media won't know."

Looking at her, Jake knew she was serious. Did she actually think they could keep their marriage a secret? And if he went along with it, just how long were they talking about? "For how long, Diamond? How long would you want to keep our marriage a secret?"

Discomfited by his question, she shrugged before saying, "I don't know, Jacob. Probably for no more than a year."

After a long, tense silence he asked, "Then what? What happens after a year? You'll still be in the spotlight. What's so magical about one year?"

Diamond shrugged. "Nothing really other than it will give us a year to ourselves. I'm not ready to share our love with the prying eyes of the world. I'm not ready for what we share to be analyzed, criticized and pulled apart by the press. I need some private time,

Jacob, to be with you whenever I can without people looking in."

Jake got out of bed and crossed the room to the huge window. Staring out, all he saw was darkness. It would be a mirror of how his life would look if Diamond walked out of it.

He turned back to her. "And what if you're pregnant now?"

There was a long pause in the room. A part of him hoped she was, but the tense bunching of her brows indicated she was hoping she wasn't.

She smiled faintly. "If I'm pregnant, then it won't be a secret for long, will it?"

She rubbed one hand over her forearm, knowing that he was thinking hard on her proposal. After moments passed and he didn't say anything, she felt compelled to ask, "What about it, Jacob?"

Jake sucked in a deep breath, wondering what choice did he have. He loved her and would continue to do so until the day he died. He walked back over to the bed and pulled her into his arms. "I love you, Diamond, and I'm willing to take you any way I can get you."

She wrapped her arms around him. "Do you mean that, Jacob?"

"Yes, I mean it."

He pulled her back into his arms and kissed her like a man who had finally found what had been missing in his life. He would love her and protect her and in time she would see that their love would truly be enough.

BOOK TWO

The Present

Chapter 13

Jake Madaris rubbed the back of his neck and looked anxiously up at the dark sky. He had been at the airstrip for more than an hour and there was no sign of Sterling's plane. He drew in a deep, ragged breath and let it out slowly as he tried to remain calm. Sterling claimed Diamond was all right, but he would breathe a whole lot easier once he saw her for himself; once he held her in his arms.

Someone had tried to attack her! He nearly choked on his disbelief that some demented person had actually broken into Diamond's home and tried to hurt her. Oh, she'd had to deal with overzealous fans in the past, but nothing of this magnitude had ever happened, and he intended that nothing like this would ever happen again.

Damn it. They were only supposed to keep their

secret for a year, but here it was nearly eighteen months later, and still very few people knew they were married. Jake searched his mind frantically to recall just how things had gotten so out of hand. Why had he allowed things to go this far? He sighed, knowing the answer to that question without really thinking about it. He had not asked her to give up anything to become his wife because he knew all about Diamond's dreams.

He of all people understood how it felt to want something so badly that you worked hard to achieve it. He of all people knew the importance of proving something to yourself as well as to others. He understood Diamond's burning desire to reach the top. She was a good actress. As far as he was concerned, the whole world knew it, but still she had not reached that pinnacle of excellence where she was satisfied.

Instinctively as her lover, husband and friend, he knew what drove her to want to be the best and not live under her father's shadow. He also knew just how much she loved being an actress. There was no way he could take away from her the only other thing that shared her love. She loved acting as much as he loved ranching.

He also understood her fears.

She was still fearful of how pulled apart and complicated their life together would become once the media found out about them. And she was fighting to protect their privacy. He didn't care what the media found out. He wanted to stop hiding the truth about their marriage and make her realize that together they could handle the media. And although a part of him wanted to push her into finally making a decision about their future, he couldn't. He would continue to do what he'd always done whenever she showed up at Whispering Pines. He would be her calm after the storm, her haven of protection, her rock of strength and her biggest supporter. And most importantly, he would continue to be the man who loved her.

He had long ago accepted the fact that the two of them would not have a normal marriage. He had gotten used to her drop-in visits, their secret rendezvous and their clandestine hideaways filled with stolen passionate moments. What he hadn't liked was keeping the news of his marriage from his family. Only one of his brothers knew the truth, and that had been by accident when Jonathan and his wife Marilyn had dropped by the ranch unexpectedly during one of Diamond's visits.

He knew other family members were worried and concerned that he was acting strangely by not spending time with the family like he used to. He had missed a couple of the family gatherings, which in the past had been so unlike him. What they didn't know was the reason he'd been absent was because he'd been somewhere having a secret illicit affair with his wife. In the beginning, he had enjoyed the thrill of outsmarting the media, who assumed Diamond and Sterling were an item. Now even that had changed.

As hard as it was to believe, Sterling, who had been a devout bachelor, had gotten married eight months ago, and he and his wife were expecting their first child. Therefore Sterling could no longer be used as Diamond's pretend lover, which had only put the media in a frenzy to discover and disclose the identity of her new love interest. News coverage on Diamond was worse than it had ever been before. The media were completely stumped as to how Colby, Sterling's wife, could become such close friends with Diamond, whom everyone assumed was Sterling's former lover. Jake shook his head at the madness.

Jake lifted his face to the sky when he heard the hum of an aircraft. In those few scant seconds of sound, a shudder rippled down his spine and he drew in a deep breath.

His wife, the love of his life, was home.

Diamond's heart squeezed inside her chest when she saw the first fragments of land. She put her face to the plane's window to peer out into the predawn sky as a clearer picture came into view.

Whispering Pines.

No matter how many times she returned, she always felt a deep connection to this place. It was here that she had found true everlasting love with a man who meant everything to her.

Jacob.

She wanted to forget about everything except Jacob and Whispering Pines. She didn't want to remember the insane young man who thought himself obsessively in love with her and had broken into her home only to get violent when she had tried getting away from him. She didn't want to think of the police's questions or the mob of reporters who had shown up after hearing about the incident.

She wanted to forget everything except for the man she loved and the land she considered as home. Easing back in her seat, a calming peace settled over her. She was home, and she knew without a doubt that when the plane landed, Jacob would be there at the airstrip, waiting for her.

Just like he had that very first time.

Jake could see the silhouette of Sterling's plane in the predawn sky. Then he watched it land. He held his breath when the aircraft came to a stop. Moments later the door opened and Diamond came out onto the top step. She saw him and across the distance their gazes met and locked. He watched as she drew a deep breath before proceeding down the steps. Her hands were tucked into the pockets of her jacket to ward off the mid-February chill. She had cut her hair for the movie she'd just finished filming. The short, curly strands covered her head like a black cap, and made the beauty of her facial features even more blatant.

He walked toward her, feeling more love for this woman than she would ever know. He met up with her when she planted her feet firmly on solid ground, the earth of Whispering Pines. When he stood in front of her, he looked at her closely, trying to detect any physical sign of harm. He reached out and tenderly ran one finger along her cheek.

"Are you all right, or do I have to go to California and hurt somebody?" he asked in a low voice and a tone that was dead serious. Diamond studied his features as closely as he was studying hers. She saw his strain, his exhaustion and his worry. She had told herself that she would not cry when she saw him; had even convinced herself that she would not break down. Now she was fighting desperately not to do both.

"No," she answered softly, in a shaky voice. "He was just a kid, Jacob, barely eighteen."

Jake shrugged broad shoulders, his gaze never leaving hers. "Doesn't matter. He had the nerve to mess with my woman, my wife. And I don't like it. I don't like it one hell of a bit."

Diamond nodded. She forced a faint smile to her face. "Neither do I, but it's over. I survived the ordeal and I'm home with my man, my husband."

Jake stared at her for the space of several heartbeats before leaning down and capturing Diamond's mouth in his. Exerting more pressure he deepened the kiss, mating their mouths, letting loose their strained emotions and their unrestrained passion. Diamond's light floral scent drifted to him, filling his mind with all the reasons why he loved her, and just how empty and lonely he felt whenever she was away. Thoughts of her fueled his dreams at night and made him rock-hard at some of the oddest times of the day. Memories of her taste, her touch and passion were things that helped him to survive life without her until she returned. He didn't think there would ever be a time in his life when he wouldn't want her completely.

Jake released Diamond's mouth momentarily to allow air to stagger into their lungs before claiming her mouth once again.

All Diamond could think about was the man kissing her, and the long, lonely weeks they had been apart. The feel of his strong arms around her made her feel safe, protected, but most of all, loved. She used every ounce of her concentration on their kiss, becoming lost in it and wishing it could go on forever.

Jake reluctantly broke off the kiss when he heard the sound of riders and horses approaching. Evidently his men, who were early risers, had gotten wind of what had happened to Diamond on the early morning news. After finding him missing from the ranch, they had put two and two together and had decided to seek him out at the airstrip.

A lump formed in Jake's throat, knowing how much his men cared for his wife. She was no longer a celebrity to them. She was their friend and they were her protectors. All of them were committed to keeping their secret.

Jake saw Diamond look over her shoulder and knew she was deeply touched by the men's show of force and support as all thirty of them filed in a single line on the horizon. When she looked back at him, he saw the tears forming in her eyes.

"It's so good to be home, Jacob. I missed you."

He swung her up into his arms and began walking toward his Jeep. "And it's good having you home, sweetheart. I missed you, too."

Diamond fell asleep as soon as Jake helped her undress and get into the bed. He had cursed under his breath and clenched his fists when he had seen the bruise that ran along her shoulder. Although she had explained it had come from her own doing when she had fallen in an attempt to get away from the intruder, that had not soothed Jake's anger.

"I'm sorry. I didn't want you to worry about me, Jacob," she'd said quietly before drifting off to sleep.

I'm sorry, too, he had wanted to say to her. He was sorry that he had not been there to protect her. And as much as he knew that his absence couldn't be helped, he felt the blame just the same.

He stood at his bedroom window and looked out, staring over the land. Whispering Pines had always been his pride, his joy, his motivator. The promise he had made to his family had assured his drive to succeed and to take care of the land that had been entrusted to him.

Jake turned away from the window and glanced across the room and watched Diamond sleep. She was safe. But for how long? When would another overzealous fan hurt her? Feeling disgusted at the thought and with himself, he rubbed a palm across his face, thinking once again that he should have been there to protect his wife.

Feeling he had failed her and that he would continue to fail her as long as their secret stood in the way, Jake walked out of the room.

"Where do you think he is, Blaylock?" Diamond asked as she paced the kitchen floor. She had awakened midmorning to find Jacob wasn't there. And he had not returned for lunch with the rest of his men.

"The boy got a lot on his mind. He'll be fine. There are things he needs to work out, Diamond."

Diamond gazed over at the older man curiously. "What things?"

Blaylock shrugged. "Things that aren't any of my business."

Diamond walked over to where Blaylock stood, stirring ingredients into a huge pot as he prepared dinner. She laid a hand on his arm. "Blaylock, everything that happens around here is your business. So please tell me what's going on with Jacob."

Blaylock stared for a long moment at the intense

plea in her eyes before saying, "The boy is blaming himself for what happened to you in California."

Diamond lifted a bemused brow. "Why would Jacob blame himself? He wasn't even there."

"And that's what's eating at him, girl. As your husband, he feels he should have been there to protect you, and he wasn't."

She frowned. She hadn't thought Jacob would feel that way. "But he couldn't be there with me. He knows we have to be discreet to keep the secret safe. He—"

Blaylock waved his hand to halt her words. "Maybe that's what's causing the problem, this secret of yours. Think about it for a minute. A man, a real man, would want to protect what's his, and Jake feels that when it comes to you, he can't do that."

Diamond looked at Blaylock, assessing and weighing everything he had just told her. "Did Jacob tell you this?"

"He didn't have to. I'm a man. Besides, I know how Jake thinks. This pretend marriage of yours is finally getting to him."

"It's not a pretend marriage," Diamond defended, raising her chin. "We have a real marriage."

Blaylock lifted a brow. "By whose definition? Definitely not by most people's. Think about it, Diamond. Then think about the kind of man Jake is. He's had to make a lot of adjustments to keep your secret. And he's had to make a lot of sacrifices. He and his family have always been close, but he rarely invites them here for extended visits since he's never sure when you might drop in."

Diamond looked at him, taken aback. She knew how close Jake and his family were. "I hadn't thought of that."

Blaylock gave a rueful shrug. "Figured you hadn't."

A quick stab of pain pierced Diamond's heart. "I only wanted to protect him from the ugliness of my career," she said quietly. "I didn't want his privacy invaded."

"I know, but what you failed to consider is that when two people marry they accept it all, the good, the bad and the ugly. Trust me. Jake can handle a bunch of annoying reporters."

"But I wanted to spare him that. I didn't want our love exploited. Nor did I want his family subjected to anything either."

"Both Jake and the Madaris family can handle their own. When you married Jake, you also married into his family. They're a family that you have denied yourself the chance to get to know. They are a good group of people who'll welcome you with open arms and who'll stand by you and Jake, no matter what."

Diamond bit her lip. "Oh, Blaylock, I never stopped to consider any of this. I've never been a part of a real family before. I think of you and the men as my family, but that's as far as I've allowed myself to take it."

"Then you're cheating yourself short. I know Jake's brothers, all five of them. They are good men and they were all lucky to marry good, decent God-fearing women who gave them, for the most part, good, responsible children. Give yourself a chance to know them."

He gazed at her thoughtfully. "They will be right proud of the choice Jake made for a wife."

Diamond ventured a smile with Blaylock's compliment. "But they may not be too happy to find out our marriage has been a secret for almost a year and a half."

"Once you explain things to them, they'll understand. The key is telling them about it."

The cool night breeze made Diamond shiver as she stood on the porch. Jacob still had not returned and his dinner sat warming in the oven. She was getting worried although a few of the men had mentioned seeing him working on a fence at the end of the north pastures.

She had thought long and hard about what Blaylock had shared with her. She could kick herself for being so stupid and so insensitive. How could she have thought that Jacob was completely satisfied with their arrangements? How could she not have known how he had really felt?

She thought of his beautiful home. She had walked through all the rooms that evening, taking stock of each one and noticing that there was nothing to indicate her presence in his life. Even in his bedroom and study, there weren't any pictures of her or them together.

And all because of their secret.

Diamond knew that her husband was a proud man who had given her the world—his world. Not only had he shared his home and land with her, he had introduced her to passion the likes of which she had never known before. From the first, he had ignited fire inside of her. It had been something they had shared from the time she had arrived on Whispering Pines. He had always been understanding and supportive when she had needed it most. He had always been there, waiting for her to return and giving her the peace and tranquility she sought, the passion she craved, the love she needed and the closeness she had wanted.

Unhesitantly. Unselfishly.

How could she not love, honor and adore a man such as that? How could she not want to publicly acknowledge her love for him, and then be strong enough to handle the consequences of doing so?

"Diamond?" Jake's whispered voice touched Diamond like a gentle wave along the ocean shore. "It's late. What are you doing out here?" he asked.

Diamond inhaled a shaky breath as she turned toward his voice. She had not heard him approach. His face suddenly appeared out of the darkness and into the glow of the starlit sky. She looked up at him. He wore an expression that she had never seen on his features before. Guarded.

She felt his gaze lock on her face and wondered what he was thinking. Staring into the warmth of his dark eyes, she thought that although his features were guarded, the look he gave her was tender.

"I was out here waiting for you, Jacob," she answered finally.

"Why?"

Why? Her mind began spinning with his single question. "Because I wanted to see you. You've been gone all day and I—"

"I had work to do."

She nodded. "Yes, I know, and I didn't expect you to change your schedule for me."

It was only after she had spoken the words that realization suddenly hit her. In the past he'd always done exactly that. Each and every time she returned to Whispering Pines, he had made changes in his schedule to spend time with her. In essence what she had done was force him to do the very thing she had not wanted— interfere with his work on the ranch.

All the things he had done he did because he loved her. He had loved her enough to make his house feel like a home for her whenever she was here. But far more important, he had done what Samuel had never done. He had trusted her when they were apart. Not once had he questioned her about any of the articles that appeared in certain magazines and tabloids, linking her with other men. She didn't know too many men who would have been able to handle that. But he had because he knew in his heart that she truly belonged only to him.

"How are you feeling, Diamond?"

Diamond's thoughts were snatched back into focus with Jacob's question. Even now he was thinking of her well-being. "I'm fine, Jacob."

He nodded. "So what's on your mind? Why were you waiting for me? What's bothering you?"

She nervously licked her lips. He could decipher her mood so easily. It always surprised her how he could sense when something was bothering her. She cocked her head to examine his features. It was obvious to her that something was bothering him as well.

"I got an idea that I want to run by you."

"What idea?"

"You haven't had a party here at the ranch in a while. You've mentioned on several occasions that you used to host an annual party for your family and close friends."

Diamond watched the subtle play of emotions cross Jake's face. He was slowly letting his guard down, she thought. Knowing that he had felt the need to put it up in the first place tugged at her heart. The knowledge of what he had been enduring because of her made regret twist and turn inside of her.

Jake crossed his arms and leaned against the porch's railing. He gazed at her speculatively. "A party? For my family?"

"Yes."

He frowned. "And just where do you plan on being while this party is going on?"

"Here. I think it's time for you to introduce me."

Jake stared at her, searching her face for some sort of explanation. "Introduce you?"

"Yes."

"As my wife?"

"I hope you don't think I'll let you get away with claiming I'm your mistress," she said lightly, trying to break the tension between them.

Jake shook his head to clear it. He then stared back at her. "Let me get this straight. You want us to come out of the closet?"

She grinned. "More like coming out of the bed-room, don't you think?"

He stared at her, not knowing what to think. He closed his eyes for a brief moment. When he reopened them relief shone in their dark depths. He hesitated for just a second before asking, "Are you sure about this, Diamond?"

"Yes."

Jake nervously rubbed the top of his head when he thought of his nieces—three in particular—Traci, Kattie and Felicia. "I may as well warn you that some of my kinfolk don't know how to keep secrets. They don't know the meaning of the phrase 'silence is golden.'"

Diamond smiled. "It doesn't matter. I'm prepared for whatever happens now. I can't continue to let things go on this way. I love you and I'm ready for the entire world to know it. I just hope you're ready, too."

Jake took a few steps toward her, closing the distance between them. He pulled her into his arms. "I've been ready. We'll handle things just fine. We love each other and we trust each other. Look at Sterling and Colby. Even with the media constantly trying to get into their business, they're making out okay. We will, too."

There was strong confidence in his voice. And when he leaned down to kiss her, a part of Diamond wanted to believe that with their love anything was possible.

Chapter 14

Diamond placed the vase filled with fresh-cut flowers on the only table in the room that wasn't already adorned with a flower arrangement. She turned a full circle around, admiring her handiwork.

"You don't think there are too many flowers in here, do you?" she asked Jake as he entered the room.

He came to stand beside her and automatically placed his arms around her waist. "No, this room looks just like you, beautiful." He leaned down and brushed a kiss across her lips. "Nervous?"

"Petrified is more like it." Diamond chuckled softly. Nearly two weeks had passed since she had approached him about telling his family about their marriage, and now the day of the party had finally arrived.

Jake pulled her closer to him. "Don't be. My family will love you as much as I do."

"Are you sure they'll forgive us for not telling them sooner about our marriage?"

Stroking her cheek with the pad of his thumb, he said, "Yeah, they'll understand. They know how the media harassed Syneda when they got wind of who her father was."

Diamond nodded. Jacob had told her how the news-breaking story of wealthy industrialist Syntel Remington's love child had made national headlines and the media, being insensitive as ever, had milked it for all it was worth without any regard for the feelings of those involved. Syneda had been engaged to marry Jacob's nephew at the time.

Leaning against Jake's hard chest, Diamond thought on all the other things he had told her about his family. His niece, Felicia Laverne, the offspring of his brother Robert who had gotten killed in the Vietnam War, and who had only been two years old when her father had died, had grown up pampered and spoiled rotten by her six uncles. Last month on New Year's Day she had married legendary football great, Trask Maxwell. The uncles were still in a daze over that match since Trask and Felicia had never gotten along. However, to all their amazement, the couple seemed to be doing quite nicely and appeared to have a solid marriage.

He had again told her about Justin, Dex and Clayton, the three nephews with whom he had a very close relationship, and that they were like brothers because of the closeness of their ages. She looked forward to meeting all of his family and some of his close friends she had never met. Invitations had been sent, and the responses they received indicated most of everyone invited would be coming.

"Your presence will definitely be a big surprise, and when they find out that you're in the family I may have to call 9-1-1 for those who won't be able to handle the excitement and shock."

Diamond shook her head, smiling. "Things won't be that bad."

"You never know. You're pretty popular with certain members of my family. Slade, one of my younger nephews even has a huge poster of you in his bedroom." Jake's eyes gleamed with amusement when he added, "Just wait until he discovers that his uncle Jake has had the real thing, not only in his bedroom but also in his bed."

He brought her closer to him and let his hand caress the warmth of her backside. "The real live passionate one." Memories of her legs wrapped tight around him, holding his body within hers as he made love to her flowed through his mind. The heated thoughts of what they had shared that morning were still fresh and ingrained on his mind.

A shiver passed through Diamond's body with Jake's touch. She looked up at him, recalling their intimate moments of that morning as well. She had memories of crying out from the sheer pleasure of having him embedded deep inside her body while they made love. Then later when he had left the bed to begin his day on the ranch, memories of how she had snuggled under the bedcovers so she could smell his scent before falling back to sleep increased her pulse rate.

When he leaned intimately closer to her and she felt his arousal pressing hard against her, she pulled back out of his arms while she had the mind to do so.

"I need to go get dressed, Jacob. Everyone will start arriving soon."

Jake nodded as he reluctantly released her. If he didn't let her go now, he would be tempted to make love to her right here in this room. It would be just his luck for a few of his family members to arrive early and walk in on him making love to her on the living room floor. No use giving any of them heart failure anytime too soon. They would go into cardiac arrest soon enough when he announced his marriage.

The plan was for Diamond to stay upstairs until everyone had arrived and until after he had made his announcement. She would then descend the stairs on his brother Jonathan's arm. He smiled. He couldn't wait to see everyone's faces when they realized the real purpose of the gathering.

Most of his family believed that he would never marry again. He knew that one particular person would be extremely overjoyed—his mother. At the age of eighty-one, his mother believed all the men in the Madaris family should be married by the time they reached their thirtieth birthday, to guarantee the longevity of the Madaris family. For a long while, she thought he was setting a bad example for his single nephews. The fact that he had been married once before didn't count.

"Jacob?"

"Mmm."

"There's another idea I have that I'd like to run by you."

He smiled down at her. "Not another party, I hope."

She returned his smile. "No, helping you plan this one was enough. It's about my name."

Jake lifted a brow. "What about your name?"

Diamond's stomach twisted. Most actresses didn't use their married name, but she wanted to begin using hers, and wasn't quite sure how he would feel about it.

"Diamond?" he prompted when she did not say anything. "What's your idea?"

"I want to start using my married name, Jacob," she said at last. "But I'd understand if you'd prefer that I didn't."

Jake stared down at her before pulling her back into the shelter of his arms. "Oh, sweetheart, why wouldn't I want you to use my name? I'm touched that you would even consider doing so. I know you didn't with your last marriage."

The tension she had felt all that day in discussing this topic with him vanished. "I never thought about using Samuel's name for some reason. But that's all I've been thinking about since we decided to go public with our marriage. I am proud to be your wife."

"And I'm proud to be your husband." A smile tugged at the corners of Jake's mouth. "Just think. By this time tomorrow, our secret will be out and our troubles will be over."

Diamond shook her head and thought of how they would have to deal with the media. *Or our troubles will be just beginning,* she couldn't help but think to herself.

One thing that everyone who knew Jake Madaris would agree on was that whenever he got the inclination to throw a party, he knew how to throw a darn good one. Since it had been a long time since he had given one, everyone decided the long wait had been well worth it. And since most of the people in attendance were family, they felt his delay in throwing one could be forgiven. After all, being the youngest of the seven Madaris brothers—Laverne Madaris's baby boy—he could be forgiven for just about anything.

Almost.

Jake discovered that "almost" as he walked around and conversed with his family then suddenly found himself cornered by three of his nephews, Jonathan's sons—Justin, Dex and Clayton. He wasn't surprised that Clayton, the youngest and most talkative of the three, had appointed himself a spokesman for the group.

"I hope you're ready to come clean, Jake, and tell us what's been going on with you for the past year or so."

He met the gazes of the three men, who almost equaled him in both height and weight. "I'm surprised you of all people noticed, Clayton, since you're still a newlywed and all."

"Oh, I've noticed. We all have." Clayton's voice then softened. "And we're concerned."

Jake nodded. He appreciated their concern. "There's nothing to be concerned about. I promise to explain things in a little while. Trust me on this one, guys," he said before walking off.

The three nephews watched as he crossed the room to talk to his friend, movie actor Sterling Hamilton, and his very pregnant wife, Colby.

"So what do you think?" Justin Madaris asked his two brothers.

"I think whatever it is, it has to do with a woman," Clayton said, smiling,

"You *would* think so," Dex Madaris said, shaking his head.

Clayton grinned. "Yeah, I would, wouldn't I?"

Justin and Dex doubted that a woman was the reason their uncle had been acting strange for the past year or so. It had been years—over twenty—since a woman had played any part in Jake's life. As far as they were concerned, the most important thing to him was the ranch. Although they were certain he didn't live a totally celibate life, you couldn't convince them their uncle would have found the time to get wrapped up in anything other than Whispering Pines.

"What makes you think it has anything to do with a woman?" Justin asked his youngest brother curiously.

Clayton shrugged. "Obvious sign."

Dex raised a brow. "What obvious sign?"

"His walk."

"His walk? What about his walk?" Dex wanted to know.

"Did either of you notice it?"

Justin frowned. "Walked like he's always walked to me. I don't see a difference."

Clayton shook his head, smiling. "That's why I'm the attorney in the family. I notice a lot of things the two of you don't. I'm more observant. It's ingrained into my makeup to notice detail. Besides, having recently turned in my player's card, I fully understand all the complexities of the single man. Especially all the physical signs."

"Really," Dex said, glaring at his brother. "So tell us, Mr. Know-It-All, what do you see in Jake's walk?"

Clayton crossed his arms over his chest as he

watched his uncle leave the Hamiltons and walk across the room to speak briefly to their parents. "I see a man who doesn't appear to have a frustrated bone in his body. Not a single one. He appears to be totally calm, relaxed and satisfied with life in general. That can mean only one thing."

"What?" Justin asked because he knew that Dex, being the stubborn one, wouldn't ask although like him, he was dying to know.

Clayton smiled. "He's getting some…and a lot of it. It's my guess it's on a pretty regular basis, too."

Justin and Dex simultaneously looked over at their uncle. He was leaving their parents' side and was now walking toward the area where the three of their wives were standing talking to two of their aunts.

"Impossible," Dex said. He knew how his uncle had always felt about any serious involvement with a woman, and making love on a regular basis with one would constitute a pretty serious involvement in his book.

"Yeah, that's impossible," Justin chimed in agreement. "Besides, we have no business standing here discussing Jake's sex life."

"Why not?" Clayton asked, grinning. "Seems like a pretty good subject to me. And I don't happen to agree with the two of you. Impossible as it may seem, we know that miracles do happen in this family." He chuckled. "And the biggest of all miracles just got here."

The three Madaris brothers watched as Jake crossed the room to greet the couple who were just arriving, newlyweds Trask Maxwell and Felicia Laverne Madaris Maxwell.

* * *

Jake checked his watch. He would give everyone another twenty minutes or so. He had sent his sister-in-law, Marilyn, upstairs to make sure Diamond didn't need help with anything. So far the party was going smoothly, he thought, as he continued to move around the room, playing out his role as host. It felt good having the people he loved and most cared about in his home.

He saw three of his nieces standing off to the side, carrying on what appeared to be an interesting conversation if the expressions they wore were any indication. Traci was doing all the talking, and her sister Kattie and cousin Felicia were getting an earful as they hung on to her every word.

He smothered a laugh when he noticed his mother, who was sitting on a sofa not far away from the three, trying not to draw attention to the fact that she was deliberately listening to every word of Traci, Kattie and Felicia's private conversation. There was definitely nothing wrong with his mother's hearing today.

Jake decided to check things out before his mother became privy to too much of whatever gossip his nieces were spreading.

"Anyway," Traci was saying as he walked up. She didn't notice him and kept right on talking. "Leigh Jones told Karen Childs and Karen told Donna and of course, she told Bobbie, who—"

Traci stopped talking when she finally noticed him. "Oh, hi, Uncle Jake. Nice party."

He lifted a brow. "Thanks. And don't let me stop you. This is all very interesting, this train of gossip that you're spreading. I missed the beginning. Exactly what did Leigh tell Karen that was so important that she told Donna, who then gave the scoop to Bobbie?"

"Nothing important, really."

"Oh." *You could have fooled me from where I was standing looking on a few minutes ago,* Jake thought to himself. He looked at the three nieces he loved and adored. But he knew they could not keep secrets no matter how many times they took the "I cross my heart and hope to die" vow.

"So tell us, Uncle Jake, why such a big splash in February?" his niece Kattie asked, smoothly and deliberately changing the subject. "We weren't expecting a party until the summer."

"Yeah, not until the Fourth of July," his niece Felicia added.

He nodded and decided to play his hand at something, which would later prove a point to his family about their inability to keep secrets. "I'll let you three in on something, but you can't say a word to anyone. It's a secret."

He smiled when the three of them leaned forward. Out of the corner of his eye, he saw his mother sitting on the sofa leaning likewise. She wasn't about to get left out of hearing anything either. "In a few minutes, I'll be making a very important announcement."

"What kind of an announcement?" Traci asked, whispering. "Are you going to announce that Whispering Pines made an extra-large profit last year?"

Jake grinned. Traci, a compulsive shopper, was anxious to know just how much extra money she would have to spend at the malls.

"I'm not saying anything just yet. And remember

what I've told you is a secret. Don't say a word to
anyone."

"Our lips are sealed," Kattie said.

A smile tugged at the corners of Jake Madaris's
mouth. *The three of your lips haven't been sealed since
the day you were born,* he wanted to say as he looked
at the earnest expressions on their faces. "I'll talk to
you ladies later. My friend Kyle Garwood and his wife
Kimara just arrived."

Jake looked at his watch as he walked off. He knew
it wouldn't be long before every living soul at the
party knew that he would be making an announcement
about something. His three very talkative nieces would
see to it.

Chapter 15

It was time.

Jake glanced around the room and noticed a number of people were eyeing him expectantly. It seemed his nieces had done a pretty good job of spreading the word that he would be making some sort of an announcement. He gave a discreet nod to his brother Jonathan, who nodded in return before slipping up the stairs unnoticed.

Jake smiled. He was not the type of person to give in to dramatics, but he had to ashamedly admit that he was actually enjoying this. "May I have all of your attention for a minute, please?" he asked the group of people assembled in his living room.

Conversation stopped immediately, and all eyes, those that were not looking at him already, turned in his direction. He took a deep breath, then let it out slowly. Other than his men; his brother and sister-in-law, Jonathan and Marilyn; and his two close friends, Kyle Garwood and Sterling Hamilton and their wives—no one else knew of his relationship with Diamond, let alone the fact that he was married to her. But now that was about to end. He would not be guarding their secret any longer.

"First of all, I want to thank all of you for coming. Someone recently reminded me that it's been a long time since I'd given a party for my family and friends, and that person was right. It has been a long time. It's been too long. There's nothing like getting the people you care about together in one place, especially on an occasion like this when I have news to share with all of you."

Jake let his gaze move across the room before continuing. "Today I am an extremely happy man, and I want to share the reason for my happiness with all of you."

From the excited looks on everyone's faces, he had a feeling that like his niece Traci, they thought he was about to talk profits. Most of them had an invested interest in Whispering Pines and knew that besides being a hardworking rancher, he was also a successful businessman. He was the financial adviser to most of them.

"A year and a half ago something happened to me that I never expected to ever happen again. I met someone and fell in love."

Everyone stared at him in disbelief. Some people blinked in surprise, others' mouths dropped open and one or two, like his nephew Clayton, wore a smug "I knew it had something to do with a woman" expression.

Jake could not help but grin at the buzz that went

around the room. He knew that everyone thought the idea of him falling in love was absurd and absolutely ridiculous. No doubt they were also wondering if what he had just told them was true, how in the world had it happen since he spent the majority of his time busting his butt on the ranch.

Before they could recover and ask questions he continued. "After realizing just how much she meant to me, I knew I had to make her a permanent part of my life. And so I did."

There was a long silence, then his nephew Dex asked, "Just what are you saying, Jake?"

Jake's gaze moved around the room before coming to rest on Dex. He had a feeling Dex knew the answer to that question, but had wanted him to clarify it for those who didn't. "What I'm saying is that the reason I invited all of you here was to let you know I got married over a year and a half ago."

"*You did what!*"

"*Over a year and a half ago?*"

"*Why didn't you tell us?*"

"*Who did you marry?*"

"*Why did you keep something like that a secret?*"

Jake raised his hand to stop the outburst of questions that started coming at him from every direction. Everyone was talking at once.

"You got married and didn't let your family know!" his oldest brother Milton roared accusingly. His voice thundered loudly above all the others.

Jake rolled his eyes and shook his head. He wasn't surprised that the main person who took offense to not knowing about his marriage was his oldest brother, Milton. There was an eighteen-year difference in their ages, and being the oldest of the brothers, Milton felt it was his God-given right to know everything that went on within the family. And usually he did.

"Yes, but there's a reason the news of my marriage was kept a secret from everyone. And once I explain things, I'm sure you'll all understand," Jake assured them.

"And I'm just as sure that we won't," Milton Madaris snorted, his feelings clearly hurt.

"Who did you marry, son?" his mother asked after her initial shock had worn off. Unlike her oldest son, her feelings were not hurt. In fact, she was tickled pink that her baby boy was no longer single. "Where is she? Where's this woman you've kept hidden from us all this time?"

Jake turned toward the stairs. "I'd like to present to all of you, the woman who has made me believe in love again, my wife, Diamond Swain Madaris."

A sudden mixture of "Wh-wh-what" and "Ohhh" murmured across the room as a beautiful and dazzling Diamond suddenly appeared on the top stair on Jonathan Madaris's arm. She was dressed in an elegant tea-length cream-colored gown and was a vision that put everyone in a daze. Even Jake was spellbound as he looked at her. A tightness gripped his throat, and his heart thumped in his chest. She was totally and incredibly beautiful.

His Diamond.

He felt so very fortunate, so very blessed to have discovered such a treasure as this diamond. And as long as he lived, he would give thanks to God for bringing her into his life.

Their eyes met and held for the longest time. It was

an automatic gesture on his part to slowly move toward the stairs. His mouth was set in a determined line and his eyes were filled with love when he came to a stop at the bottom stair and stood there. Like everyone else, mesmerized, he looked up at the woman standing next to his brother.

The room went completely silent. Whether it was in awe or in shock, Jake wasn't sure, nor did he care. The only thing he cared about was the woman returning his stare from under long lashes and who was smiling down at him. He gave her a long look, from the top of her head down to the bottom of her feet. His gaze moved back up again and followed her gown's tempting neckline and the split that ran down the front.

He swallowed. Breathtaking. She was simply breathtaking. A part of him trembled when she left Jonathan's side and began slowly walking down the stairs to him. Alone. It was as if she was giving herself to him again, fully and completely. And she was taking it a step further by giving herself to him publicly.

Unable to stand still, he began moving up the stairs to meet her.

They met on the middle stair.

"You are," he started saying in a voice that was deep and husky, "everything that any man could ever hope for. You are more than I could ever hope for."

Diamond felt like she couldn't breathe with Jake's words. Her heart was beating with the amount of love she felt for him. Her entire body was pinned in place by the intensity of his gaze. He reached out and captured her hand in his and brought it to his lips.

Her body slightly trembled with the emotions that overwhelmed her from his touch. Everyone else in the

room faded in a haze the moment he released her hand
and his arms slipped around her and he pulled her to
him. She moaned when he captured her mouth in a
searing kiss that nearly stole the very breath from her
body. She wrapped her arms around his neck and clung
to him as the solid rock in her oftentimes-hectic world.
Her body was filled with joy. Complete joy.

Ignoring their audience, Jake kissed her more
deeply. Holding her tight in his arms he leaned back
and lifted her feet off the stair.

"Well, Lordy, look at that. I don't believe it. Jake
got himself a diamond," Jake heard one of his brothers
say from the crowd below.

"And she got herself a Madaris," one nephew's wife
added proudly.

"And we got a movie star in the family," a third
person, a teenager, piped in.

Catcalls, wild applause, whistles and shouts thundered loudly in the room, but all of that was lost on
Jake and Diamond. Neither took them as interruptions. A hard wind could have blown the house down
and they would not have noticed. For the moment,
nothing else mattered to them but each other.

Their secret love was not a secret any longer.

Jake stood across the room, leaning against the
wall, watching while Diamond stood comfortably
talking to the women in his family. It was evident that
everyone was completely taken with her. She had been
so sure his family would not forgive her for holding
him to their secret. But she had been wrong.

Together he and Diamond had given his family and
close friends the complete story. He knew that after lis-

tening to Diamond explain why she had wanted to keep their marriage, their special love, from under the media's scrutiny, everyone had understood because they knew her fears of what the media would do were justified.

His family had thought it amusing how they had eluded the media by letting them continue to assume that there was more between Diamond and Sterling than friendship. It had been a ruse that had worked until Sterling had gotten married.

Jake was about to walk off, to go claim his wife when he found his way blocked by his nephew Dex.

"You surprised the hell out of us, Jake," Dex Madaris said as a slow smile touched his lips.

Jake crossed his arms over his chest, and his own lips curved into a grin. "Figured I did. I guess I'll be thanking Sterling for the rest of my life for sending Diamond to Whispering Pines to rest and relax."

Dex nodded. "Yep. Just like I'll always be grateful to you for Caitlin. It was sheer luck that you had to go out of town on business that day, and I'm the one who had to interview her for that summer job here."

Dex looked across the room at his wife. Like most of the other women present, she stood in a crowd surrounding Diamond. "I think I fell in love with Caitlin the moment I laid eyes on her. I just didn't know it at the time." He chuckled. "It took me all of a little over two weeks to find it out, and with a little help from Clayton."

Jake chuckled, remembering. He looked over at the group when he heard Diamond's throaty laugh. The rush of sexual desire that made him tremble from just looking at her didn't surprise him. Only Diamond could do that to him. "I was a goner the moment Diamond walked off that plane onto Whispering Pines land," he said to Dex. "Because of Jessie, a city woman was the last person I wanted to be attracted to. But after a mere few days, I came to the stunning realization that my mind was saying one thing but my heart had its own private agenda."

Dex studied his uncle for a long spell before asking, "So now that chances are high that your secret is going to get leaked to the press, how are you planning on handling the media? You may want to come up with some sort of game plan. None of us were prepared for what happened to Syneda. What the media put her and her father through was totally uncalled for."

Jake nodded in agreement. "Yes, and I've prepared myself. I'm just about ready to deal with anything. I've had to put up with a lot of garbage being written about Diamond, and none of it will stop just because she's married to me. In fact, I've got a feeling things will get worse. Everything she's tried to avoid and protect us from will happen once the secret gets out."

It wasn't going to be easy, Jake realized. No doubt the media would not be too happy with them for fooling them these past eighteen months. Some facets of the press felt it was their God-given right to invade people's privacy. They cared more for profits than they did people's feelings.

"If you ever need any of us, you know you can call at any time," Dex said to his uncle. "Hopefully the media frenzy will eventually die down and you and Diamond will be able to have a normal marriage."

Jake chuckled. "A normal marriage with Diamond is too much to hope for, Dex, as long as she's in the spotlight. But I'm determined that whatever we have to go through, whatever we have to endure, will make our love that much stronger and our marriage that much more solid."

Dex studied his uncle. Jake's voice held the patience, willfulness and tenderness of a man hopelessly in love; a man who was determined to hold on to what he had, no matter what the cost because he had a woman he felt was well worth it. Dex knew firsthand how that felt.

"If things get too rough around here and the media get the nerve to invade your space, remember your family and that no matter what, we stick together."

Jake met his nephew's gaze, proud of the man he had become. "Thanks. I'll remember that."

Jake fought back another yawn. It was time to rescue his wife, yet again. First it had been the women in the Madaris family demanding her time, now it was the men.

Determinedly threading his way through the cluster of men surrounding his wife, he headed straight toward her. Finally reaching her, he came to a stop directly in front of her. "I came for my Diamond," he said, moments before sweeping her into his arms, ignoring her gasp of surprise and the men's startled looks.

"Sorry, this conversation is over, guys," he said, smiling.

Milton Madaris shot his brother a hard glare. "Who says?"

"I do, Milt. It's late. Besides, whether any of you noticed or not, the party ended hours ago. Good night." Jake then proceeded to leave the circle of men.

"Wait a minute, Jake," his brother Lee called out to him. "You can't leave before your guests. Where're your manners?"

Jake shot his brothers and nephews a mellow grin. "Upstairs. And if all of you will excuse me, I'm on my way up there to join them."

He walked a little ways before turning back to the group. "If you leave to return to Houston tonight, do have a safe trip back. If you decide to spend the night, please make yourselves at home. Just don't disturb me or Diamond. It was hard work planning this party and we're completely exhausted."

Jake's smile widened. Not for one minute did he think any of the men believed he was taking Diamond upstairs so the two of them could rest.

Chapter 16

"Did you get all the rest you needed last night, Jake?"

Jake's smile faded the moment he walked into his kitchen the next morning and found his nephew Clayton sitting at the table, drinking a cup of coffee. He walked over to the counter to pour his own cup. Ignoring Clayton's question, he drawled teasingly, "I guess it was too much to hope that all of you had left last night."

"Yep," Clayton said with a somewhat cocky grin. "Some of us decided to extend our visit for a day or so. It's every man's dream to be able to claim that he slept under the same roof as Diamond Swain."

"Diamond Swain Madaris," Jake corrected, slanting a glance in his nephew's direction. "She's going to start using her married name."

"And you're okay with that?" Clayton asked, studying his uncle while he sipped his coffee.

Jake lifted a brow as he walked over to the table and sat down. "Why wouldn't I be? She's my wife, and that's her name."

Clayton shrugged. "If for no other reason than for simplicity's sake. She's been Diamond Swain for so long, how do you think her fans will feel about the change?"

Jake looked pointedly at his nephew. "I'm sure they'll get over it. I would hope they can. And for those who can't, tough."

Clayton shook his head. "With that kind of attitude, it's good to know you're very supportive of her career."

"And what's that supposed to mean?"

"What it means, Uncle dearest, is that the woman you've chosen to live the rest of your life with is a woman who happens to bring countless hours of joy to millions of people with her acting abilities, not to mention her heart-stopping beauty."

"So?" Jake asked, still not understanding where Clayton was coming from and most importantly, just where he was going with this. For some reason, Clayton's attorney mind was at work. "What's the big deal, Clayton?"

Clayton took another sip of his coffee before answering. "The big deal may not be just the media. Oh, I think they'll cause you some problems at first, but I see a bigger problem that neither you nor Diamond have thought about."

Jake leaned back in his chair and stretched his legs out in front of him, crossing them at the ankle. "Which is?"

Clayton met his uncle's stare. "Her fans. Her very devoted fans. They can be just as bad with invading your privacy as the media."

Jake frowned as he leaned forward. "Diamond always had fans. So I'm asking you again, what's the big deal?"

Clayton sat up straight in his chair. "The big deal is that those same fans will probably want to latch on to you because now you're an extension of Diamond. Not only will you have the media to worry about, but you'll have to deal with Diamond's adoring fans, as well."

Not all of them are adoring, Jake thought, remembering the young man who had forced his way into Diamond's home a few weeks ago. He sighed as he sank back onto his chair. "Is there any reason you're telling me this?" he asked coolly, narrowing his eyes to slits. He had a feeling he was not going to care for Clayton's answer.

"The word is out, Jake. I don't have the slightest idea which one of our family members was so overjoyed at the thought of Diamond becoming a Madaris that they shared the news with friends—who evidently thought nothing of leaking it to the press. Take your pick as to who the culprit might be. You have several of your talkative kinfolk to choose from. But the fact remains that someone did, and news of your marriage to Diamond made the front page in the newspapers this morning across the country."

Jake shrugged. He and Diamond knew that news of their marriage was bound to leak out once he had told his family. Like he had warned her, there were some Madarises who didn't know how to keep secrets. "So it made the front page. That's all?"

"No."

"No?"

"No. The sheriff called to let you know that he stopped a convoy of reporters and fans who were headed out this way. He told them that Whispering Pines was private property and if they set foot on it un-invited, they could be arrested."

Clayton chuckled. "Let me rephrase that. He told them that they *would* be arrested."

Jake nodded. He would definitely have to remember Sheriff McCoy at reelection time. He got up and moved over to the sink to pour out his coffee. He'd suddenly lost the taste for it. "Sounds like everything's under control then."

"Not quite."

Jake turned from the sink and met Clayton's gaze. "What else is there?"

When Clayton didn't answer right away, Jake walked back over to the table. "I asked, what else is there?"

Clayton took a deep breath before handing Jake the high-tech digital phone recorder. "You need to get your phone number changed as soon as possible. This call came in early this morning. I thought I'd better save it. It's up to you as to what you do with it, although I'd be glad to offer suggestions."

Jake frowned as he took the tape player from Clayton. He pushed the button and a husky, somewhat muffled, male voice filled with anger began talking. *"If you're the Jacob Madaris who married Diamond, you'll be sorry. I stood by and let her make a mistake by marrying that race-car driver but I won't risk her being hurt. Get out of her life and leave her alone, or you'll pay a price that could cost you your life."*

The message ended, and Jake turned off the tape player.

"Well?" Clayton asked as he strained to watch the emotions that crossed Jake's face. There weren't any. Like Dex he was an expert at hiding them.

"Well, what?" Jake responded, taking the microchip out of the phone recorder and slipping it into the pocket of his jeans.

"What are you going to do about that call?"

"Nothing."

Clayton frowned. "If that's your position, then I think you're making a mistake. A big one. That caller sounded pretty serious. At least to be on the safe side, you should report that call to the police."

"Why? So the media can have a field day with it? Just because one lovesick fan of Diamond's threatens my life? The man's a quack. He had something to get off his chest, and he did."

Clayton shook his head. He refused to dismiss the call as easily as Jake wanted to do. "You need to be careful, Jake," he said, looking up at his uncle over the rim of his coffee cup. "That guy evidently took your marrying Diamond as something personal."

Jake looked annoyed. "Since you've gotten married, you worry too much, Clayton. You're becoming a pain in the—"

"Jake," Clayton interrupted. "In my profession you learn not to take everything with a grain of salt. Some things are worth worrying about. Just humor me and be careful. That episode with Trevor in South America took years off my life. I don't think I could handle anything major like that again."

Jake nodded slowly. Trevor Grant was a very close

childhood friend of his nephews, and the entire Madaris clan considered him as family. He had gone out of the country on a business trip several months ago and had ended up escaping into the jungle to elude terrorists. The only good thing that had come out of Trevor's adventure was the fact was he had escaped into the jungle with a woman—a woman he had ended up falling in love with and marrying. And now they were expecting their first child.

"All right," Jake finally said. "If it makes you happy, then I'll be careful."

"Thanks. I'd appreciate that." Clayton stared long and hard at his uncle before asking, "Are you going to tell Diamond about that call?"

"No." Jake stood. "She doesn't need to know. Like I said, the man probably just wanted to get some things off his chest. He'll get over it. Now if you don't mind, I have work to do."

"You should tell Diamond about that call, Jake. You know what they say about keeping secrets. Nothing is safe as a secret forever."

Jake frowned. Diamond had once told him that very same thing. "I am not telling her, Clayton, so forget it," he said firmly.

He turned and walked out of the kitchen.

Sunlight, in all its radiant glory, came pouring into Jake's bedroom window.

In a semiconscious state, Diamond stretched her naked body before cuddling up under the covers once more. The bed seemed larger, colder and emptier. Opening her eyes just a little, she stared at the vacant spot next to her. Deciding that if she couldn't have the real thing, then she would gladly settle for a substitute, she pulled Jake's pillow to her, burying her face in the richness of the scent of his masculinity that was entrenched there.

She didn't want to get up and wasn't sure she could even if she wanted to. Her body was sore and aching something fierce. Jacob's lovemaking last night had been hot, hungry and hard. She was grateful that his bedroom was off to itself, on a different wing away from all the other bedrooms. That had given them total and complete privacy.

She would not have been able to face any of his relatives again if she thought for one minute that they heard the primal moans, some louder than others, that had escaped her lips. She had not been able to stop herself from becoming wanton, desperate and wild in Jacob's arms last night, surrendering all to him. Nor could she stop herself from letting the heat and need pour out while he made love to her with everything that he had and then some. Their need for each other had been raw, rough and rippling.

Diamond sighed deeply as she lifted one hand to cover her eyes from the golden splash of sunlight propelling its way into the room. Instantly her mind flashed back to the party when Jake had introduced her to his family—and later when she had spent some time trying to get to know most of them, and enjoying every minute that she had done so. They had been more than understanding when she and Jacob had explained the reason they had kept their marriage a secret for a year and a half.

She shook her head. Jacob's family definitely had been more understanding than her father had been when she'd called him early yesterday morning to tell him about it. She knew he was upset about her marriage because it had effectively terminated any chance of her and Samuel ever getting back together. Not that there had been any chance of that anyway, but her father had felt that she should have forgiven Samuel for his one time of infidelity, but she hadn't agreed with his way of thinking. As far as she was concerned, by having that affair Samuel had destroyed the very essence of their marriage vows.

Diamond glanced down at the third finger of her left hand and the ring she now proudly wore. Finally, after eighteen months, she could wear the beautiful diamond ring Jacob had placed there on their wedding day.

Last night when she had stood on the top stair and looked down at him, he had stood tall and looked gorgeous dressed in his dark slacks and white dress shirt. Dressed much too formal for a family gathering, the sight of him had sent a rush of simmering need up her spine and had literally weakened her knees. But it wasn't just his physical appearance that she totally appreciated, it was his sense of honor that she loved and admired the most. Unlike Samuel, Jake would keep the vows they shared.

Her hand dropped to her stomach. A warm sensation settled there at the thought that even now she could be carrying Jacob's baby. They had not used any sort of protection since she had returned to Whispering Pines. She smiled to herself at the thought of being pregnant. More than anything, she wanted to give him a son or a daughter. In fact, she wanted at least three children if he was willing. There was no doubt in her mind that he would make a wonderful father.

That one night long ago, the night they had confessed their love for each other and had had unprotected sex, Jacob had wanted her pregnant, and he had hoped that she had gotten so. But she'd had mixed feelings about it. She had not been ready to settle down to a full-time life on his ranch. She had still been chasing her dream.

But now the life she knew didn't hold that appeal and excitement it once had. She was getting tired of jet-setting all across the country, filming movies, living out of a trailer with a dozen or so people hovering over her all at once. There were the makeup artist, the hairstylist, the manicurist, her script coach and the photographer, just to think of a few. All of them had a job to do on the movie set and contributed to the outcome of the movie.

She sighed. After talking with her father and having to deal with his unpleasant attitude, she had realized she had nothing to prove to him or anyone. The only person that mattered in her life was Jacob, the man who loved her and believed in her. He had unselfishly given her so much love and trust and now added to that was the family he had given her—a big wonderful family. She felt that she was a truly blessed woman.

Diamond heard the sound of the knob turning on the bedroom door and didn't have to wonder who was entering the room. She felt Jacob's presence in every cell of her body. His vibes flowed through every artery.

She lifted her head and fixed her gaze on her husband the moment he entered and closed the door behind him. He looked wonderful dressed just as he had been the first time she had seen him. He was wearing a Western shirt that covered his muscular chest and shoulders, and a pair of snug-fitting blue jeans that stretched neatly across every physical attribute he had. She tried not to notice the curvy firmness of his backside when he turned to lock the door behind him. He turned back around and gave her a heart-stopping and appealing smile.

"Good morning, sweetheart."

The husky rasp in his voice made Diamond's skin tingle. She smiled as she boldly stretched her body. Doing so made the covers slip off her breasts and down to her waist. She didn't bother to recover herself. "Good morning to you, Jacob. I'm convinced that I'd like this bed a whole lot more if you were in it with me."

Jake inwardly groaned at the sensation that seeing her breasts was doing to him. He remembered all the attention he had lavished on the twin peaks the night before. His breathing quickened as he remembered every little detail about last night. Every nerve in his body had sizzled with an inner fire that had subsequently blazed out of control.

He thought about the number of times during the course of the night that he had made love to her. Each time he had entered her body, pushing himself deep into her warmth, had nearly blown his mind with desire. His body had repeatedly rocked against her, desperately claiming her, completely possessing her, over and over again. And she had been just as wild and out of control as he had been, matching him move for move, stroke for stroke. They had thrashed about on the bed as their pace had grown faster and faster, and their mating had become harder and harder.

Jake leaned against the door, thinking that there

was no way her body wasn't sore this morning. It had to be after the intensity of that kind of lovemaking. He walked over to the bed. Reaching down he uncovered the rest of her body. Leaning closer he touched her.

His fingertips gently stroked her breasts before moving lower, skimming across her abdomen and moving lower still to caress the area around her inner thighs. From the look in her eyes, he could tell that this part of her body was sensitive to his touch. The part of him that had become so attuned to her felt the discomfort she was trying hard to hide.

"You're sore, baby," he said gently, tenderly.

Not giving Diamond a chance to respond to his comment, in one smooth sweep he picked her up in his arms. Walking through doors that led into rooms extending from his bedroom, he entered the room where he'd had workout equipment and a hot tub installed several years ago. He had discovered nothing soothed his tired, sore, aching body more after a long, tiring day spent on the range than relaxing in his hot tub.

Gently placing Diamond on her feet, he quickly began removing his own clothes. After that was done, he picked her up again and climbed the few stairs and carefully stepped into the water. He cradled her into his lap as he sank lower in his seat, allowing the hot water to completely cover their bodies. His hands gently massaged her body, kneading her flesh, as he tried to help release its soreness.

"I didn't mean to hurt you this way," he said tenderly, regretfully. "But last night I wanted you something awful, sweetheart."

Diamond settled against him, loving the feel of the hot water swirling around them, over their bodies. She loved the feel of him caressing her body. "I wanted you just as bad, Jacob, so you don't have to apologize. That's one bad thing about us being apart so much."

"What's that?"

"When we do spend time together, we try making up for lost time."

Jake nodded, knowing that was true, at least somewhat. He had a feeling he would probably want her just as much and just as often even if he looked in her face every single day.

"I may have a remedy for that," she said quietly.

Hearing the sedateness in her voice, Jake looked down at her curiously. "What's your remedy?"

"After I wrap up things in California with the project I'm presently working on, I want to move home permanently."

Instant spirals of happiness surged through Jake's entire body. He fully understood what she was saying, what she was offering. In his heart he knew that she had long ago accepted Whispering Pines as her home, which was something his ex-wife had never been able to do. Diamond had once explained to him that her home was where her heart was, and her heart would always be with him.

Although he knew what she was saying, he wanted to be absolutely sure nonetheless. "Is that really what you want, sweetheart?" he asked, his voice husky with emotion.

She turned in his arms to look at him. "Yes. What I want is to stop being hounded by the media. I want to stop having my private life the main topic over breakfast in homes around the country. I want that same private life—the one I'm sharing with you—off limits."

Diamond then tilted her chin up and met his searching gaze. "But most of all, Jacob, I want to build a future, a solid future with you here at Whispering Pines. I want to be your ranch mate as well as your soul mate. I want to always be here when you come home after spending a day on the range. I'm tired of feeling like a drop-in lover."

She draped her arms around his neck. "And more than anything, I want your baby. Boy or girl, it doesn't matter as long as it's from your seed. One that you've released inside my body while loving me."

Tears began misting her eyes. "You have been so wonderful, Jacob. You have been so very understanding. You've been my beacon of light during the storm and my calm after the storm. All the while I was jet-setting around the world, you were here waiting patiently every time I came home. I know how hard that must have been on you, to love me, sometimes from so far and not be able to acknowledge the fact that I was your woman, that I was your wife. You had to put up with reading garbage about me and other men, although you knew in your heart it wasn't true. I had selfishly asked a lot of you, and convinced myself it was for the best for the both of us. But now it's over. Whatever happens, we'll deal with it. The next time I come home, I don't plan on leaving again. I love you, Jacob, so very much."

Jake pulled her to him and cradled her in his arms. For the moment, he couldn't say anything. He just wanted to hold her and feel her tucked in his arms.

"And I love you," he said moments later. His heart was about to burst with all the love he felt for her. He lifted her chin with his fingers to meet her gaze. "But what about your chance at winning an Oscar? I don't want to take that away from you. I don't want to stand in the way of you fulfilling your dream."

Diamond smiled at him. "You won't. Winning an Oscar doesn't matter anymore." Drawing her legs up, she twisted around in his lap. "I think *Black Butterfly* has a good chance of winning Oscars for both me and Sterling next year. I believe our performances were just that good."

Jake nodded, knowing that anything she and Sterling starred in together was of excellent quality. *Black Butterfly* was a movie about early Spain under Moorish power, and the black Spanish queen that had ruled the country during that time. It was based on Spanish history that very few people knew about, but one that would be brought to the big screen with Diamond and Sterling in its leading roles. The movie was due to be released in June, and already critics were predicting it would be the hit of the summer.

Sterling and Diamond had filmed the movie together in Spain several months ago, right after Sterling had gotten married. The media had caused quite a stir, trying to figure out how Sterling was going to balance his recent marriage and his alleged affair with Diamond. Unfortunately Sterling had not explained his and Diamond's true relationship to his wife Colby, but she had trusted him enough not to believe the newspapers and tabloid headlines.

"Will you accompany me to the premiere showing?" Diamond asked, interrupting Jake's thoughts.

"Of course I will. I wouldn't miss any chance to be seen in public by your side."

Sighing happily, Diamond settled more deeply in Jake's arms.

"So you want a baby, huh?" Jake asked, reaching down and running the tips of his fingers over her flat tummy. The thought of his baby growing inside of her definitely felt right. The knowledge that he was in his forties, when most men ended rather than began fatherhood, didn't bother him.

"In all honestly, Jacob," Diamond said, looking directly at him, "I want babies, but I'll be more than happy to start off with just one."

Jake chuckled. "That's fine with me just as long as you don't get any ideas about having a tribe like Kyle and Kimara are intent on doing. With the twins she gave birth to on Christmas Day that makes six."

Diamond smiled. "I heard Kimara tell your mother last night that she wants another baby."

"What! They're nuts!"

Diamond laughed. "They like babies."

Jake snorted. "Kyle and Kimara like doing what you do to get babies. They need to stop spending so much time at Special K," he said of Kyle and Kimara's beautiful cabin in the North Carolina mountains. "Every time they spend time there is a pregnancy just waiting to happen." He frowned. "As Kyle's financial adviser, maybe I need to persuade him to invest heavily in a pharmaceutical company that specializes in developing birth control."

Diamond shook her head. "Leave them alone, Jacob. Let Kyle and Kimara have all the babies they want."

He reached out and cupped her face between his two hands so she would look into his dark eyes, bringing her mouth just inches from his. "If you insist."

"I do insist, and I think we should concentrate on

making a baby of our own." Diamond twisted her body around to straddle his thighs. When she did, the core of her femininity rubbed intimately against him, making his body harden.

"You're playing with fire, Diamond," he growled in her ear. The feel of her pressing against him was driving him insane.

"But I like your fire, Jacob," she whispered, fitting her body even closer to him, enjoying the sound of his uneven breathing, his quick intake of breath.

Jake's gaze moved lovingly over her features as hot, throbbing passion shook his body. "You're sore, baby, and if we do what people do to make babies, I'll have to carry you around the rest of the day because you'll be unable to walk."

"Big deal, carry me around. I like being in your arms."

"How will we explain things to my family?"

"What's there to explain? From the little girl-talk I had with one particular woman in your family, it seems most Madaris men are in heat most of the time anyway. So they'll understand the reason for my inability to move around comfortably."

"You don't say," Jake said, wondering which woman in his family she'd had that conversation with, and then having a pretty good hunch. He let out a slow breath as he moved his hands down Diamond's back and over her hips to hold her firmly to stop her from rubbing rhythmically against him.

"I'm just repeating what I've been told," she said, leaning forward to kiss the flat, dark nipples on his chest, and feeling his body respond as her tongue swept across it.

"Behave yourself, Diamond, or you'll be sorry later," he muttered thickly, trying to retain control of their situation. He couldn't think straight when she outright disobeyed him and the tip of her tongue continued to trace a path across his chest, moving from one male nipple to the next.

"You'll be sorry later," he repeated warningly, his voice husky, his breath catching in his throat.

Diamond shook her head, smiling. "No, I won't be sorry later. I'll be very satisfied later. We'll both be."

She brought her face to his and gave him a kiss that immediately made him forget everything except for pleasing her and giving her everything she wanted.

Chapter 17

Justin Madaris tried to hide his grin as he watched the play of emotions on his uncle Jake's face. Usually Jake was an expert at hiding his emotions. But not this time and definitely not today: emotions or no emotions, Jake was no match for the group of women surrounding him.

It would be interesting, Justin thought, what the outcome of the confrontation would be. His wife Lorren, Dex's wife Caitlin, Clayton's wife Syneda, his two sisters—Traci and Kattie—and his cousin Felicia were not going to give up and back down. They were intent on being just as stubborn as Jake.

Justin glanced around the card table at the husbands of those women. Fully aware of what was happening across the room, none of them seemed inclined to go to Jake's rescue or aid him in his cause. The only thing they were intent on doing was finishing their poker game. They were willing to let Jake deal with their wives the best way he could. After all, the women were his nieces. Besides, they knew Jake's fight was a losing one and that pretty soon, being the smart man that he was, he would realize it, too.

Justin smiled. Because he loved his uncle and because he knew this power play of woman versus man could last the rest of the day, Justin took a deep breath and decided to intervene, taking on his role of peacemaker in the family. "Give it up, Jake, and give in. You may as well because you're fighting a losing battle. Give them what they want, and come join us. The game's getting pretty interesting over here."

Jake sent Justin, as well as the other men who were seated across the room at the card table, a hard glare. "It wouldn't be a losing battle if all of you put more effort into controlling your wives."

"Our wives are your nieces," Daniel Green reminded Jake, not bothering to look up from his close study of the cards he held in his hands. "Surely you can get them to do something simple like going along with your way of thinking. That should be easy enough for you since you had a hand in raising Felicia, and everyone knows how controlled she was before Trask married her."

Felicia Madaris Maxwell rolled her eyes upward. "Thanks a lot, Dan."

"Don't mention it."

Felicia looked at her uncle, who was only a few years older than she was. "Really, Jake, all we're asking for is one night, a girls' night at the cabin, not an entire week's leave of absence. You've had Diamond for eighteen months, surely you can miss her presence for one night."

Jake crossed his arms over his chest. "Why can't you do this girls' thing right here? This house is plenty big enough. Why do you want to spend a night at the cabin?"

"For privacy," Caitlin Madaris said.

"For bonding," Traci Madaris Green added.

"To cultivate sisterhood," Lorren Madaris threw in.

"To get Diamond away from you for one night to give her body a rest."

Jake frowned. Not surprisingly the last statement was made by Clayton's wife Syneda. She was known to not bite her tongue about anything. She wouldn't hesitate to lay her cards on the table and play what she thought was a winning hand, something her husband was probably doing across the room at that very moment. Jake had a feeling she had been the one to share that information with Diamond about the Madaris men constantly being in heat.

Jake cleared his throat. "I don't have a problem with the privacy, the bonding, the cultivating of sisterhood or," looking pointedly at Syneda he said, "giving my wife a night of rest, but I still don't understand why you need to do it at the cabin and not here."

"Come on, Uncle Jake, a girls' night at the cabin won't hurt anything. Then you guys can play poker all night," his niece Kattie said.

Jake almost told her it was their plan to do that anyway. He let out a sigh and had to admit Syneda was right. His wife did need a break from him. She deserved at least one restful night. Right now she was upstairs sleeping off the exhaustion from their full morning of lovemaking. But still, he wasn't ready to give up his fight.

"Don't you ladies have children to take care of?"

"No," Caitlin answered quickly. "Mama Marilyn and Poppa Jonathan took the kids back to Houston with them, so all of us are children-free."

"And I don't have a child to worry about yet," Syneda added, smiling.

Jake lifted a brow. "Maybe that's your problem. Maybe you need a child to worry about so you can settle down and stop being everybody's advocate." He glanced across the room at his nephew. "Clayton, you need to work on getting your wife pregnant."

To Jake's surprise, and to the annoyance of the men at the card table who were intent on finishing the game, Clayton placed his cards down and stood up. He held out his arms and Syneda walked across the room into them. He wrapped her in his arms and lovingly kissed her on her lips. "My wife *is* pregnant. She found out this morning."

At first shocked silence, then earth-shattering elation followed Clayton's surprise announcement. The women raced over and pulled Syneda from Clayton's arms.

"Oh, Syneda, that's wonderful," Caitlin Madaris said in a choked voice. "Have you told the folks yet?"

Syneda was crying now, getting all emotional. So were all the other women. "Yes, Clayton and I told them before they left to return to Houston. They were very happy for us."

"I can't believe you're pregnant," a teary Kattie was saying. She was next in line to give Syneda a hug. "You and Clayton just got married eight months ago."

"This is a planned pregnancy, and at least we waited until *after* the wedding," Clayton said to his sister, playfully pulling one of the many braids on her head, and reminding her of how her situation had been.

"Tell Clayton to shut up, Raymond," Kattie said to her husband as she gave Syneda a hug.

"Shut up, Clayton," Raymond Barnes said teasingly to his brother-in-law. "So we goofed. Everybody isn't as fetishistic about birth control as you were," he added. "You're the only man I know who kept a case of condoms in his closet."

"Oh, Syneda, we're so happy for you," Traci and Felicia were saying together, giving Syneda double hugs.

Next came Lorren Madaris. She stood in front of Syneda for the longest time without saying anything. She didn't have just a few tears, she had an entire bucket of them. And everyone in the room understood why. Lorren and Syneda were childhood friends who had grown up together in the same foster home. There was a strong bond between them. Through the years, they had always been there for each other and now by marrying brothers, they were blessed to be in the same wonderful family.

Lorren finally gave her dearest and closest friend a long hug and burst into more tears.

"You ought to do something before Lorren has us floating out of here, Justin," Dex leaned over and whispered to his brother.

Knowing Dex was right, Justin stood and walked over to Syneda and Lorren, who were hugging and crying at the same time. Gently pulling Lorren into his arms, he handed Syneda over into Clayton's.

"Congratulations, baby brother. Welcome to father-hood," he said to Clayton before placing full attention to consoling his wife.

Jake walked over to his nephew by blood and his niece by marriage. He cared deeply for the both of them and like everyone else, he was caught up in the happiness and the excitement of their news.

He shook his head. Clayton and Syneda had been the least likely two to get involved with each other, and had shocked the hell out of the family when they had announced that they were getting married. Now they were surprising everyone again with Syneda's preg-nancy. He thought they were the two least likely people who'd want to become parents, at least this soon. He'd figured they would wait at least four to five years. He had always thought they were more into es-calating their professional careers than their family status. Now it seemed that starting a family meant a whole lot to them. There was no doubt in his mind that they would make good parents.

"Have you told your father yet, Syneda?" Jake asked.

Syneda looked up at Jake, smiling at him through her tears. "Not yet. Clayton and I are going to Austin as soon as we leave here tomorrow. We'll tell Dad then. I can't wait."

"I wish Diamond was awake so she could share in your good news. She and I are very happy for you and Clayton."

"Thanks, Jake."

The card game forgotten, the other men stood and walked over to console their wives, who seemed intent on staying emotional.

Dex Madaris let out a huge chuckle. "Heaven help us all. That kid will be the most argumentative child on earth."

"And one of the best-dressed," Kattie piped in, thinking about Clayton's and Syneda's flair for fashion.

"Heaven help the future women of Houston if it's a boy," Raymond Barnes said, laughing. "Especially if he turns out to be a chip off the old block. You may want to put that case of condoms somewhere in storage."

"And heaven help the future gents if it's a girl," Jake added, grinning. "She'll have no pity on the opposite sex."

Trask Maxwell pulled his wife into his arms. "I wonder what's going to happen next," he said. "With my and Felicia's wedding last month, news of Jake's secret marriage yesterday and finding out Clayton and Syneda are going to be parents today—shows that there are never dull moments in this family."

At least that was something everyone in the room agreed with.

Jake tipped into his bedroom and found Diamond still sleeping. The sun was shining brightly into the room through the blinds—however, the way they were angled kept any direct sunlight from hitting her.

He walked over to the bed. She was lying atop the covers in a short, very skimpy nightshirt that was un-buttoned. His breath caught in his throat when he looked down at her. He thought of his family down-stairs, celebrating Clayton and Syneda's news and wondered just how he would feel when the day came and Diamond told him she was carrying his child.

Jake knew that would be the happiest day of his life. He knelt beside the bed and reached out to touch her. Being careful not to wake her, he pushed her shirt aside and let his hands touch her flat belly. It was a belly that would one day grow with his child. He had never given much thought to fatherhood until he had met Diamond. Now he couldn't help but think of anything else than them sharing a love and a product of their love.

He caressed her stomach, imagining a child growing inside of her. His child. He would love it, protect it and be the kind of father his father was to him, his brothers were to their children and his nephews were to theirs. He bowed his head in silent prayer, thanking God for sending this woman, this very special woman, into his life. And he made a vow that if they were ever blessed with a child, he would always be there for his son or daughter. Sealing his promise, he leaned over and placed a special kiss on her stomach.

Diamond mumbled in her sleep. "Jacob." His name was whispered off her lips while she slept.

Jake placed a kiss on her lips. "I love you."

Standing, he walked across the room and eased out of the door, knowing if he stayed he would be tempted to wake her and make love to her again and again and again.

The man was angry. He was more angry than he had been in a long time. He crushed the newspaper in his hand. If Jacob Madaris thought he was going to get away with this, he had another thought coming.

The man pushed himself back from the table, disgusted with the way things were going. If what he had read was true and Diamond had been secretly married eighteen months, then she had been at risk all that time. He could not let any man hurt her. Men could be physically brutal to women like her, and he would protect her with his life if he had to. He was determined that he would protect her the way he had not protected his sister.

"A girls' night at the cabin?" Diamond asked her husband excitedly. "Oh, Jacob, that's sounds wonderful. Whose idea was it?"

Not mine, that's for sure, he thought as he sat across the bedroom in a chair and watched his wife get dressed. Damn, she looked good. She had slept most of the morning, and it was a little past noon. He watched as she struggled with the zipper on her jeans, thinking just how tempted he was to walk across the room to peel the things off her again.

Jake forced his mind back to what they were discussing. "I think it was Syneda's idea, but then all the others jumped on the bandwagon about it.'

Diamond looked up from snapping her jeans at the irritation in Jake's disgruntled tone. She studied his features. "I take it you're not too crazy about the idea."

One corner of Jake's mouth lifted into a smile. "I'm not crazy about any idea that takes you away from me, even for a night."

After slipping into her blouse, Diamond walked across the room and eased into her husband's lap and wrapped her arms around his neck. "It's just for one night, Jacob. Besides, you had mentioned that you and the guys would be playing poker all night anyway."

He sighed heavily. "I know, but I still wanted you close by."

"And I will be." Diamond snuggled closer into his arms. "I've never been to an all-girls' sleepover before. I think it will be fun."

"You're kidding—you've never done the pajama party thing? I thought all girls did something like that at least once in their lifetime. I know for a fact that all my nieces used to have sleepovers all the time."

"Well, I didn't. My father wouldn't allow it. He never wanted me to have close girlfriends."

Jake frowned. He couldn't help but wonder what other things she had missed out on during her childhood by being the daughter of Jack Swain. "But I thought you spent a lot of time with your grandmother while your father traveled."

"I did, but Dad had given her strict rules and she knew better than to break them and put her at risk of losing me. So the only friends I had were the ones he selected for me."

Intrigued and more curious about her childhood, he said, "Like Kyle and Sterling?"

"Yes. Dad thought friendships with men were safer. He claimed women befriended each other one minute then couldn't stand each other the next. It was natural for me and Kyle Garwood to become friends since our families were well-acquainted. In fact, Kyle's grandfather is the one who financed my father's first movie. As a child growing up, I occasionally spent my summers at Kyle's grandfather's cabin in the mountains."

"Special K?"

"Yes, Special K. I met Sterling through Kyle when I was in my teens. The three of us—Sterling, Kyle and I—became best buddies and have remained so over the years."

She looked at Jake. "So there were never girlfriends around to have fun with, to discuss our coming-of-age and all the things that went with it, to share breathy revelations or earth-shattering secrets. You know, just someone to hang out with.

"And," she said, pulling in a deep breath, "it's been only recently that I've realized what I missed out on. Just the little time I spent with your nieces has shown me how close they are and just how much fun they have together. I think it was nice of them to include me in their group."

Jake cocked his head to look at Diamond carefully. Again he was reminded of what Sterling had told him about her in the beginning. She was a person who loved people and who enjoyed being around them. But because of her status in life, she'd been denied that. Now it seemed her father had denied her other things as well. Something as elemental as having another woman for a friend.

"Of course they would include you," he said. "You're a part of the family, and they think you're special. Not only because of your accomplishments in the movie and film industry, but because you're also the one who captured my heart."

He chuckled. "Everyone had pretty much given up on me in the love department. But you came along and changed that."

Diamond smiled at him. "So you don't have a problem with my staying at the cabin tonight with your nieces?"

"No, I don't have a problem with it." *Not anymore,* he thought. *You really need that time to formulate friendships you've been denied.*

Jake stood with her in his arms. "Oh yeah, before I forget, I need to let you know that I'm having the telephone number here changed."

Diamond lifted a brow. "Why?"

"Because it's accessible to the public. Since the news of our marriage appeared in the morning paper, anyone can call here." *Someone already has,* he didn't bother to add.

"Oh, I didn't think of that," she said, as he placed her on her feet. "And we do want all the privacy we can get, don't we?"

He reached out and let his thumb caress her cheek. "Yes, baby, we do."

Chapter 18

The next day, Diamond stood at the window in Jake's bedroom and gazed out. As far as her eyes could see, there were endless plains of lush green peaks and valleys. This was her home, the home Jacob Madaris had given her to be shared with him and his family.

This was Whispering Pines. It was Madaris land that had been in the family for six generations. She could just imagine the hard work, labor and tiring days that had gone into keeping the land out of the hands of others. Jacob had once told her that there had been a number of African-American families in Texas who had been fortunate to own spreads such as this over a hundred years ago, but very few of them still owned them today. The Madarises were in that few.

Diamond stood spellbound. The beauty of the setting sun nearly took her breath away. She didn't think she would ever get tired of such a beautiful view, and from this window you could see it all. She wondered if that was the reason Jacob had placed his bedroom on this side of the house and at this angle so that at any given time he could stand at this window and be reminded of all he owned—all the land he had been blessed to inherit from his family.

"Home," she said softly. Whispering Pines was home. No matter where she went or what other places she traveled, here with Jacob was where she preferred being above all else.

She didn't bother to turn around when she heard the bedroom door opening. As always, she sensed her husband's presence. After his family had left to return to their homes, he had gone riding the range to help his men look for a few strays.

Gently grabbing her by the shoulders, he slowly turned her around to him. "What are you thinking?" Jake asked her.

Diamond sighed and looked up at him. "Everything. Too much. Not enough."

He dropped his hands from her shoulders and raised a questioning brow. "Translate."

She couldn't help but chuckle. "I'm thinking of everything because this place is so beautiful and I love it so. Then I'm thinking too much, because no matter how much I try I'd never be able to fully appreciate just what you have given me here. And I think not enough because I don't think there will ever be enough words to tell you just how I feel. I have so much to be thankful for. You, your family, Blaylock, the men who work for you. All of you are so special to me, Jacob. For the first time in my life I feel so very blessed."

She smiled up at him. "Like last night, for instance, when I spent the night at the cabin with your nieces. That time was very special for me."

Jake gently pulled her into his arms. "You never told me what you all did last night and what all you talked about.

Diamond laughed. "Because, Jacob Madaris, you never gave me the chance."

He joined her in laughter. "No, I didn't, did I?" he said, remembering how he had arrived at the cabin on horseback right after breakfast to claim his wife. A night at the cabin was all he had agreed to. He'd had no intention of his nieces imposing on his day with Diamond, as well. He had walked into the kitchen, nodded good-morning to all those present and walked straight over to Diamond and picked her up in his arms saying, "I came for my Diamond." He had carried her outside and placed her on his horse behind him and had ridden off, totally ignoring the surprised and shocked look on his nieces' faces.

Instead of taking Diamond back to the ranch like he'd originally intended, and where he knew his nephews were still sleeping off a long night of playing poker, he had taken her to his private place where he had shown her just how much he'd missed her.

"Well, what did you ladies talk about?"

"Umm," Diamond moaned contentedly. "You know, girl stuff. Movies, fashions, trips we've taken, the men we love, Syneda's pregnancy, our weight…that sort of stuff. We had such a good time that we're planning on doing something like that again. I invited them to spend some time at our place in California since we've decided to keep it even after I move here permanently."

Jake nodded. Ever since their marriage, everything that had been "his" and "hers" had automatically become "theirs" and "ours." There had never been any discussion about it. There was a silent understanding between them that they would share their love and everything else that came with it.

"I would love for them to go with me to Jackie's Spa and Resort," Diamond was saying. "You know, the place I told you about that's tucked away in the heart of the California mountains. I think it would be a perfect place to relax, enjoy a little bit of pampering and unlimited use of the spa's facilities and activities."

Diamond paused, lifted her gaze to his and smiled. "What do you think?"

Jake leaned down and kissed her lips. "Besides thinking you're beautiful, I think the ladies will enjoy it." A somewhat serious expression then crossed his features. "And I think that we need to talk about something."

Diamond saw his expression and immediately became concerned. "What is it, Jacob?" She touched his arm. "What's wrong?"

"Clayton just called. He thinks it would be a good idea for us to hold a press conference tomorrow."

Diamond's heart slowed for one tiny millimeter of a second. "A press conference?"

"Yes. We need to either confirm or deny what everyone has been reading in the papers for the last two days. Since we've had this phone number changed and Sheriff McCoy is doing a good job at keeping reporters away, the media are in a frenzy. There are a lot of questions on everyone's mind. You disappeared seemingly off the face of the earth, right after that

incident in California. Your multitudes of adoring fans
are concerned. Now they read in the papers, two weeks
later, that you're married to me, who just happens to
be a very close friend of Sterling Hamilton's, the man
who's been your alleged lover for the past two years."
Jake couldn't help but chuckle. "To some people, all
of that is more interesting than the most top-rated soap
opera."

Diamond nodded. "There's something else, too,
isn't there? What aren't you telling me, Jacob?"

Jake took a deep breath and captured Diamond's
hand in his. "It seems that when some of my family
returned to Houston they found reporters camped out
on their lawns."

He felt Diamond tremble and tightened his hold on
her hand.

"Oh, Jacob, I'm sorry. This is what I didn't want
to—"

"Shh, baby. It's okay. My family knows how to
handle this. They dealt with the media before with
that incident involving Syneda."

"But I wanted to protect all of them from this. I
wanted to protect you."

"Don't worry about it, sweetheart. Like I said, the
Madarises can handle the heat, trust me. But I think
you and I need to officially announce our marriage so
people can stop guessing and stop hunting for answers."

Diamond nodded, knowing he was right. "I'll
contact Robin and let her set up things." Robin Weston
was her publicist. "Do you have a preference as to
where you want to hold the press conference?"

"Let's hold the first one in Houston. Then we'll

fly out to California and hold another one there the following day.'

Diamond's shoulders sagged. "But that will take you away from the ranch."

Jake shrugged. "Doesn't matter. Getting this done is more important."

She nodded as she reached up and slipped her arms around his neck and gazed adoringly into his eyes. "You're a wonderful man. Do you know that?"

He pulled her into his arms. "Only because you're constantly telling me that I am. You, Mrs. Madaris, are pretty good medicine for my ego."

She smiled. "And you, Mr. Madaris, are fantastic medicine for anything and everything that ails me."

"I think you're making a very wise decision, Diamond," Robin was saying over the telephone. "I didn't want to call and bother you about what's been happening here, but it's been crazy ever since the story of your marriage broke. Reporters are calling every three seconds. I spoke with Edward Stewart, Sterling's attorney, and he said things are just as crazy over there. It's a good thing Sterling is at his home in the North Carolina mountains so the reporters can't get through to him."

Diamond nodded. "I'll give Sterling a call to give him a heads-up as to what Jacob and I will be doing. Make all the arrangements, Robin. Jacob and I want to hold the first press conference in Houston."

"Got it. I'll call you back after everything is set and ready to roll."

"Thanks, Robin."

"And Diamond?"

"Yes?"

"For all it's worth, I think it's about time you let the world know about that gorgeous hunk of Texan you've been hiding. The two of you make a beautiful couple. Every time I'm around you and Jacob, I feel so much love radiating between you two. You are a very blessed woman. And I'm sure everyone who sees you two together, especially all of your adoring fans, will be happy for you."

"Thanks. It's not my fans I'm worried about, Robin, it's the media. You know how they can be at times."

"Well, I think with Jacob Madaris by your side, you have nothing to worry about."

After Diamond had hung up the telephone she took a long, deep breath, not understanding why she was feeling so nervous. She had done press conferences before, numerous times, first with her father, then later alone or with other actors and actresses. She and Sterling had done several in the past two years, denying rumors of their alleged affair. She couldn't understand why she felt so uneasy about this one.

In her line of business, press conferences were expected. Whenever celebrities had major changes in their lives, the media felt they had a right to know about it. It was better to face a ton of them in an organized and formal setting than being cornered by them at the airport or on your front doorstep.

She and Samuel had done a press conference to announce their engagement the day before the Indy 500, in which he was a participant. They had done another press conference three months later to announce their marriage. The media had asked probing questions, which she thought were none of their business. But Samuel had answered them anyway. That had been the cause of their first argument. She had later learned that he enjoyed the media attention and that he would use anything, including the intimate details of their marriage, to get it.

Diamond took another deep breath. She needed all the strength she could muster for the press conference.

Jake had known exactly what he was doing in setting up their first press conference in Houston, where most of his family resided. It was decided it would be held on the campus of Texas Southern University in the Barbara Jordan Auditorium; an auditorium that Dex's company, Madaris Explorations, had provided funding to build.

As expected the place was packed. Among the members of the Madaris family in attendance were community leaders, members of the Cattlemen Association and long-time friends. All had been specifically invited and were there to give their support.

Jake and Diamond walked into the auditorium together holding hands and appearing to everyone like the epitome of a picture-perfect couple. He was dressed in a dark gray suit, and she was wearing a very chic, very stylish tailored blue pantsuit and looking like she had just stepped off the cover of a magazine. Even before they had stepped in front of the microphone it was obvious that they had dazzled the members of the media.

The reporters went into action and began firing their questions amid the flashbulbs exploding all around them. Conrad Ammons, a reporter known for his tenaciousness and hostile interviewing skills, started off by asking, "Is it true that you and Jacob Madaris are married and have been for nearly a year and a half? If so, why did you hide that fact, and why did you and Sterling Hamilton deliberately make fools of the media by leading us to believe the two of you had a thing going on?"

Before Diamond could respond, another reporter asked, "And if you are married, how does your father feel about it since to this day he still maintains a relationship with your ex-husband?"

A third reporter requested, "And could you please give us details about that attack on you in your home in California."

Diamond smiled up at Jacob and took a deep breath. When she faced the crowd to everyone's eyes she looked totally ravishing and in complete control. "One question at a time, please," she said in a deceptively calm voice. "First, to answer your questions, Mr. Ammons."

She glanced again up at Jacob and gave him an adoring smile. He smiled back at her and tightened his arms around her. "Yes, Jacob Madaris and I are married and have been for eighteen months, four days, three hours and—" after glancing at her watch added, "—twenty-four minutes and twelve seconds."

At everyone's chuckle, she continued. "The reason Jacob and I decided to keep the news of our marriage a secret was to preserve our privacy for as long as we could. And as for Sterling Hamilton, he's a very close friend to the both of us. Jacob and I hold him responsible for bringing us together, and we will be indebted to him for the rest of our lives."

She then glanced around the room, letting her gaze light on the numerous reporters present before speaking again. "Sterling and I have told all of you on numerous occasions that there was nothing between us and that we were just friends. But a number of you didn't believe us and wanted to make it out to be more. You couldn't accept the idea that a man and woman could be close friends without there being anything sexual between them. So we gave up trying to convince you otherwise. You printed what you wanted to believe and nothing Sterling and I ever told you. I didn't lie to you, Mr. Ammons. You lied to yourself and your readers by printing the untruth."

Diamond knew that she had effectively put Conrad Ammons in his place. She also knew that doing so would probably come back and haunt her one day. The man had a history of holding grudges against various members of the entertainment industry if he felt they had crossed him in some way. She took a deep breath in accepting that she was now probably on his list. She blinked when what she thought was a smile curved his lips. She quickly thought she must have been mistaken.

She swung her head toward the reporter who had asked the second question. "As for my father, you're right. He does have a close relationship with my ex-husband, Samuel Tate. However, although I can't speak for my dad, I believe he's very happy for me."

Looking at the reporter who had asked the third question, she said, "There's nothing to add about the young man who broke into my home other than to say that I wasn't injured, just scared out of my wits."

"Mr. Madaris, how do you feel about being married to Diamond Swain?"

Jacob's arms around Diamond tightened even more. "I feel like an extremely lucky and happy man."

"Ms. Swain, there's a rumor that you're thinking about giving up acting to become a rancher's wife."

Diamond smiled at the reporter who had asked the question. "I'm already a rancher's wife, and I am thinking about it," she said, not ready to tell them of her decision. It would be her and Jacob's secret for a while. Telling them would lead to too many other questions. "It is my and Jacob's dream to one day have a family. And when that time comes, I will gladly trade my role as an actress to become the mother of his children."

"So you want more than one?"

"Yes, I was an only child, so I want my child to have a playmate. Jacob says we'll have at least two, maybe three."

"What do you have to say?"

She glanced up at Jacob and gave him a brilliant smile. "I'm going to try my best to convince my husband that we need at least four."

After that a number of other questions were asked. Some of them were directed at Diamond, others to Jake and some to the both of them. The final question was asked before it was decided to wrap up the press conference.

"Mr. and Mrs. Madaris, I'm sure there are a number of magazines that are just dying to do an exclusive story on you two. Everyone is interested in knowing how you met, fell in love and managed, quite nicely I might add, to keep the news of your marriage from the press." The reporter shook his head, smiling in admiration. "I must take my hat off to you two for a job well done. Have the two of you made any decisions as to what magazine will be doing that exclusive story? I'm sure your fans are dying to know."

Diamond looked up at Jake. "I think we'll keep that information a closely guarded secret for as long as we can."

After that statement, Robin Weston announced to everyone that the press conference was over. Afterward the photographers had a field day, taking numerous photos of the stunning couple.

"Well, how do you think I did?" Diamond asked Jake.

Instead of answering her, he kissed her in front of the cameras, among all the flashing lights. When he released her, she smiled at the photographers.

"I guess that's Jacob's way of saying that I did okay."

The news conference in California the following day went just as smoothly, although Diamond was asked more detailed questions regarding the incident of the irate fan breaking into her home.

As usual, Conrad Ammons was again one of the reporters. Diamond had hoped that she had answered enough questions to suffice for the reporter at the press conference in Houston, but evidently, that had not been the case.

"I'm glad that's over with," Jake said when they had returned to their hotel room in Beverly Hills. He ripped the tie from around his neck. "What it is with that Ammons guy? He's like a dog with a bone. Once he gets a hold of something, he can't let go. He needs a life. Does he usually follow you around like that from press conference to press conference?"

"Yes, a number of reporters do. It's their job." Diamond smiled, then yawned. "Today was a hectic day, and I am tired." Diamond wasn't too tired to notice the agitated look on Jacob's face. "What is it, Jacob? What's bothering you? Is there anything you want to talk about?"

Jake shook his head. "There's nothing bothering me. Like you, I'm just tired." He walked over to her and kissed her nose and pulled her into his arms. "Come on, let's get ready for bed. We both need a good night's sleep. I have a feeling that tomorrow will be just as tiring."

Later that night Jake lay awake for a long time, holding Diamond in his arms. He watched the moonlight that was peeking through the curtains shimmer softly across her sleeping features.

He sighed deeply. He hadn't wanted to tell her earlier how the press conference they had been a part of that day had grated on his nerves with the relentless questions the reporters had asked. He wondered how in the world she could spend her life enduring something like that constantly. He'd had to bite his tongue not to tell one or two calloused reporters to take their questions and shove it.

No wonder Whispering Pines had been a haven for Diamond. While there she didn't have to worry about reporters harassing her. Jake's mind thought of one reporter in particular by the name of Conrad Ammons. There was something about the man he didn't like, and from the direct eye contact the man had cut his way several times, evidently the feeling was mutual.

Not that he cared, thought Jake. But he was curious

as to what was Ammons's problem. Deciding the reason was insignificant and not enough to lose sleep over, he pushed the thought to the back of his mind.

Jake pulled Diamond closer into his arms, and a short while later, he joined her in sleep.

The ringing of the telephone woke Jake. He reached for it on the nightstand next to the bed before it could wake Diamond.

He said hello as he glanced over at the clock. It was three in the morning.

"You're not a smart man, Jacob Madaris. I've given you fair warning to leave Diamond alone," the muffled male voice said. "Take my advice, and do what you're told. You two don't belong together. Although I would never hurt Diamond, I wouldn't hesitate to do harm to you. Remember that."

Fury consumed Jake. "You can go to—"

The caller hung up before Jake could finish telling him exactly where he could go.

Recognizing the muffled voice, Jake knew the caller was the same person who had called the ranch a few days ago. It was a caller he had dismissed as being a quack, but now…

Jake couldn't help but wonder how the person knew that he and Diamond were staying at this particular hotel. He could only guess that the information had somehow gotten leaked to the press. He raked a hand across his face. Should he be concerned with the caller like Clayton thought he should be?

He pulled Diamond into his arms. At three in the morning, he was too tired to think straight. He would give it more thought tomorrow. Right now the only thing he wanted to do was to get some more sleep in the arms of the woman he loved.

Conrad Ammons took another long swig of liquor directly out of the bottle. He knew one thing for certain. If Jacob Madaris was a smart man, he would eventually take heed of his warnings.

He remembered the first time he had seen Diamond, sitting next to her father at a press conference. She had been only seventeen at the time, and Jack Swain was announcing his daughter's emergence into the entertainment arena. There had been such a freshness about her, such a young innocence. It had struck him that day that she'd had a striking resemblance to his baby sister Caroline when she had been that age.

Caroline had left their parents' home in a small Ohio town and had come to California to live with him after graduating from high school. There had been this sweet small-town innocence about her. And as hard as he had tried, he could not protect her from the men who had been determined to take advantage of it. Maybe if he had tried harder, Caroline would still be alive today with the acting career she had always wanted. Instead his sister had fallen in love and married some wealthy guy who appeared to be treating her like a queen, but in reality, behind close doors he was physically abusing her.

Ammons took another swig out of the bottle. By the time he became aware of what his sister was going through, it was too late. The man killed Caroline senselessly one night in a bout of jealous rage.

Remembering what had happened to Caroline, he had left the news conference that day determined to protect the seventeen-year-old Diamond from marrying a man who would claim to love her and would only hurt her. It was apparent to him that her father had no intention of offering her any such protection. The only thing Jack Swain wanted was to advance his daughter's acting career.

Now eighteen years later, he was still obsessed with protecting Diamond. It had been hard over the years to treat her with indifference at press conferences. He couldn't pamper her in front of the other reporters without running the risk of their getting suspicious of his role in her life. So as not to give anything away, he'd had to use his hard-nosed line of questioning with her just like he did with all the other celebrities he interviewed.

He took another drink, thinking that she didn't need to be married. She could do just fine without a husband. All a man would eventually do was hurt her, and he wouldn't let that happen. He was determined to do for her what he didn't do for Caroline.

It had angered him when she had married that race-car driver, Samuel Tate. Twice he had managed to sabotage Tate's car before a race, and twice Tate had miraculously walked away unharmed. He was about to make his third attempt when Diamond had released a statement to the press, announcing her pending divorce from Tate. It was lucky for the man that she had done that.

He hadn't felt threatened by her alleged involvement with Sterling Hamilton. Since not all love affairs ended in marriage, Hamilton had been spared his anger. One could walk away from an affair—but when you were married to someone, you were doomed for life to take all kinds of abuse.

Now Diamond had gone and hitched herself to a rancher. That would never do since she was even thinking of leaving California to live permanently on the man's ranch in Texas. No telling what the man would do to her on that isolated stretch of land out there in the middle of nowhere. She would not have anyone around to protect her.

He couldn't let what happened to Caroline happen to her. He had to do something to protect Diamond. He would stop at nothing to keep her safe from overbearing and abusive men.

From both press conferences, he could tell that she actually thought Jacob Madaris was the love of her life. Unfortunately, Caroline had thought the same thing of Spencer Campbell.

He would give Madaris another warning. If that didn't work, he would put into action a plan to rid Diamond of him forever.

Chapter 19

When Jake awoke the next morning, he was surprised to find Diamond was already up and moving about. Lifting himself up on one elbow, he watched her move around the room, getting dressed.

"Good morning. Going someplace?"

Diamond looked up from slipping into her shoes and smiled. "Jacob, I'm sorry. I didn't mean to wake you. I wanted to let you sleep for a while longer," she said, putting on her jacket. "Robin and I are meeting downstairs in the coffee shop to work on the press release that will be going out later today. I was going to leave a note on the dresser."

Jake nodded as he eased out of bed. Every muscle in his body ached. Because of his height, he and hotel beds did not always get along. He stretched his body to work some kinks out of it. "What time do you think you'll be ready to fly out of here today?"

Diamond heard Jake's words, but her mind and her gaze were focused on his body, which was clad only in a pair of briefs. No man, she thought, should be that well put together and that built. Nice chest, muscular shoulders, tight buns, flat tummy.

Interesting. Sexy.

Her gaze left his flat tummy and moved up to his face. She saw his pupils darken and his nostrils flare when he sensed her interest. The air surrounding them began to sizzle with stimulating awareness. She wondered if this sudden heat, this spontaneous attraction, would always be there between them.

She ran her tongue lightly over her lips. Now was not a convenient time for her and Jacob to go rolling about between the sheets. Robin was probably downstairs, waiting for her at this very minute, and Diamond knew if she didn't leave the room in the next five minutes, she never would for the balance of the day.

She took a step back when Jake took a step forward. "Jacob, what did you ask me about leaving today?" she asked quickly, taking another step back.

He flashed her a smooth smile as he gave her one of his long, heated looks. "I forgot. My mind is on other things right now."

Diamond nodded slowly. "All right, Jacob, you will behave yourself, won't you?"

Jake shrugged. "I suppose," he said without much conviction in his voice.

"Okay, then, what were you asking me?"

With a smile that was oozing with not-so-hidden promises, he said, "I asked what time do you think we'll be ready to leave for Texas?"

Diamond swallowed past the lump in her throat

and replied, "Anytime after lunch. Do you want me to order up breakfast for you?"

"Not really. As far as I'm concerned, I have a pretty tasty morsel within arm's reach if she'll just give me the chance to—"

"Jacob, stop it," Diamond said, shaking her head, grinning.

"If you insist."

"I do."

"In that case, no, you don't have to order me anything. I'll order it myself after I take a shower and get dressed. I need to call Gary to let him know the time we'll be leaving so he'll have the plane fueled and ready to go."

At that moment, someone banged loudly on the door. "Wake up you two lovebirds and let me in before I get thrown out of this place."

"Kyle!"

Diamond raced to the door and opened it for their friend. She threw her arms around him for a huge hug. "What are you doing here? Where's Kimara and the kids?"

Kyle Garwood entered the hotel room, closing the door behind him. Like Jake he was a tall man, and his imposing stature nearly filled the room. "After we left Whispering Pines, we followed Sterling and Colby to their place in the mountains. I left Kimara and the kids there since I knew I had a business trip out here," Kyle said. "What I didn't know was that you two were here until I read it in this morning's paper. Then I ran into Robin downstairs in the lobby and she gave me your room number." Kyle smiled. "Oh, by the way, the two of you made the front page."

Jake shook his head. "Figures." He looked over at the man whom he had known for a number of years. First as a business associate and then as a friend. Like Sterling, he considered Kyle as one of his most trusted and loyal friends. Kyle was also very objective when it came to making sound decisions, business or otherwise. Maybe it wouldn't be such a bad idea to discuss with Kyle those two phone calls he had received to get another opinion on them.

"Have you had breakfast yet?" Jake asked Kyle.

"No."

"Good. Diamond is meeting Robin downstairs, and I was going to be eating breakfast alone. Now you can join me."

Kyle smiled and gave Jake a thumbs-up. "That sounds like a winner to me, partner."

Jake held the cup tightly in his hand and inhaled the scent of the strong black coffee. He heard Kyle's chuckle.

"I take it you need that, Jake."

Jake glanced up. "If only you knew how much." He slowly took a sip and shook his head frowning. "Blaylock's coffee is better."

Kyle chuckled again. "I wouldn't doubt that."

Jake glanced over at Kyle's plate. They had ordered room service. "Eating for two, Kyle?"

A corner of Kyle's mouth curved slightly. "No, actually I'm eating for six. It's not easy trying to keep up with six little ones. How Kimara does it, I don't know. Whenever I'm home, I try giving her a break by helping out with them all I can."

"Yet the both of you want more kids?"

"Just one more."

Jake rolled his eyes upward. "But there's a chance you two run the risk of having a third set of twins, right?"

Kyle smiled. "Yeah, the doctors claim there is a slim chance," he said. He paused and lifted his brow. "Although my and Kimara's breeding habits may be an interesting subject, that's not what's really on your mind, is it, Jake? So what gives?"

After taking another sip of coffee, Jake provided Kyle with all of the details of the two phone calls he had received. Afterwards he watched Kyle's mind silently at work. "So, Garwood, what do you think? And don't tell me to go to the police. I don't want the media to get ahold of this."

Kyle gave a slight nod of his head. "I understand. And you're sure this person who's calling isn't the same guy who broke into Diamond's home three weeks ago? According to the papers, he's out on bail."

Jake shook his head. "Diamond said he was an eighteen-year-old. I'd put the age of the person who called those two times in their middle thirties or early forties."

Kyle nodded. "What I wouldn't do, Jake, is ignore this person's threats. From what you've told me, it doesn't appear that Diamond is in any danger—just you are. Fans of entertainers can get downright possessive, and whoever this guy is he doesn't like the idea of you and Diamond being married."

Kyle picked up his coffee cup and took a sip. "Have you mentioned this to Sterling?"

"No."

"Maybe you should. A lot of Diamond's fans thought the two of them were having an affair for the last two years. It would be interesting to see if Sterling received similar threats. And what about Samuel Tate, her ex-husband? Did you ask Diamond if he received similar threats?"

Jake hesitated in answering just long enough to make Kyle raise his brow knowingly. "You haven't asked her about it, have you? In fact, I'll bet you haven't mentioned those calls to her."

Jake gazed intently into Kyle's face when he said, "No, I haven't and I would appreciate it if you don't either. I don't want her to worry."

"Jake, you're her husband. Don't you think she has a right to know?"

"You know Diamond, Kyle. She'll not only worry, but she'll start blaming herself. The caller may be all bluff."

"And what if he's not? Don't take a chance on your life, Jake. If anything happens to you, Jack Swain may as well have Diamond committed someplace. For the first time in her life, she loves someone who loves her in return not because she's Diamond Swain, the movie star, or Diamond Swain, who's Jack Swain's daughter, but because she's Diamond Swain, the woman with a heart of gold."

Jake tipped his head back and gazed up at the ceiling. He was torn with a mixture of wanting to do the right thing and tell Diamond about the calls, and wanting to protect her peace of mind by not telling her about them. "I love her so much, Kyle."

"I know you do, man," Kyle said quietly. "Whether you tell her what's going on or not tell her is your decision, but as a friend to both of you, I want you to take every precaution, Jake. If you don't want to question Diamond about her ex-husband, at least talk to Sterling about it to see if he knows anything. And I think you need to meet with him face to face and not talk to Sterling over the phone. That way you can be assured that you have his complete attention."

Kyle's lips eased into a smile. "Sterling is acting downright silly with this first baby he and Colby are having."

Jake raised a brow and looked pointedly at Kyle. "He can't be acting an sillier than you did when Kimara was pregnant with your first."

Kyle chuckled. "I did act kind of crazy, didn't I?"

"Crazy isn't the word for it, Kyle. You acted down-right foolish," Jake replied, laughing.

Kyle couldn't help but laugh himself upon remembering that time. "Hey, I've gotten better."

"After six kids, I should hope so."

"Let me get this straight, Jacob," Diamond said, looking up from packing. "You want us to go to visit Sterling and Colby before we go home?" At his nod she asked, "Why? We just saw them at Whispering Pines when they came to the party last weekend."

"I know, but I need to talk with Sterling about something. You don't mind, do you?"

Diamond shook her head. "Of course not. I just assumed you would want to get back to the ranch to check on things."

"Percy is a good foreman. He can handle things without me for a few more days."

Diamond nodded as she closed the lid to their luggage. "Should I call Colby to let her know we're coming?"

"There's no need. Kyle left for the mountains and said he would mention to Sterling that we might be coming. Tomorrow is Kamry's birthday, and Sterling is giving a birthday party for his fourth godchild at his home."

Diamond nodded. Kamry was one of Kyle and Kimara's kids. "It's been a year already?" Diamond said, remembering how she had held the newborn baby in her arms. She and Jake had been secretly married for only six months then. She couldn't help but recall their secret, intimate meetings and how Kyle and Sterling had gone to great lengths to keep the media in the dark as to her whereabouts. A lot of times when the media assumed she was visiting Kyle and Kimara or was with Sterling at his home in the mountains, she had been somewhere in Jacob's arms. She couldn't help but grin, remembering the fun she'd had sneaking around to sleep with her own husband.

"What are you grinning about?" Jake asked, coming across the room to her.

When he stood by her side, she looked up at him, smiling. "Oh, I was thinking about our earlier days when we were closely guarding our secret. We could probably make a pretty good pair of undercover cops." Her smile widened. "You get it, Jacob?"

Jake chuckled. "Yeah, I get it. *Under cover.*" He understood where she was coming from. Most of their time had been spent under bedcovers.

The grin on Diamond's face flickered again. "We'd make a dynamite team. I wish that—"

Jake's lips came down to swallow her words and as usual Diamond became putty in his arms.

At that moment, someone knocked on the door. "Bellman to take your luggage down."

Jake refused to release Diamond just yet. "Do you know the one thing I don't like about this place?" he asked her, placing short kisses on her lips.

"What?" she asked in a ragged whisper.

"The untimely interruptions."

Chapter 20

Jake and Kyle sat on opposite ends of the sofa as Sterling Hamilton paced back and forth across his immaculate office.

"Do you have to pace while you think?" Kyle asked him. "I'm getting a disjointed neck just watching you wear down the carpeting."

Sterling stopped and smiled. "Oh. Sorry." He eased into a nearby chair. After a few moments of silence, he said, "I've been wracking my brains but I can't recall Diamond ever mentioning Samuel being threatened by anyone. And as for me, I know for a fact that I never received any threats."

He frowned. "However, come to think of it, I do remember two incidents of Samuel's car catching fire during a race. The officials ruled it as mechanical failure, although they could never find the cause."

Sterling shook his head. "Samuel was pretty hot about it."

Jake stood. "But you don't know for certain that his car was tampered with."

"No," Sterling agreed. "Samuel never mentioned that he thought his car had been tampered with, so he must not have been threatened."

"Would he have mentioned it if he had?"

Sterling grunted. "Who, Samuel Tate? If you knew him, you wouldn't be asking that question. The man would have blasted that information to the media in a heartbeat. He loved getting media attention of any kind." Sterling's expression then darkened. "Even so far as to use Diamond to get it if he had to."

Jake nodded. Diamond had shared information with him about her marriage with Samuel Tate and how insensitive he was.

"But I go along with Kyle, Jake. You should not dismiss those calls you've received. If you don't feel comfortable about taking this to the police just yet, then you need to consider hiring a private detective to look into it. Maybe this guy is nothing but a crank, as you seem to think, but you don't know that for sure."

"And I agree," Kyle added.

Before Jake could respond there came a soft knock on the door. Moments later, Sterling's very pregnant wife Colby stuck her head in. "All right, you guys, the birthday party is outside and not in here." She chuckled. "Nicholas is beginning to panic being surrounded by so many kids."

Sterling shook his head, smiling. His half brother, Nicholas Chenault, was a bachelor and was not used to being around children. Sterling had talked Nicholas into dressing up as a clown for the party. "We'll be out in a minute."

Colby nodded and closed the door behind her.

"So, Jake, what do you plan to do?"

Jake raked his hand down his face, feeling disgusted with the entire turn of events. "I'm going to do as the two of you suggested and hire a private detective to check into those calls. I'm just hoping there's nothing to them."

A half hour later, Jake settled onto a bench on Sterling's patio and watched Diamond. She was helping Colby, Colby's sister-in-law, Cynthia, and Kimara coordinate the activities for the children. He looked around at everything, all the expenses Sterling had spent on his fourth godchild, and personally thought this was a bit much to celebrate the kid's first birthday. But what a cute kid she was, he thought, seeing Kyle walk around holding his daughter, Kamry, who had not yet begun walking. The little tyke was the spittin' image of her mom, which Jake thought was about time since their first three children looked so much like Kyle. Not far away, resting in outdoor cribs, were the newest members of the Garwood household, eight-week-old twins, Kellum and Keenan. Born on Christmas Day, they were both sleeping peacefully through all the noise.

Jake held his breath when he watched as Cynthia handed Diamond her son to hold. In talking earlier with the little boy's father, James Wingate, who was Colby's brother, Jake knew that the baby was five months old. Diamond was smiling and cooing to the little boy as he smiled back at her and tried to reach for a lock of her hair.

Jake thought she looked so beautiful standing there with the baby in her arms. She was such a natural. In his mind, he could see her holding their child that very same way.

"Wishful thinking, Jake?"

Jake didn't bother to look up when Sterling came and sat down beside him. "Yes. Diamond and I want a baby. I'm sure she's told you that she wants to stop acting for a while."

Sterling lifted his brow. "For a while? She gave me the distinct impression that she was ready to leave Hollywood permanently."

"Yes, she thinks that's what she wants."

"And you don't believe her?"

"I believes she wants to spend more time at the ranch, but Diamond's heart is in acting. She's very good at what she does." What he didn't say to Sterling was his deep inner fear was that although he knew how much Whispering Pines meant to Diamond, he was afraid that there would come a time when she would want to move away back to the West Coast.

Sterling nodded. "Yes, but people can be very good at a lot of things, not just at one thing. Now Diamond wants to be very good at being a wife to you and a mother to your kids. Give her that chance, Jake. Believe that she knows what she's doing."

"I just don't want her to feel like she has to give up anything because of me."

"Knowing Diamond, whatever she's giving up she's doing willingly. I'm going to miss her. She's one hell of a leading lady, but all of us have to shift priorities at some time or another."

Sterling's gaze shifted across the patio to his wife,

who would be bringing his first child into the world anytime within the next few weeks. He felt such a profound love for the woman who had been bold enough to make him take a good look into his inner self. "I've done it and don't regret doing so. I can't imagine my life without Colby."

"So you enjoy being married?"

"Yes, but unlike Diamond I'm committed to being a Hollywood star, spouse and parent. Other than my time away from home, things are working out fine. However, I'm sure when the baby comes, although he'll provide company for Colby when I'm away, I will miss out on a lot of things. That's why I plan for Colby and Junior to travel with me every chance they can."

"Junior?" Jake couldn't help but smile. "So you still think your wife is having a boy?"

"Yes, although she's convinced it's a girl. I keep telling Colby there hasn't been a female born into the Hamilton family in over a hundred years."

"Colby thinks she's carrying the first."

"I know, bless her sweet heart. She even has Nicholas and my mother believing that she's having a girl."

Jake watched as Diamond reluctantly handed the baby over into his father's arms. James took the little boy from her proudly. Diamond looked over in Jake's direction, saw him watching her and smiled.

Jake took a quick breath. Although he had been watching her, when Diamond looked over at him, she had caught him off guard. He smiled back at her, his lips curving in a predatory grin. One that he knew she would recognize.

She did and blew him a kiss that held promises. They were promises he definitely planned on holding her to when they were alone later.

Before daylight the next morning, the Hamilton household was in an uproar when Colby suddenly began having labor pains. The doctor arrived and assured the expectant father that his wife was not in any danger of dying—although she was behaving as if she were—and that unfortunately it would be a long labor.

It was.

Twelve hours later, Colby gave Sterling his first child—a girl. Chandler Hamilton became the first female to be born into the Hamilton family in over a hundred years.

When Jake and Diamond left to return to the ranch two days later, Sterling was still in shock.

Conrad Ammons handed the postal worker the box that was addressed to Jacob Madaris at Whispering Pines. He was sending it as priority mail.

Leaving the post office, he knew what was in the box would be his final warning to the man. The next time, he would be removing him from Diamond's life for good.

Chapter 21

"Blaylock wanted me to let you know that Alex is at the big house to see you, boss."

"Thanks, Ray." Pulling off his work gloves, Jake tossed them down on the twenty-pound bale of hay he had just moved into the stall. Shading his eyes against the dazzling morning sunshine, he walked out of the barn and glanced in the direction of the ranch house.

Jake suddenly felt uncomfortable about the meeting he was having with Alexander Maxwell. Sterling and Kyle had convinced him the meeting was needed. He understood that. But he still didn't like it. It bothered him that there was a possibility that someone he didn't know had such a problem with him being married to Diamond that he'd made threats against him.

When Jake entered the house he heard movement upstairs, the sound of furniture scraping across the pine floors. He shook his head, smiling. With Blaylock's help Diamond was determined to add a feminine touch to his bedroom—which she had reminded him three times since they had returned home that it was now *their* bedroom.

Knowing Blaylock would have Alex wait for him in his office, Jake turned down the long hallway in that direction. He walked into the room and found Alex standing with his back to him, looking over his collection of prized family photographs he had collected over the years and were now framed on one wall of his office. "Alex."

Upon hearing Jake call his name, Alexander Maxwell turned around. He was at least six feet four inches tall, and if such a thing were possible, he was impeccably dressed in a chambray shirt and blue jeans. His massive shoulders filled the shirt. Brilliant and observant dark eyes held Jake's.

Jake was reminded of the man's intelligence and skill and felt good in knowing he had chosen the right man for the job. "I'm glad you could meet with me on such short notice."

"No problem," Alex replied as the two met in the center of the room and shook hands.

Jake tried to remember how long he'd known Alex and decided he had known the young man all twenty-nine years of Alex's life. Alex had grown up in the same neighborhood as his nephews Justin, Dex and Clayton. Over the years as youngsters growing up, a lot of kids from that neighborhood had managed to spend quite a number of their summers at Whispering Pines. At one time he'd thought Dex, Justin and Clayton had turned the ranch into a summer camp for their friends.

Alex's older brother, Trask, former football legend, had married Jake's niece Felicia last month. Instead of following in his brother's footsteps and playing sports, it was discovered at an early age that Alex had a brilliant mind when it came to solving things. After graduating from high school early at the age of sixteen, he had gone to Howard University to major in criminal justice and graduated in three years instead of four. He went on to obtain a master's degree in computer engineering from MIT. At the age of twenty-two, Alex became the youngest person to work for the FBI in their Most Wanted division, solving some of the Bureau's most difficult cases. Instead of taking a high promotion with the Bureau, at the age of twenty-six he decided to go into the private sector and start his own security and investigative agency.

Everyone knew what a good detective Alex was. He'd been the one Dex had turned to when he wanted to know who was interested in buying Caitlin's father's land, and the one Clayton had turned to when he wanted to learn the identity of Syneda's long-lost father.

Now, Jake thought, the job he wanted to give Alex was to uncover the identity of the person responsible for making those two threatening phone calls to him.

"I understand congratulations are in order," Alex said, smiling. "I guess I don't have to tell you that you're the envy of every man in this country with Diamond Swain as your wife."

Jake couldn't help but smile as he indicated a chair to Alex then went to sit down behind his desk. "Well…yeah, I'm sure that's true, but I have reason to believe that to at least one person in particular, I'm the most hated."

Alex raised a brow at Jake's serious tone. "Would you care to explain what you mean by that, Jake?"

Jake provided Alex with as much information as he could regarding the two phone calls. He then played the first call to him off the digital phone recorder. "Well, what do you think, Alex?"

Alex sat back in his chair. "I think you did the right thing by contacting me. If you don't mind, I want to replay this tape again and concentrate on something."

Jake frowned. "Something like that?"

"Background noises."

Jake sat and listened to the tape with Alex again. He watched as Alex jotted a number of things down on a pad that he had taken out of his expensive leather briefcase. At the end Alex cut off the recorder.

"What did you hear, Jake?" Alex asked him.

Jake shrugged. "Just a lot of different sounds. Why? What did you hear?"

"I heard enough to let me know the caller was not calling from his home. I heard distant conversations, the clinking of silverware and faint music playing. It would be my guess that the call had been made from some restaurant. And since the tape indicated the call was made at seven in the morning, it was probably made from a place that serves breakfast."

Alex flipped a page on his notepad and kept talking. "I also noted the caller tried to cover up his voice and that he was using a cell phone."

"A cell phone? How you figure that?"

"From the static that was occasionally popping through with the call. Some cellular phones don't transmit as clear as land phones. The one the man used was causing him to talk louder and in a more muffled voice."

Jake watched as Alex leaned forward in his chair, his gaze unwavering. "Now I want you to try and recall any background noises you may have heard during that second call."

"Okay, although I don't know just how well I'll be able to recall anything. It was late and I was tired. The call woke me up from a sound sleep."

Jake was silent as he tried to recollect his memories of the call he had received in his hotel room. His jaw clenched tightly as he remembered the man's threat. "I don't recall any of the sounds you recognized in the first call," he said. "But instead of sounding muffled, the voice sounded kind of slurred, like the guy had been drinking, but there was nothing in the background to indicate he may have been calling from a bar."

Jake shook his head and added, "But then I'm not as observant as you are," forcing his voice to sound cheerful.

Alex grinned. "I'm paid to be observant."

Jake nodded. "What I've told you is not a whole lot for you to go on, is it?"

"No, but at least it's something."

At that moment there was a knock at the door, then Blaylock walked in to deliver the mail. He placed the pieces of correspondence and a small rectangular box on Jake's desk.

After Blaylock left, Jake said to Alex, "Excuse me while I sort through this. A lot of the men receive letters here and are always anxious when the mail comes. I like to get any letters they receive to them right away." As usual whenever Jake sorted through the mail, he took the time to get rid of any junk mail.

He was about to open the box when Alex stopped him. "Wait, Jake. Do you usually get unmarked boxes through the mail?"

Jake frowned. "Unmarked boxes? What do you mean?"

"I mean that I happened to notice there isn't a return address on that box. May I look at it for a second?"

Jake nodded and handed the box over to Alex.

Alex looked at the postal stamp. "Do you know anyone in California who would be sending you a package?"

"Not right offhand. Do you think it's something I need to be concerned with?"

Alex shook his head. "Not if you were expecting this box, but yes if you weren't. After the information you just shared with me earlier about those two calls, I don't think we should take any chances."

Jake watched as Alex took what appeared to be an ink pen out of his top pocket and taking it apart, he reassembled the ink pen into what appeared to be a hand-held scanner. He ran the instrument all over the box.

After a few minutes, he said to Jake, smiling, "False alarm. But I like being safe rather than sorry."

Jake nodded, shaking off the feeling of looming paranoia. He slowly opened the box. Pushing the tissue paper aside, he came to a group of photographs. He picked them up and looked at them one at a time. The hair on the back of his neck began to rise when he noticed they were pictures of him and Diamond taken at the press conferences in Houston and Los Angeles.

All of the photos were close-up shots of him and Diamond. And in each one, someone had taken a razor

and slashed out his face. Not believing what he was
seeing, Jake passed the photographs over to Alex.

He heard, without looking up, Alex release an angry
hissing sound through his teeth. When he passed the
last photo to Alex, he leaned back in his chair, his own
anger barely contained.

"Whoever this guy is, Alex, I want him found. I'll
never do what he wants. I'll never give Diamond up,
no matter what."

Jake stood at the window of his office, looking out.
Behind him Alex was busy on the phone making calls,
establishing contacts and following up on leads. One
lead Alex thought he might have was linked to the photographs.

According to Alex, the camera used to take those
photos was not one a typical consumer would own.
The camera was one of high quality and could possibly
belong to someone who was a photo buff or a professional photographer. He was having someone check
out that lead with various camera manufacturers.

Since all of the photographs that had been sent to
Jake were taken at the two press conferences, that had
narrowed the scope somewhat. Alex had not dismissed
the possibility that someone had posed as a reporter
or photographer to get inside both meetings. Alex had
ordered a listing of the names of every reporter and
photographer who had been in attendance.

"Okay, that about does it for now," Alex was saying.

Jake turned around. He couldn't help but admire
how efficiently and professionally Alex was handling
things.

"Although I don't think Diamond is in any danger,

I'm not going to take any chances, Jake. Since you don't want her to know what's going on, I promise to be discreet. My men will begin watching her twenty-four hours a day after she leaves to return to California the day after tomorrow. I'll make sure they remain in the background. At no time will she know she's under their protection."

Jake nodded. That was the way he wanted things.

"What about this place, Jake? Is this ranch as airtight as it used to be?"

Jake couldn't help it when his face broke into a leisurely smile. As kids growing up, his nephews' friends swore that no one could sneak on or off Whispering Pines without Blaylock or Jake's father knowing about it.

"Yeah, it's even more so with all the modern monitoring equipment I use to keep up with things like strays and trespassers," Jake said. "I feel Whispering Pines is safe. But under no circumstances will I become a prisoner to this ranch."

Jake stretched his neck and rotated his shoulders. He was exhausted, not particularly from all the work he'd done around the ranch that morning but for lack of sleep. The last few nights since returning home he had tossed and turned, wondering what demented person wanted him out of Diamond's life. Luckily since she was a sound sleeper, his tossing and turning had not disturbed her. In fact, he doubted that she had even noticed.

"I didn't think you would let me keep you a prisoner here, Jake, so the same discreet protection I'm setting up for Diamond is being set up for you, too, whenever you're off the ranch."

"Do you think that's necessary?"

"Yes, Jake, as a private detective as well as a friend, I honestly think so. Until we know exactly what we're up against, I hope you let me handle things my way. No one other than me and you will know about the men I'm posting in the background. I doubt very seriously that you'll even notice them. They're just that good."

Alex glanced down at his watch. "I've taken up enough of your time already, Jake. I'll get back with you as soon as I get anything I think you need to know about. And I'd appreciate it if you'll prepare a list of any appointments you have away from the ranch."

Before Jake could say anything against his request, Alex said, "I need you to cooperate with me on this, Jake."

Reluctantly, Jake nodded.

With the business part of their meeting concluded, Alex walked back over to the wall where he had been earlier when Jake had entered the room. He kept staring at one framed photograph in particular. "When was this photo of Christy taken?"

Jake came to stand next to Alex to see just what photo of his niece that Alex was referring to since he had several of her on his wall. The one Alex was asking him about was one of those glamour-type photos Christy had taken over the Christmas holidays.

"Christy took that one at Christmas. She looks good, doesn't she? It's hard to believe she's all grown-up now and is a junior in college. It seems like it was just yesterday that her brothers and I were teaching her how to ride a horse."

"Yeah, and I'm the one who taught her how to ride

a bicycle," Alex said, chuckling. He couldn't get over just how grown-up she looked. Nor could he dismiss just how beautiful she was. "How old is Christy now?"

"She'll be twenty-one in a few months."

Alex nodded. "She's become a very beautiful young woman."

Jake studied the photograph. "Yes, she has become a beautiful woman," he agreed. "I expect she'll get even more beautiful as she gets older. I feel sorry for the man who takes it in his mind to pursue her."

Alex frowned. "Why?"

"Because that man will have to deal with her brothers."

Alex nodded. He knew just how overprotective Justin, Dex and Clayton were when it came to their baby sister. A couple of years ago, Clayton had asked him to run a background check on some guy Christy had started dating during her freshman year in college.

Alex shrugged, thinking that how the three Madaris brothers protected their sister wasn't really his concern. Unlike most men, getting seriously involved with a woman was not in his future plans. He honestly didn't have the time. He had the career he'd always wanted and was working hard to be a success at it. Instead of dividing his time and energy into doing two things halfway, he wanted to focus and center his energy on one thing and do it well.

"Alex, how would you like to meet Diamond?" Jake asked, interrupting his thoughts.

A huge smile spread across Alex's mouth. "I was wondering when we were going to get around to that."

* * *

Conrad Ammons tried to appear sympathetic to the photographer who had accompanied him to the press conferences in Texas and California. "Are you saying that some of your film is actually missing? What happened?"

The man's frown deepened. "I have no idea, but I know for a fact that I took more pictures than this. I took a lot of good shots of Diamond Swain and her husband."

"Did you keep the negatives?"

"No. Whoever took the originals also took the negatives. I can't believe it."

Conrad Ammons thought to himself, *Believe it, I had to make sure that you didn't run those same exact prints in the paper and run the risk of Jacob Madaris recognizing them as the same ones that had been sent to him.*

"At least you didn't lose every single photo that you took."

Like he knew it would, his comment angered the man. "I didn't lose any of the others, Ammons. Someone took them."

Conrad Ammons shook his head. "Who would want to take a few pictures of Diamond Swain and her husband?" he asked, wanting to make sure he squashed the thought from the man's mind. "Have you thought of the possibility that those shots may not have come out?"

The man frowned as he considered the idea. "Hey, you think that's what happened?"

"It's a good possibility. You know how they sometimes screw up things downstairs in the photo lab."

The man nodded. "You're probably right."

Conrad Ammons chuckled. "Of course I am. How about if we leave here for a while and go grab something for lunch?"

"Good idea. Just give me a second to grab my camera." The man smiled. "A good cameraman never leaves home without it."

Chapter 22

Jake looked across the table at Diamond. He had not been able to take his eyes off her all through dinner. She had that type of effect on people. He smiled when he remembered introducing her to Alex that day. For the first time ever, Alexander Maxwell had been at a loss for words. He understood. Even after almost two years, she still had a profound effect on him.

Besides her stunning beauty, both inside and out, she was simply irresistible, fascinating and intelligent. There was also a controlled calm about her, one he could always break through once he had her in bed. Then he could turn her into a fiery, passionate being. One that he was intensely in love with.

Even now dressed simply in a celery-colored lounging outfit, she looked gorgeous as always. But there was something else about her tonight. She had some sort of radiant glow. He couldn't stop the flow of ideas that went rushing through his head. Ideas of undressing her, piece by piece, running his fingers through her short, curly hair. And then he would...

"Jacob, sweetheart, are you listening to me?" Diamond asked softly, lifting her brow.

Jake smiled at her, lifting his. No, he hadn't been listening to her. His mind had been on an entirely different subject than the one she'd been discussing. "Oh, sure I'm listening."

Diamond raised a glass of iced tea to her lips and smiled before saying, "Yeah, right."

Her smile, Jake thought, was sexy as hell. And the look she gave him immediately kicked his hormones into gear—not that they needed much kicking around her. He shook his head, amazed at what the woman could do to him. Over the years, he had done everything possible to safeguard his emotions against women. No other woman, he had decided after his fiasco with Jessie, would wrap herself round him. No other woman would get her claws into him. Jake inwardly laughed. Not only did Diamond have him wrapped pretty tight, but her claws were in him pretty deep, as well.

The phone rang loudly—repeatedly.

"Aren't you going to answer that, Jacob?" she asked quietly.

Thinking it was probably just one of his family members, he said, "No. I prefer sitting here and getting turned on looking at you. Whoever it is can call back if it's important. Tonight is your last night here with me, and I don't want to be disturbed unnecessarily. Even Blaylock had the good sense to take a hike."

The phone stopped ringing.

Jake and Diamond stared at each other across the table, saying nothing. A taut, sensuous silence stretched between them, and neither wanted to break it.

The phone began ringing again.

Diamond cleared her throat. "I guess you better answer it this time."

Thinking it could possibly be Alex with some news for him already, Jake said, "I guess I'd better."

Standing up, he walked across the room to answer the phone. "Hello?"

Diamond stood and began clearing up the remnants of their meal. As always whenever she was spending her last night at Whispering Pines for a while, she felt sad. Although she felt good this time in knowing that at least when she returned to the ranch within the next couple of weeks, she wouldn't have to leave again on any extended trips.

She had no regrets with the decision she had made to walk away from her life as a movie actress. The man she had chosen to live the rest of her life with was a man who had demanded little but deserved much. He was a man who lived by a special code of honor. During her thirty-two years she had dedicated her life to pleasing her father and never fully reaching that goal. In the one and a half years she had been with Jacob, first as his lover then his wife, he had taught her all about pleasing herself. During those secret and private rendezvous they had shared, they would meet and love the night away. Afterward he would hold her in his arms while she told him of her insecurities and her fear of failing the people she cared about. He had lovingly told her how much she meant to him and that she didn't have anything to prove to him or anyone. Somehow Jacob Madaris had convinced her that she was special. And she believed him because he always made her feel that way. She knew in her heart that she would love him forever, and by his side on Whispering Pines was where she wanted to be. She couldn't wait to see his face when she told him what she'd been dying to tell him since morning.

Jake watched Diamond move around the kitchen. He tried to keep his mind on what the caller was saying, but was having a hard time doing so. His mind preferred concentrating on the way Diamond's hips swayed beneath her outfit when she moved around the table collecting their plates, and the way her breasts tilted upward when she leaned over and straightened the placemats on the table. The room smelled of her enticing scent, light, feminine and alluring. His body began throbbing with the want of her. His body hardened with the need of her.

"I'm sorry, Cole, come again," Jake said to the caller, Cole Wells, as he tried to get control of his thoughts and body. Cole was a fellow rancher whose land bordered Whispering Pines. He was also a member of the Texas Cattlemen Association and was calling to remind Jake of their annual banquet in two weeks and to make sure he planned on attending.

Jake shook his head. Cole had never felt the need to phone him with a reminder before. Jake knew Cole was really calling to make sure he brought Diamond with him to the black-tie affair. This was the third call he had received that day making him regret giving a few of his close neighbors his new phone number. He shook off the thought. One thing the neighbors did for one another was to keep an eye out on things and because of the distances between ranches, the telephone was the primary way.

"I'm not sure Diamond will be back from California then, Cole, but if she's here, I'm sure she would love to come." Jake's smile came and went. "Sure, Cole, I'm sure Diamond is looking forward to meeting everyone, as well."

Jake glanced across the room at Diamond—his mouth literally dropped open. She was bending over, seemingly stretching her body for lack of anything better to do. Her lithe body was extended downward in such a graceful manner, almost like a ballerina but more so like a body ripe for loving, he thought, as his gaze traveled the length of her and zeroed in on her rear end.

He wondered just what the heck she was doing. After a few minutes, she straightened her body and glanced over at him and smiled. That flirty gesture of hers made him forget just what he was about to say to Cole.

"Uh, look, Cole. I'm going to have to catch you later." Without saying goodbye to his neighbor, Jake hung up the phone. He crossed his arms over his chest. "Diamond, just what the heck were you doing a few minutes ago?"

Diamond's eyes lit up, and she made a half circle of the room as if she was tidying up things. He watched the seductive sway of her body as she did so. "Do you want to know the truth, Jacob?"

"Yes," he managed to say. His mouth felt dry. His throat tightened.

"Trying to get your attention."

His body hardened even more. "You got it, baby. Come here."

Diamond slowly began walking over to him. He smiled thinking no man should have it this good, no man should be this blessed. He studied her face, saw the love shining there. He also saw her blatant invitation. It was one he definitely planned to accept. Tonight was her last night with him, and he didn't want to think of the nut who wanted him out of her life; the man who'd been crazy enough to threaten his life.

When she came to a stop in front of him, he reached out and gently placed his arms behind her head and pulled her toward him. Parting her lips with the tip of his tongue, he leisurely and thoroughly mated his mouth with hers. The feel of her breasts pushing against his chest fueled his fire, increased his need. He could make love to her mouth forever, he thought as he continued to plunder it like the hungriest of men.

At the moment he felt like he was.

His hand moved downward to cup her bottom, and to bring her closer to the hard fit of him. He thought of how his next two weeks would be without her and began missing her already. He would miss her scent, her taste, the feel of coming apart in her arms, the feel of entering her body, his body hard and thick inside of her, and then the release, an earth-shattering, rippling explosion.

Tightening his hold he lifted her into his arms. He wanted her now but didn't want to waste time taking her up the stairs, nor did he want to make out with her in the kitchen in case Blaylock decided to come back to the ranch unexpectedly.

So Jake carried her to the closest room that could give

them privacy—his office. They would start there, and sometime before the breaking of dawn, before he had to take her to the airstrip, he would make love to her several times, in several rooms. He wanted the memory of her everywhere, so later after she was gone he would be able to draw on those memories and bring her close.

After locking the office door behind him, he had barely placed her on his desk before he began quickly removing her clothes, and then his own. His breathing was short and aching. The need to mate with her was so strong he instinctively reached out and cupped her hips and opened her thighs.

Her body arched forward to wrap her legs around him and to receive him. Their joining was as fierce as the need that encompassed them. Tomorrow she would be gone away, but tonight she was where he wanted her to be. Tonight he was where he wanted to be— inside of her. He didn't want to think about what the next course of action would be if they did not capture the person who was threatening him before Diamond returned to the ranch. He didn't want to place her in danger by being around him even if that meant putting distance between them to keep her safe. Jake didn't want to think about any of those things now. He wanted to think about and concentrate only on tonight and the woman he was making love to.

His woman. His wife.

Being inside of her, loving her this way, sharing this gift of love with her took him right over the edge as the tempo of their lovemaking increased. And when she became bold and let her mouth become aggressive, his heart pounded three times its normal rate.

"Diamond." He whispered her name when she

released his mouth for a moment—it was only for a moment—then she was weaving her magic on his mouth again, branding him with strokes of her tongue. What she was doing was making him groan.

"I'm going to make sure you miss me, Jacob," she whispered in a sweet, achy voice. The rhythm of their bodies was hard, silken, fast, slow. It was prolonging what awaited them. It was complete torture that heightened the pleasure and they tried to hold back, neither wanting the moment to end. It was more than either of them could handle or could stand.

But it still wasn't enough.

Jake closed his eyes as his emotions swamped him, making his thrusts harder, firmer and deeper. Diamond's head fell back and she lifted her hips off the desk to draw him in further. He gritted her name and felt every shiver of passionate tremors that suddenly ripped through her body. And then that same passion tore through him. He felt himself lose control and not once thought of claiming it back as he pulled her face toward his and clamped his mouth to hers, devouring everything.

When completion shattered them and Jacob spent himself deep within her, they both felt replete and content in the languorous glow of fulfillment.

Somehow after regaining his strength Jake scooped Diamond up in his arms and carried her upstairs to their bedroom. Later, they lay quietly in bed for a long time, their bodies still tingling in the aftermath of the passion they had shared downstairs.

"I don't think anything can get better than this," Jake said in a voice that was husky and dazed.

"Oh, I think it can," Diamond said lightly, rising up

on her elbow and looking down at him. She reached out and stroked his cheek with loving care. "Try this one on for size. I'm pregnant."

Jake froze. Slowly he shook his head, certain he had heard wrong. "Come again. What did you say?"

Diamond's smile widened. "I said I'm pregnant," she repeated. "You, Jacob Madaris, will be a father.'

Jake closed his eyes for a moment, hoping he wasn't dreaming. He opened his eyes. "Are you sure?"

Diamond grinned. "Yes, Jacob, I'm sure. I took a pregnancy test last night and another one this morning. Both say that I am." Waves of pure happiness were surging through her. It had taken all she could to keep her news from him until now.

"But…how? Where did you get pregnancy kits from?"

"I brought them with me the last time I was here. Well, are you happy about it?"

"Oh, yeah, I'm very happy about it." He wanted to laugh, cry and jump for joy, all at the same time. But most of all he wanted to kiss her and show her just how much both she and their child meant to him and how much he loved them.

He stared at her, thinking how through it all with their unorthodox relationship, their secret love, their hidden marriage, he had been the happiest he had ever been in his entire life. Reaching up he caught her hands and interlaced her smaller fingers with his larger ones. He then leaned down and captured her mouth in a long, languid kiss.

And then he made love to her again, this time in controlled yet fluid movements. He wanted to go slow, he wanted to be gentle but thorough. The intimacy of what they were sharing now and what they had shared over the past eighteen months touched him deeply. And knowing that his child was resting within her body made an all-encompassing feeling of love rip through him. The love they shared for each other had created another human being. Now he knew just how Sterling and Kyle must have felt. What could be more joyous and more right than this?

For the second time that night, passion overtook them and sensation after sensation tossed them both over the edge of sanity and into unadulterated ecstasy.

Jake pulled his Jeep up to the airstrip just as dawn was streaking across the sky. He glanced over at Diamond, who was sitting quietly next to him. Although she hadn't said anything, he knew her thoughts. Last night hadn't been long enough. Morning had come too soon.

Instant memories of the night before flitted through his brain. Those memories would be the ones he would hold on to until she returned. He shook his head. He was going to be a father. It was still hard to believe. They had decided to wait until she returned to the ranch before officially announcing the news to anyone, including his family. They wanted it to be their own private secret for a while. They wanted it to be something only the two of them shared for now.

"Jacob?"

He turned to her when she said his name.

Diamond took a deep breath and studied her husband's face with her heart in her throat. She loved him so much and now she was carrying their child and felt very happy about it. "Can you believe it? I'm going to be a mother."

Jake smiled. "Yeah, and I'm going to be a father."

Tears glistened in Diamond's eyes. "I think we're going to make pretty good parents, don't you?"

He lifted a finger and wiped a tear from her eye. "Definitely the best," he said, swallowing back the rushing tide of happiness inside of him. He pulled her into his arms. "I can't wait to tell everyone."

He held her tighter. Everything he ever wanted was here in his arms. And no matter what, he would never let her go.

Over the next few days after Diamond left, Jake settled into his regular routine of running the ranch. He got up early to make sure the working stock was fed, the stalls were mucked out and the cattle were moved from one section of the ranch to another. Alex checked in with him about the leads they were following, but so far, he had not been able to tie anything together.

February turned into March and with that change of months had come longer days and shorter nights. To Jake it seemed his shorter nights were even lonelier with Diamond gone.

One afternoon a very tired Jake was about to take the stairs to his bedroom for a shower when he heard Blaylock call to him from the living room. "Come quick, Jake. Diamond's on television."

Instantly Jake went to where Blaylock was. Upon entering the room he glanced over at the television set. He took a seat on the sofa. Beautiful as ever, Diamond was surrounded by reporters as she answered their questions.

"You heard wrong," she was saying to one reporter, but her voice was carrying to all the rest. "The main reason I'm back in California is to take care of some unfinished business, and not because I've left my husband or that we're having marital problems."

Jake shook his head, wondering just where the media got some of its garbage. He watched as Diamond's smile widened as she added, "Jacob and I are doing just fine, and I can't wait to take care of things here to return home to him."

"Are you still thinking about giving up acting to go live on a ranch?" another reporter asked.

"Yes, my plans about that haven't changed."

"And what does your father think of your decision?" a third reporter asked.

Jake watched Diamond's features closely. Only someone as close to her as he was could detect the pain hiding behind the smile. He knew her father was not at all happy about her giving up her acting career.

"I'm sure he'll support my decision. My marriage to Jacob is a dream come true and my husband means more to me than anything, even an acting career."

"Is your husband forcing you to give up acting?" another reporter asked.

The camera hit the reporter's face who was asking the question, and Jake frowned and sat forward, leaning his forearms on his thighs. The reporter was Conrad Ammons. Although Diamond had explained to him that Ammons was a reporter who had been assigned by his magazine to cover her and that he had been doing so for quite a number of years, Jake didn't like the idea of anyone, including Ammons, constantly following her around. His jaw tightened and something inside him twisted. He couldn't explain it, but there was something about Ammons that he just didn't like, but it was nothing he could put his finger on.

"No, Jacob isn't forcing me to do anything," Diamond was saying. "And that's the reason I love him so much. He's always given me a choice. Now if you gentlemen will excuse me, I don't want to be late for dinner."

"Well, Diamond sure set those guys straight, didn't she?" Blaylock was saying.

Jake only nodded. He then stood and left the room.

Two days later, Jake received an unmarked letter. Recognizing the California postmark as the same one that had been on the box he had received nearly a week ago, he called Alex.

Alex came to the ranch immediately and after scanning the letter he gave Jake the okay to open it. The letter read: *"I won't let Diamond give up her career for you. No more warnings. You're a dead man, Jacob Madaris."*

Chapter 23

Just like all the other warnings Jake had received, Alex Maxwell was taking this one seriously. He sat on the sofa in Jake's office and closely studied all the reports he had gotten back over the past week.

He shook his head. One thing was for certain, the individual wasn't doing a whole heck of a lot to cover his tracks, which meant he had a few screws loose or he just didn't care. Pushing the last of the papers he'd been reading aside, Alex concluded the person fit both categories, and nothing was worse than dealing with someone who felt he had nothing to lose.

Alex glanced across the room at Jake, who was standing looking out of the window. Beneath the tan Stetson was a man who was a brilliant businessman, an expert rancher and a person with nerves of steel. He was also a man who had a stubborn streak a mile wide.

It was that stubborn streak that Alex hated dealing with most of all. Jake was determined to protect Diamond, but was bucking all of Alex's pleas to protect himself. He was putting his life on the line for the woman he loved. Alex shook his head. He would never, ever understand that kind of man-woman love.

"All right, Jake, I'm ready to discuss what I've come up with," Alex's deep voice said in the quiet room.

The broad brim of Jake's hat shadowed his eyes when he turned away from the window. Walking across the room he sat down on the sofa, slumped back against it and scrubbed his hand over his face. "Okay, what do you have?" he asked wearily, annoyed. He didn't like this digging, searching and the not knowing. Never in his forty-three years had he been in this sort of predicament. It was a bloody uncomfortable feeling, one he didn't care for. He'd been in danger before of getting trampled by a herd of spooked cattle or getting buried under shifting boulders, but not from the insanity of a madman.

"I have information on a number of things," Alex said. "Let's start with the camera that was used to take those pictures." He shifted in his seat. "I was right. The camera used to take those photos is one that would be owned by a professional photographer. It's a very sophisticated model that has a scope that's great for close-up shots. It's the latest model. I've asked the manufacturer to provide me with a list of everyone who filed a warranty deed on that particular brand of camera within the last three years."

Alex met Jake's gaze. "The type of shots that were taken leads me to believe that those photos were originally taken to be printed in the newspaper or a magazine. The poses were too precise for anything else."

Jake nodded. "What else do you have?"

"The next thing I checked out was the post office where the box and letter were mailed. Lucky for us a number of the larger post offices have installed video cameras for security purposes. I was able to determine exactly what post office in Beverly Hills the items were mailed from and the date. I have someone checking footage of that film to see if they recognize anyone as being someone who also attended those two press conferences."

Alex opened his briefcase. His eyes rested meaningfully on a stack of papers he pulled out and handed to Jake. "This is a list of the persons who attended both press conferences. As you can see there are a number of names appearing on both lists, which isn't unusual since a number of the same reporters and photographers are assigned to cover certain celebrities."

Jake lifted a brow. "So you've ruled out the possibility that the person is an avid fan?"

Alex nodded. "Only because those press conferences weren't open to the public. The one in Houston was a little more lax because you requested that certain family members and friends be included, but from the look of the list here, the one in California admitted only members of the media."

Jake stared at Alex. "Are you trying to tell me that you suspect someone who is part of the media?"

"What I'm trying to tell you is that I'm leaving nothing to chance. I even had her father and her ex-husband checked out as well as every member of her staff. As far as I'm concerned, no one is above suspicion." Alex leaned forward. "The way I see it, Diamond's life isn't in any danger, Jake, yours is. I think the person who wants you out of the picture is someone who has appointed himself as her protector."

Jake sat up. "What makes you think that?"

"The words the person used when he called and the way the letters were worded. The tone was easy to decipher. Someone is very angry that you married Diamond. However, instead of directing that anger Diamond, it's being directed at you like you're completely to blame."

Jake sighed. He felt some comfort in knowing he was the one in danger and not Diamond. But he also knew it was important to keep Diamond away from Whispering Pines for a while longer. He would call Sterling for his help on that. Hopefully the two of them could put their heads together and come up with a plan, claiming Colby could use Diamond's help with the baby or something. Once she got to Sterling's mountain Jake knew his good friend would make sure she stayed there until the danger was over.

"I've looked over your schedule for the coming weeks, Jake," Alex was saying. "It might be a good idea if you were to cancel going to the Cattlemen's Ball."

Jake's eyes narrowed. "Forget it, Alex, I'm going."

"With Diamond?"

"No. I'm going to do everything in my power to make sure she's not here."

Alex nodded as he stood. "You may not want to hear this, but I'm going to tell you anyway. We may be dealing with a dangerous person with a warped mind. Don't make things easy for him." A slow grin crossed his face. "Or harder for me. Once again I'm asking for your full cooperation. We'll get this guy, but I don't want you to make yourself a walking target. I want to get him before he can do anything to you."

Alex shook his head, chuckling. "Can you imagine what Gramma Madaris will do to me if I let anything happen to her baby boy? Not to mention me having to deal with those brothers of yours.

"And," he continued, oblivious to Jake's silence, "it may not be a bad idea to let your family know what's going on. If not all of them, at least some of them. You can't protect everyone, Jake, and you can't keep what's happening a secret forever. Sooner or later, we may need police and FBI involvement."

Silence hung heavily in the room. Jake glanced across the room at the pictures that hung on the wall— pictures of nearly everyone in his family. His gaze then shifted to the framed photograph of Diamond that now sat on his desk. All of them were people he loved and people who he would protect with his life if he had to.

"No one needs to know just yet, Alex," Jake said. "Once we know just who we're dealing with, then I'll let certain people in on what's going on and I'll get Sheriff McCoy involved."

Alex nodded, knowing that was all the cooperation he would get out of Jake for now.

Diamond had been surprised to receive a phone call from Casey Williams, the man who had been her father's personal secretary for a number of years. Casey advised her that her father had returned to California from his six-months' stay in Europe and wanted to meet with her at his home in Beverly Hills.

Diamond had accepted the call for what it was—a summons. Like all the other times when she'd been asked to meet with her father, she knew it was because he was not pleased with something she had done.

Diamond rang the doorbell once before it was opened by Casey. She was glad the reporters and photographers who had been following her had been stopped at the entry gate to her father's estate.

"Casey," she greeted the man who opened the door.

The man nodded. "And how are you today, Miss Swain?"

Diamond smiled. She'd always liked Casey. "It's Mrs. Madaris now, Casey, and I'm doing fine," she replied, stepping into the massive foyer. "Where's my father?"

"He's in his study, awaiting your arrival," he said, leading the way. "I guess I don't have to tell you that he's pretty upset with you."

Diamond hung her head to hide her widening smile. Through the years, Casey had always tried to prepare her for Jack Swain's roller-coaster moods. "Then things should be rather interesting since I'm pretty upset with him as well."

Casey stopped walking and turned around to stare at her. He gave her a smile that clearly said "It's about time." He turned back around to lead her to the room she could probably find in the dark.

The door to her father's study was open and she saw him immediately as he sat drumming his fingers on top of the huge oak desk. She glanced to her right and frowned when she saw Samuel sitting comfortably on the sofa while he sipped a glass of Scotch. She couldn't help wondering what reason her ex-husband had for being here.

Deciding not to even be nice and acknowledge Samuel's presence, she turned her full attention to her father. "I understand you wanted to see me, Jack." Her father had ordered her to begin calling him by his first name when she had begun her acting career at seventeen.

Jack Swain nodded. "First of all, Diamond, I want to say you're looking well."

"Thank you." She was used to his approach. First give a compliment then go in for the criticism.

"Now I want you to explain this foolishness I hear about your giving up acting."

Diamond met his glare. "It's true. I'll be spending much of my time on the ranch with Jacob. We want to raise our family there, and I want to be a stay-at-home mom."

From her right she heard Samuel's snort before he said, "See what I told you, Jack. This rancher has her mind all screwed up. Take my advice and have her marriage declared illegal."

Diamond frowned and turned to Samuel. "Illegal? And just how is he supposed to do that?"

Samuel shrugged. "Jack Swain has the power to do anything."

Except give his daughter the love she's needed over the years, she thought. She turned back to her father. "I'm not underaged, so you can't have the marriage annulled. Jacob and I got married in a very private, very secret but very legal ceremony. There will be no divorce in our future, only happiness."

"You think you've found the perfect man?" Samuel sneered.

Diamond turned back to Samuel. She hadn't failed to notice that although her father had been the one to call the meeting with her, it was Samuel who seemed to be doing most of the talking. "No, I don't think Jacob is a perfect man, but I do believe he's an honorable man. But being honorable is something you wouldn't know about, Samuel."

Jack Swain cleared his throat. "I think the both of you have said enough." He then turned his direct attention to Diamond. "I want you to call a press conference and retract everything you've said this week about giving up your acting career. I'll tolerate your marriage to that rancher, but I won't tolerate your giving up acting. You're a wonderful actress. All of your performances have been nothing but excellent. I've even seen a sneak preview of *Black Butterfly* and it's superb. There's no doubt in my mind it's a performance worthy of an Oscar nomination."

Diamond stood speechless. Her father had never lavished her with such compliments before. She shook her head. It was sad that his praise had come a little too late. She no longer cared what he thought of her acting abilities.

"I happen to agree with you, Jack. I am an excellent actress, and I believe my role in *Black Butterfly* won't just get me an Oscar nomination—I believe I'll have a good chance to bring home the Oscar. And that's why I *can* walk away now. That's why I *will* walk away. I have nothing left to prove to anyone."

A frown covered Jack Swain's face as he stood. "Don't do it, Diamond. You'll only be ruining your life."

Diamond met her father's gaze. "No, actually I'll

just be beginning to really live my life. One day you'll realize just what a good man Jacob Madaris is and how blessed I am to be married to him. If you don't want to get to know him it will be your loss. Goodbye, Jack."

Without glancing in Samuel's direction, she turned and walked out of the room.

Chapter 24

For one brief moment, Alex thought he saw a flicker of some deep emotion cross Jake's face. Surely what he had just told him had had some effect. Being given the name of a person who was out to kill you would garner some type of reaction from most people.

But not from Jake Madaris.

After hearing the report he had given him, Jake hadn't yet made a comment or shown any type of physical emotion. Alex shrugged. If he was in Jake's boots, he'd be ready to hit something or hurt somebody.

Alex cleared his throat. "Now that we have a suspect, especially one who can't be found at the moment, I think we need to alert Sheriff McCoy in case Ammons is in this area. I have a few contacts at the Bureau who'll help me on this one, and who'll agree to keep things quiet for now."

Jake nodded. *Conrad Ammons.*

Somehow, he thought, it all fit. The pointed questions, the cold looks, the hard stares. Alex's report, his very thorough report, had provided everything. The camera manufacturer's information had led to the magazine publisher Ammons worked for, not to mention his face had shown up both times on the video obtained from the post office where he mailed both the box and the letter. And if that wasn't enough, Alex had obtained a handwriting analysis of handwritten articles Ammons had turned into his publisher against the handwritten letters that Jake had received. The result of the analysis had indicated the handwriting was that of the same person. Also, further checking into Ammons's background revealed he'd had a younger sister, who would have been a few years older than Diamond had she lived—a sister who had died a brutal death from a beating at the hands of her husband; a sister who from the photo Alex had obtained, bore a startling resemblance to Diamond. It seemed that Conrad Ammons had a crazy notion that he was protecting Diamond from what had been his sister's fate.

"I don't think you should leave the ranch until Ammons is apprehended, Jake."

Jake raised his gaze quickly to Alex, although he really wasn't surprised by his request. "That's impossible for me to do, and you damn well know it, Alex. I have a business to run and nobody, sane or insane, is going to stop me. Diamond is safe at Sterling's place, and that's all that matters."

Alex knew to argue with Jake would be pointless. "All right, but at least let some of your family members know what's going on. Let me arrange a meeting here to brief them."

After a few minutes, Jake nodded. "Okay, arrange the meeting with my brothers and include Clayton and Dex. Justin's in town so make sure he's included, too."

Alex nodded. "I'll set up the meeting."

Diamond turned off the light in the baby's nursery and closed the door. Taking the stairs she found Colby in the kitchen sitting at the round oak table, drinking a glass of warm milk. "The baby is asleep," she said, smiling. "I may have rocked her too much."

Colby smiled. "No baby can get rocked too much. Come sit down. Sterling asked you to keep me company while he's away. He didn't ask you to be a nursemaid to Chandler."

Diamond's smile widened. "I know but I enjoy her so much. She's so tiny."

Colby chuckled. "Tiny? I don't think there are many people who would consider a baby born weighing close to eleven pounds as tiny, Diamond."

Diamond shook her head. "I guess you're right, but she still looks tiny to me." She took the chair across from Colby at the table. "When did Sterling say he'll be back?"

Colby smiled. "Antsy to get away from here already, are you?"

Diamond shrugged, grinning. "I miss Jacob."

"That's obvious. I act the same way you do when Sterling's away and I begin missing him something awful."

Diamond lifted an amused brow. "And just what way am I acting?"

"Like a woman who wants to be with the man she loves."

Before Diamond could agree, they heard the sound of the front door opening and closing. Moments later, Sterling walked into the room.

"How's my girls?"

Diamond watched as he quickly crossed the room, pulled Colby into his arms for one heart-stopping kiss. Releasing her, he leaned over and kissed Diamond's cheek before turning to run up the stairs to the baby's nursery.

Diamond grinned. "Was that a whirlwind that just breezed through here?"

"I'm afraid so," Colby said, chuckling.

"Well, now that he's back I'm no longer needed here. I may as well start packing."

"Are you going to leave in the morning?"

Diamond shook her head. "If Sterling can make the necessary arrangements with John to get the plane ready, I prefer leaving tonight. I want to surprise Jacob and get home a few days earlier than planned."

A warm California breeze rustled through the nearby palm trees and drifted onto the veranda where Jack Swain sat silently. A medley of Duke Ellington tunes being played throughout the entire house, from a very sophisticated intercom music system, mingled with the other sounds of the night.

"I'm an old fool, Casey," he finally said to the man who was sitting across from him and who was also enjoying the soothing music.

"Don't expect me to disagree with you on that, Jack."

"You do like your job, don't you, Casey?"

Casey Williams couldn't help chuckling at that question. "I guess so since I've been at it for over forty years. If you're thinking about firing me, don't bother. No one else will put up with you."

After a long moment of silence, Jack Swain spoke again. "I think I've lost her, Casey."

Casey looked over at him. "If I didn't know just how much Diamond meant to you, I'd say you got just what you deserved. I was proud of her for finally standing up to you."

A small but definitely wry smile curved the corners of Jack Swain's mouth. "So was I."

Casey dipped his chin and peered at Jack from beneath one bushy brow. He was one of the few people who understood Jack and why he'd always kept Diamond at arm's length. "Don't you think it's time for you to began showing Diamond all that love you've got stored in your heart for her? You're seventy-two years old. Although you're in pretty good shape physically, there's no telling just how many good years you have left."

Jack Swain glared at Casey. "You're not a young man yourself."

"True. But I'm not the one who has a daughter who is starving for her father's love."

After a silent moment, Jack said, "I do love the girl."

"Yeah, I know it, but she doesn't know it. I think Diamond believes in her heart that you have some feelings for her but…"

"I didn't want to lose her, Casey. I wouldn't have been able to handle it if I'd lost her like I lost Nell."

Casey nodded in understanding. Jack had lost his first wife, who had been the love of his life, to cancer after ten years of marriage. He had married Diamond's mother, Emerald, a year later. Emerald, an actress-wannabe, had been a mere twenty-four when she had married a forty-year-old Jack Swain. Wild and reckless, she had been just what Jack thought he needed to get over losing Nell. But it soon became apparent that no woman would be able to do that. The only good thing that resulted from Jack and Emerald's marriage had been Diamond. There was no doubt in anyone's mind that although Jack didn't love Emerald, he did love the child they had conceived together. That was the main reason Emerald had tried using Diamond to get whatever she wanted from Jack. However, it was a tactic that failed when Jack took her to court for custody rights and won. Over the years, Jack had convinced himself that if he loved someone too much he would suffer tremendously if he lost them like he had lost Nell. Therefore he had never shown his daughter any sign of his true feelings. Instead, the main focus of their father-daughter relationship had been centered on her acting career.

Casey raised his head and met Jack's stare. "The way I see it, Jack, you're going to lose her anyway. Life is too short to waste it on foolishness. When people live to be our age, we need the people who love us and the people that we love around us. There is nothing worse than being old and alone."

Jack hung his head, knowing Casey was right.

When it came to his daughter he had made a complete mess of things.

"It's not too late, you know, Jack. It's not too late."

Jake Madaris sat in the swivel chair at his desk. He glanced around the room at his brothers' and nephews' reaction to what Alex had just told them. Unsurprisingly, it was Clayton who spoke up.

"Let me get this straight. That nut who called you that morning we were here nearly three weeks ago is actually some news reporter who has appointed himself Diamond's protector?"

Before Jake could respond there was a bombardment of other questions being thrown out by his brothers, and all of them were directed at Clayton.

"Three weeks ago?"

"What are you talking about?"

"You knew about this nut, Clayton?"

"And you didn't tell us about any of it?"

Clayton glanced around the room at the men shooting the questions at him all at once. "Calm down, please," he said. "At the time, I didn't say anything because Jake told me not to," he said, providing the first smile since the meeting had begun. "I was taught at an early age to respect my elders, and that includes Jake."

Clayton's smile widened when one of his uncles snorted. Which one, he wasn't sure. "The important thing," he said, "is finding out what we can do to help."

Jake stood and faced the brothers and nephews he loved and respected. "Alex is working with Sheriff McCoy and the FBI on this. They have everything under control."

"Where's Diamond?" Jonathan Madaris asked.

"She's visiting Sterling and Colby in the mountains. He's aware of what's going on and has strict orders from me to keep her with him until I give the word that it's safe for her to come home."

Jonathan Madaris shook his head. "I wouldn't want to be in Sterling's shoes, or yours for that matter, when Diamond finds out what's going on and the fact that you've kept it from her, Jake."

Jake shrugged. "I'll have to worry about that when all this is over. Right now the most important thing is keeping her safe."

He took a deep breath before continuing. "Which is the main reason I wanted to meet with all of you today." He came around and sat on the edge of his desk to face the men in the room. "Diamond is pregnant. We've known for only a little more than a week, and were waiting for her return next week before letting everyone know."

His gaze moved around the room but focused intently on his five brothers. He was about to ask the same thing of them that his brother Robert had asked the day before he'd left for Vietnam. It had been a tour of duty that he had not returned from alive.

"I have complete confidence that Ammons will be caught," he said slowly. "But should anything happen to me, I want your promise that you'll do everything in your power to make sure Diamond and my child are taken care of."

The room became deathly quiet. He knew they were thinking about Robert and remembering his similar request. Jake stood. "Don't get me wrong, you guys.

I have all intentions of getting out of this alive, but just in case, I need to know. I need to be assured."

"You have our word, Jake, that we'll do what you've asked of us," Jonathan Madaris finally said, speaking for himself and the others. He then met his brother's stare. "But don't get us wrong either. You're our brother and we intend to keep you alive, even if we have to watch your back twenty-four hours a day, seven days a week."

"Jonathan, look—" Jake started to say.

"No," Jonathan interrupted. "*We* have to know. *We* have to be assured."

Jake was deeply touched with his brothers' stand, but he couldn't help but smile. Although he knew that Jonathan, being the closest to him in age, was still pretty physically fit to kick a few butts if he had to, Jake couldn't see his other four brothers being of much help. Although from the stories he had heard, in their younger days they were a rough and tough group. That was then. This was now. They were in their late fifties and early sixties, for heaven's sake! He shrugged. It was the thought that really counted.

"Although appreciated, your assistance is not needed," Alex decided it was best to say. "Just like Jake has said, I have everything under control. I'll be the one who'll be watching Jake's back. Besides, if all of you suddenly began following him around, your mother is going to get suspicious, and the last thing we need is for Gramma Madaris to know what's going on. The best thing all of you can do is to go back to your homes and discuss this with no one, not even your wives. It has to be a secret."

"Just like the tea recipe?" Lee Madaris asked.

Alex smiled. "Yes, sir, Mr. Lee—just like the tea recipe."

* * *

Diamond stared at Sterling. "Pardon me? What do you mean, I can't leave?"

Sterling inhaled deeply. He had a sinking feeling in his stomach that Diamond would not be a cooperative hostage. He leaned against his desk. "I mean just what I've said, Diamond. I was hoping this mess would have been taken care of before I had to detain you, but it hasn't been. Therefore you're here until Jake gives me the word that it's okay to take you home."

Diamond shook her head. "Just what is going on, Sterling? I want answers, and I want them now!"

Sterling rubbed a hand over the top of his head. "All right, Diamond, please sit down and I'll explain things to you," he said, knowing he had no other choice now.

Seeing she would not get anywhere with Sterling until she did what he asked, she angrily took a seat on the sofa.

Hesitating before he spoke, Sterling took a quick glance around the room to make sure there was nothing within Diamond's reach that she could throw at him. He had a feeling she was just that angry right now.

"Jake's been receiving threatening calls and letters, Diamond. They started the morning after word got out that the two of you were married. This person threatened his life unless he got out of yours."

Diamond stared at Sterling, speechless. Her hands balled into fists in her lap. "Why wasn't I told about this?" she asked, not even trying to hide the anger in her voice.

Sterling's heart twisted at the hurt he also heard in her voice. "I think at first Jake thought it was a joke.

But when other warnings began coming, it soon became apparent it wasn't a joke."

Sterling came across the room and sat down next to her on the sofa. "He wanted to keep you safe and protected as much as possible. He also wanted to keep things from the media as long as he could."

He then provided all the facts to her that Jake had given him.

"Conrad Ammons?" she asked quietly, unbelievingly. "The reporter?"

"Yes, Conrad Ammons. The authorities are looking for him now, and as soon as he is picked up this nightmare will be over."

Pain welled up inside Diamond at the thought of what Jacob had been going through for the past three weeks. His life had been in danger, and she hadn't known anything about it. She had spoken to him on the phone earlier that day and he hadn't given any kind of hint that anything was wrong. "But when will another nightmare begin, Sterling? This should not have happened. It's all my fault."

"It's not your fault, Diamond. It's not your fault that Ammons is someone who wanted to protect you because you resembled his sister."

"But placing Jacob in danger is my fault. I've only turned his life upside down since I've been in it. It's not fair. All I...I wanted," Diamond sniffed, fighting back her tears "for once was a special love. For once I wanted to love a man who would love me just as much with no strings attached, no harm and no worries. I should have known better than to believe in love ever after. Even giving up my career as an actress isn't helping matters."

"Jake loves you, Diamond."

She smiled up at Sterling through her tears. "Yes, I know. He loves me so much that he's willing to put his own life on the line to protect mine. I can't have him doing that. I love him too much." She inhaled deeply before saying, "I guess our problem is that we have too much love."

"There can never be too much love."

"For me and Jacob there is."

Without saying another word Diamond stood and walked out of Sterling's office.

Chapter 25

Diamond stretched out on the bed and turned her head on the pillow to stare out of the window. She always thought the view of the mountains surrounding Sterling's home was beautiful, but today she didn't want to think about anything but Jacob and what he was enduring because of her.

Sighing, she placed an arm over her forehead and shifted her gaze to the ceiling. A single tear rolled from the corner of her eye. What would she have told her child if anything had happened to Jacob? *I'm sorry, but your father is no longer alive because of me...*

More tears filled her eyes as she gently rubbed her stomach where their baby rested. Why was the world so cruel? Why couldn't people—fans, media, photographers—just leave her and Jacob alone to love each other in peace?

Blast it! They would never have peace whether she was Diamond Swain Madaris, the movie star, or Diamond Swain Madaris, the ex-movie star. They'd had more peace from the prying eyes of the news-hungry press when their marriage had been a secret. Now their secret love was no longer a secret and with the revelation came complications. And she had a deep feeling that this would only be the beginning.

Diamond glanced toward the bedroom door when she heard a soft knock. "Come in."

The door opened, and Colby appeared in the door-way. "Hi. Sterling just told me what's going on. Are you all right?"

Diamond nodded and swung her legs off the mattress to sit up. Colby crossed the room to sit beside her. "Is there anything I can do?" she asked.

Diamond smiled through her tears. "Not unless you've got another planet for us to go live on."

Colby smiled gently. "Sorry. I can't help you there." After a few moments, she asked, "Are you upset with Jake for not telling you what was going on, Diamond?"

"Yes, somewhat. But I'm more upset with myself for having placed him in that position in the first place. We should never have married."

"Oh, Diamond, surely you don't mean that."

"I do. This is the main reason I didn't want to marry him. I knew if he married me that his world would be turned inside out."

"Why are you blaming yourself? You know as well as I do that Jake is not blaming you. He loves you."

"But look what loving me has gotten him. I couldn't handle it if anything were to happen to him because of me. I would never forgive myself, and our child wouldn't forgive me either."

Colby reached over and hugged Diamond. Right now words would be useless. What her friend needed now more than anything was a hug.

Conrad Ammons walked out of the food mart to the car he had rented. He had taken two weeks of vacation time from his job to do what he felt had to be done. From the information he was able to garner from the locals, Jake Madaris rarely left his ranch.

Ammons knew that more than likely Madaris would be attending the Cattlemen's Ball that would be held in a few nights. He would make the hit then. Everything was set and in place. Getting rid of Jacob Madaris would be a piece of cake, especially since Diamond wouldn't be around and there wouldn't be any chance of her getting hurt. Word had it that she was visiting Sterling Hamilton and his wife and new baby and wouldn't be making it home for the ball. No doubt she would mourn the loss of her husband for a while, but later she'd be thankful that he had spared her a life of abuse. Something he had not done for Caroline.

Ammons was about to open the door to his car and get in when suddenly out of nowhere two men dressed in dark suits appeared by his side. He relaxed, knowing thieves didn't usually dress so neat and clean. "Can I help you guys with something?" he asked in a friendly tone.

"That depends," the taller of the men said. "May we see some identification, please?"

Ammons's expression froze. "Why? Who are you?"

The shorter man answered, "FBI. May we see some

identification please?" He repeated the same question the taller guy had asked earlier.

Shifting his grocery bag to one arm Ammons pulled out his wallet from his pants pocket and flipped it open for the two men to see.

"Mr. Ammons, you're under arrest."

"I'm glad it's all over, Jake," Sterling was saying into the telephone receiver. "Yeah, Diamond's okay, but she's pretty upset about everything."

Sterling shook his head. "It's not so much that you didn't tell her what's going on, Jake. She's on a pretty bad guilt trip right now."

Sterling nodded. "Okay, I'll see you then." He placed the phone back in its cradle on the nightstand. He then pulled Colby closer into his arms.

She lifted her head and looked up at him. "Did they capture that guy?"

"Yes. They picked Ammons up at a food store a couple of miles from the ranch. He'd been clueless that the authorities were on to him and that there was a warrant out for his arrest."

Colby nodded. "So what does Jake plan on doing about Diamond?"

Sterling released a deep sigh. "He'll be here to get her as soon as he can wrap up things with the authorities there."

It was all over the television and on every network, the newsbreaking story that someone had been arrested for planning to kill Diamond Swain's husband. And to some the most interesting part of it all was that the man had been part of the media. A fully loaded high-powered rifle and a box of ammunition had been found in the trunk of his car, which meant Conrad Ammons had meant business.

Not wanting to hear anything more, a teary-eyed Diamond turned off the television set. She turned at the sound of the knock on her door. "Yes?"

Colby entered the room with the baby in her arms. "You have a phone call, Diamond."

Diamond inhaled deeply, hoping it wasn't Jacob. She didn't want to talk to him right now. The last thing she needed was to be weakened by the sound of his voice. She had made up her mind about what she had to do. She had made up her mind to return to California and not go to Whispering Pines. Jacob's life would be better without her in it. That was her decision and she couldn't let anyone, especially Jacob, change it. "Is it Jacob?" she asked quietly.

Colby shook her head. "No, it's your father."

Diamond frowned. "My father?"

She quickly walked out of the bedroom and into Sterling's empty study and picked up the phone. "Jack?"

"Diamond? Are you all right? I heard the reports. It's been all over the television about what Ammons had planned to do. I've been worried sick."

Hearing the concern in her father's voice comforted Diamond somewhat. It felt good to know that even after their cross words a few days ago, he had cared enough to call. "I'm fine. It wasn't me that he was after, Jack. It was Jacob. He wanted to hurt Jacob." Diamond couldn't control the trembling in her voice.

"Yes, I know, sweetheart."

Diamond swiped at the tears in her eyes. "Jacob

knew all along and made sure I was safe." She gulped back a sob. "Did you hear what one reporter had to say? He said that Jacob had hired a private investigator because he didn't want to take it to the police because he thought the media coverage might make the guy turn on me. Jacob was even going to let the FBI use him as live bait the night of the Cattlemen's Ball to lure Ammons out."

Her throat contracted in another gulp, and she said, "He didn't want to take any chances with my life, but he was willing to take plenty of chances with his. He was doing everything to protect me and wasn't thinking of himself. Oh, Daddy, what am I going to do? It's all my fault."

Jack Swain heard the pain, agony and distress in his daughter's voice. His heart wrenched painfully. He doubted if she was aware that she had called him Daddy. He regretted that he had ever stopped her from doing so.

The lines of strain and worry he felt etched into his face made him feel a lot older...if that was possible. "Everything is going to be all right, Diamond. I want you to come home. I'm coming to get you to bring you home."

Chapter 26

Sterling took one look at Jake as he descended the helicopter and knew the man had come to the mountain intent on claiming his wife. He shook his head, wondering just how Jake was going to handle the news that Diamond was no longer there. The closer Jake came toward him, the more Sterling saw his tired eyes and haggard face.

"Where's Diamond?" Jake asked when he finally reached where Sterling was standing.

"She's gone, Jake."

Jake lifted a dark brow. Sterling also saw the anger that suddenly appeared in his eyes and how his jaw tightened. "What do you mean, she's gone?"

"Like I told you on the phone, Jake, she was upset. She wanted to leave and short of tying her up and gagging her mouth, there was no way I could keep her here against her wishes any longer."

"So why didn't you bring her to Whispering Pines?"

"I offered to do that," Sterling finally answered. "But she said that Whispering Pines was the last place she wanted to go to right now."

Sterling's words were like a knife to Jake's heart. Whispering Pines had always been her haven. Jake raked a hand down his face. He hadn't had any sleep in over twenty hours. Once the authorities had apprehended Ammons, there had been numerous questions to answer and a multitude of paperwork and reports to complete since both the local and federal authorities had been involved.

"Where did she go?" he asked, trying desperately to keep his head on straight. The weight of everything that had happened over the last three weeks was beginning to take a toll on him. It seemed he might have made a mess of things by not telling Diamond what had been going on. But even if he had, she would be doing the same thing she was doing now and that was blaming herself.

"She went to her father's place in Beverly Hills. The old man actually came for her himself."

Jake scowled fiercely. "That figures." If Jack Swain thought for one minute he would keep Diamond away from him, the old man had another thought coming.

Sterling sighed. "Maybe her going with him was for the best right now, Jake. I know Jack Swain. He can be a hard man at times, but I truly believe that he loves his daughter."

Jake snorted. "If that's true, he has one hell of a way of showing it."

"I have a feeling that he wants to change his way of doing things regarding Diamond," Sterling said quietly.

Jake rammed his hands into his pockets and stared out into the distance. "I love her, Sterling."

"I know you do, Jake. I also know what could have happened to you had the authorities not captured Ammons. Diamond knows, too, and the thought of your life being in any sort of danger really freaked her out big time. She's been crying ever since I had to tell her what's going on, and she's blaming herself."

Sterling said nothing for a while, hoping Jake would listen to what he was saying. "Think about it, Jake," he said, as he began to talk again. "Over the past three weeks, you've done everything in your power to make sure Diamond was protected. Now it's Diamond's turn to want to protect you. She feels she has to do whatever she has to do to keep you safe as well. Give her time to think things through. She'll eventually come around."

"I'm going to make sure she does," Jake responded stubbornly. He then turned around and walked off back toward the helicopter.

"Let's go," he said to the pilot once he had gotten inside and was strapped in.

The man glanced over at him. "Where to, Mr. Madaris?"

"Get me back to the airstrip. My pilot will be flying me to California."

Jack Swain looked up from the papers he was reading when Casey walked into his office. "What is it, Casey?"

"Security just phoned. Jacob Madaris is at the entrance gate."

Jack Swain leaned back in his chair. He had spent

most of the morning going over the report he had
ordered on Jake Madaris, which was something he
should have done the moment Diamond had told him
she was married to him. *Ebony* magazine had declared Jacob Madaris as an excellent businessman.
Black Enterprise magazine had called him an investment genius, with his ability to play the stock market
as easily as a gambler was able to shuffle a deck of
cards. *Time* magazine had applauded his efforts in
aiding the British government with England's cattle
industry's "Mad Cow" epidemic. But what impressed
Jack even more about the man was that he was a man
dedicated to his family, and more importantly he was
a man Jack knew without a doubt loved his daughter.
His actions over the past three weeks were clear evidence of that.

"By all means, Casey, let him in. I think it's time
that Mr. Madaris and I have a nice, long talk. We need
to clear up a few things."

A few minutes later, Jack Swain stood when a
towering Jacob Madaris walked into his office. Before
giving Jake a chance to say anything he said, "I was
wondering just how long it was going to take you to
get here to claim your wife. You're earlier than I
expected, which really doesn't surprise me at all."

Diamond spent the first day she arrived at her father's
house in abject misery. As much as she didn't want to,
she missed Jacob. It didn't help matters that she felt she
was doing the right thing—that without her in his life
his world would get back to normal and that he would
be safe.

She knew that because of the baby, there would

always be some sort of bond between them, but she'd learn to deal with that. She had eight months to learn how to live without him.

She sat down on the bed and patted her stomach. Lowering her head, she bit down on her lips to keep from crying again. "Oh, baby Madaris, how on earth are we going to make it without your daddy? I love your daddy so much. So very, very much."

"That's good to hear."

Diamond jerked her head up to see Jake standing in the doorway. She quickly came to her feet, fighting the urge to tell him how glad she was to see him, and fighting a bigger urge to race across the room and throw herself in his arms. "Jacob! What are you doing here?"

The look he gave her was concentrated, absolute, determined. He crossed the room to stand in front of her. "I came for my Diamond," he said in a deep, husky voice.

Taking a deep breath, she shook her head and bit down on her bottom lip. "You shouldn't have come, Jacob. I'm not going with you. There's no way I'll be able to go through something like this again. And there's no way I'll let you go through it either."

Jake folded his arms across his chest so he wouldn't reach out for her. They had to talk. There would be plenty of time to hold her in his arms later. "Oh? And just who made you God, Diamond? Who gave you the authority to dictate what happens in either of our lives?"

Tears sprang into Diamond's eyes at his harsh words. "You don't understand," she said, trying to hide the tremble in her voice. "I love you more than life itself. If anything were to happen to you because of me, I'd never forgive myself, and your child would grow up hating me."

Jake frowned. Sterling was right. She had really freaked out big time over this. "So what do you want, Diamond? Some guarantee that I'll live forever? Well, sorry, babe, that's tough because I can't give you one. In life there are no guarantees. The only guarantee I'll give you is that I'll love you until the day I die, and that as long as I live I'll continue to do whatever I have to do to protect you."

"But you shouldn't have to do that."

"Yes, I do. You belong to me. It wouldn't matter if you were a secretary, nurse, teacher or a housewife, I'd still make it my business to put you and my child first. To ask me not to do that would be asking me not to be a man who takes care of his own. Any man would want to protect those he loves."

"But my life will make it difficult for you. It'll put you more at risk. Even giving up acting may not help. The media will still find a reason to hound us since I'll still be Jack Swain's daughter."

"Fine. Whatever happens, we'll deal with it together. We can't allow the world to dictate how we should live our life. I never have, and I won't start now. And don't ask me to give you up because I won't."

He reached out and gently touched her cheek. "For more than twenty years, I thought Whispering Pines was all I needed and all I ever wanted. Then you came into my life, and I found out just what real happiness meant."

His gaze continued to bore into hers. He saw the tears that flowed freely from her eyes and let his thumb brush a few of them away. "That night I asked you to marry me, I knew the risks. But I didn't care. The only thing I could think about was just how much I loved you and that there was no way I could let you walk out of my life," he said more softly now. "And I knew our marriage would not be a normal one, but what I did know was that it would be forever, because diamonds are forever, and you are my Diamond. Your radiance shines bright within my heart, so bright that it overwhelms me at times. When we married, it was for better or for worse."

He took her hands in his. "So we're just beginning to taste a little of the bad times, but it could get even worse. Should we throw in the towel and give up? No, I don't think so."

Jake's hands moved to cup her face. "Love is risky, Diamond. But so is my getting up in the morning and herding five hundred head of cattle across an open range. So is your getting on a plane and jetting across the country each and every time you go to shoot a movie. Do I worry about you when you're not with me? Damn right I do. But I have to believe that the same God that brought you into my life will keep you there until he's ready for things to be different. He's the one calling the shots, Diamond. Not me, nor you, nor Ammons nor the media."

Jake's lips moved closer to hers. "What we share is a gift from heaven. I believe it, and you have to believe it, too." He touched his lips to hers. "Come home with me, Diamond," he said tenderly. "Home to Whispering Pines." He reached down and laid a hand over her belly. "I came to take you and our baby home."

He kissed her then. Several times. He mated his mouth to hers slowly and gently. When he felt her response he deepened his kiss and his hold. It was only when they both needed to breathe did he release her mouth.

"Oh, Jacob, I was so afraid."

He heard the anguish in her voice and pulled her slender form against his chest, holding her tight. "I know, sweetheart. But it's over now."

She leaned back out of his arms and looked up at him. "You should have told me what was going on."

He nodded. "Yeah, maybe I should have, but I made the decision not to because I didn't want you to worry about it…or blame yourself."

He pulled her back into his arms. "Our life together won't be easy, Diamond. But we knew that in the beginning and chose to love each other anyway. We can't and we won't let anyone change our plans on that."

Diamond looked up at him. He was right. They had to believe their love was strong enough to endure anything. "No, we can't and we won't."

Jake kissed her again. He then released her and walked over to the door and locked it. He hadn't slept all night. He had tried closing his eyes on the plane, but each and every time he did so he'd seen Diamond. He walked back over to her.

"I love you," he whispered softly.

"And I love you, too."

He picked her up and placed her on the bed. Turning her into his arms he kissed her again. He wanted to remove her clothes, but she wanted to keep right on kissing him, so he obliged her. She wanted to take the lead and set the pace for them and so he decided to grant her her wishes there, too.

She began unbuttoning his shirt. Once that was

done she opened it up and ran her hands lightly down his chest.

He shivered at her touch and sucked in a deep breath.

She then began unfastening the fly of his jeans, slowly easing down the zipper. Kneeling above him on the bed she tugged the denim down his legs. She made sure his briefs quickly followed them. She settled back on her heels and looked at him, her expression passionate, serious. "For always?" she asked quietly, softly.

He met her gaze for the longest moment before reaching behind her head and bringing her mouth down to his. "And forever," he responded hoarsely. "Diamonds are forever." And then he kissed her again, long and hard.

After he released her mouth he watched as she leaned back and untied her robe and removed it. Her gown soon followed. Then she once again rose above him until she was covering him with her body, straddling his hips. He inhaled deeply when her body touched his, surrounding him. And when she joined their bodies, sheathing him inside of her, he shivered uncontrollably at how she was making him feel. He clutched at the bedspread, wadding the material in his hand as she rode him into a place where mindless sensation after mindless sensation awaited him. What she was doing to him and the way she was making him feel was pure ecstasy.

She held his gaze and looked into his eyes as she continued to move over him, stroke him, love him, pleasure him. When her movements became faster, hotter, wilder, he gently flipped her on her back and took over the dominant role, taking them to a place where total fulfillment and utter abandonment dwelled.

His breathing quickened when he felt her femininity clench him and hold him tight within her. "Sweet heaven," he moaned. He couldn't think of any other place he would rather be at the moment but inside of her. He no longer felt tired. He felt like he was being plunged straight into an earth-shattering abyss. The primitive rhythm of their mating accelerated until there was only one place to go.

And they went there together as ripples of fulfillment and shocks of passion tore through both of their bodies.

They knew that even without being at Whispering Pines that they had come home. Home was where the heart was, and at the moment it was in each other's arms.

When Jake awoke it was daylight outside the window, and Diamond was no longer in bed with him. Before he could clear his sleepy mind to wonder where she had gone, the bedroom door opened and she came in carrying a tray loaded with food.

She looked up and saw that he was awake and smiled. "All during the night you and I pretty much took care of one type of hunger, and I thought I'd better take care of the other while you were sleeping. Since I'm eating for two now I ate breakfast with my father. Here's something for you to eat."

She placed the tray of food on the nightstand next to the bed. "You've been sleeping for a long time."

Jake sat up in bed. "What time is it? How long have I been sleeping?"

Diamond sat on the edge of the bed and faced him. "It's past noon and since you last made love to me around four this morning, you've been asleep ever since."

Jake's brow lifted. Nearly nine hours? He'd been asleep that long? To a rancher that was almost an entire workday. He hadn't been aware of just how tired he had been.

"Are you ready to eat?" Diamond asked, interrupting his thoughts.

He smiled over at her. "It depends on what you're feeding me," he said huskily.

Diamond sighed as she stood and removed her robe and gown and crawled back in bed with him. "Daddy's cook prepared you a tasty lunch since you missed breakfast."

Jake wrapped his arms around her. "Yeah, but nothing is more tasty than this," he said, kissing her.

After his long, deep kiss Diamond pulled herself out of his arms and looked at him. "I understand you and my father had a long talk last night."

Jake stared at her. "Who told you that?"

"He did," she said, studying him. "You want to tell me about it?"

Jake reached out and fingered a curl that had drooped down on her forehead. "What did he tell you?"

"Only that the two of you had talked."

Jake smiled at her. "Yeah, we talked. And we both understand each other's position. He's your father, and I'm your husband. Our roles in your life are different."

Diamond nodded and snuggled against him. "I think he likes you."

Jake chuckled. "That's good to hear, although I'm not going to lose much sleep over it if he doesn't. He made you unhappy a few times, and I can't forget that."

Diamond looked up at him with pleading eyes. "Please try. I think he's regretting some things, and I'm willing to meet him halfway. He's my father, and I love him. Our child is his grandchild."

Jake nodded. He knew from his conversation with the man last night that he loved his daughter and intended to make a number of changes in his relationship with Diamond. They were changes that Jake approved of. "We'll talk more about your father later," he said, pulling her into his arms.

"Are you ready for lunch?" Diamond asked, smiling at him.

"Not yet."

He pulled her into his arms to show her exactly what he was ready for.

Epilogue

It seemed that all of Hollywood had come out for the premiere of the predicted summer blockbuster movie, *Black Butterfly,* that had Diamond Swain and Sterling Hamilton in the starring roles.

A number of stars attended the pre-premiere reception. Afterward they began migrating from the plush and elegant restaurant in limousines to the theater where the movie would be shown. Sterling was throwing an after-premiere party at his home in Malibu Beach, and everyone was definitely looking forward to that.

Movie critics had given the film excellent reviews. Some considered it Sterling and Diamond's best work yet, and a number of them predicted their performances had guaranteed them Oscar nominations. Movie tickets were to go on sale within a week. Already ticket lines had begun forming at various theaters around the country. There were those who predicted the movie would be even more successful that last summer's blockbuster, that featured Will Smith and Julia Roberts in the starring roles.

The photographers had a field day when the tall, handsome and dashing Texan, Jacob Madaris, and his gorgeous, sophisticated and beautiful wife, actress Diamond Swain Madaris, descended from the limo. Smiling for everyone, they dazzled the crowd of people that greeted them at the theater. Diamond returned the thumbs-up sign a number of her fans gave her for encouragement.

Amid the glow of bright lights and photographers' flashing bulbs, a number of poses of Jake and Diamond were captured on camera, then the reporters began throwing out their questions.

"Mrs. Madaris, is it true you're pregnant?"

Diamond smiled up at Jacob before answering the reporter's question. "Yes, it's true. I'm almost three months along. And according to my doctor I'm doing fine, and if all goes well Jacob and I will have a little Madaris this November."

"Mr. Madaris, how do you feel about your wife's pregnancy?"

Jake thought that was a pretty dumb question for the reporter to have asked but decided to keep his opinion to himself as he held Diamond's gaze. Her smile widened to let him know that she'd known just what he'd been thinking about the reporter's question. "I feel like a very blessed man. What man wouldn't feel that way with a beautiful and talented wife—and a baby on the way."

Another reporter asked, "Mrs. Madaris, what do you think of Conrad Ammons's attorney's insanity plea?"

Diamond took a deep breath as she looked out over the group of reporters. For a number of years she had grown accustomed to seeing Ammons among them. "I read the article in the paper. What happened to Mr. Ammons's sister was unfortunate. And although it wasn't his fault, he loved his sister deeply. A part of me understands him for wanting to blame himself for it all these years," she said sadly. She didn't add that she understood because a few months ago she had been ready to walk away from her true love because of misplaced blame.

"So," she continued, "I have no problem with it if the court goes along with the plea. If they do I just hope he gets the proper medical treatment to recover. I believe he was a fine reporter." She couldn't help but grin. "He certainly kept me on my toes with his questions whenever he interviewed me."

Jacob's arms around Diamond tightened. His wife was such a warm, caring and forgiving person. He was glad the reporter hadn't bothered to ask him that particular question. He would have told him straight out that it would not have bothered him in the least if they locked Ammons up and threw away the key. But then, he thought, that was why he loved Diamond so much. It had been her incredible ability to care so much for others that had made him realize just how different she was, and had made him fall head-over-heels in love with her.

"Mr. Madaris, is it true that you and Kyle Garwood have formed some sort of a production company and that Sterling Hamilton will take the role of producer and put together a movie that will be filmed on parts of your ranch, Whispering Pines?"

Jake lifted a brow, wondering if there was anything that could be done without the media finding out. He smiled. Yes, he knew of one thing—his and Diamond's marriage. Their secret love. For eighteen glorious months, they had outsmarted the news-hungry press.

"It would be premature for me to discuss any business deals regarding me, Kyle Garwood and Sterling Hamilton, especially since nothing has been finalized yet."

He then smoothly and tactfully changed the subject by asking, "Have any of you seen *Black Butterfly* and if so, what do you think of it?"

Diamond smiled at the positive responses they received and how Jacob was expertly handling the reporters. He was not a person to let anyone, including the media, get an upper hand. She shook her head, thinking how at one time she actually thought she had to protect him from them.

"Only one more question, you guys," she said cheerfully. "We don't want to be late for the movie. The opening scene is one of my favorite parts."

"Mrs. Madaris," a reporter jumped in. "Are you still giving up acting?"

Diamond looked up at Jake and smiled warmly. "Yes, I'll be too busy raising our family for a while, but I'm not going to say I'll never venture into acting again. If Sterling does trade in his acting shoes for a pair of producer's boots, then I'd love doing a project for him. Sterling and I enjoy working together."

A few minutes later, Jacob escorted his wife inside

the plush theater. "Well, how did I do?" She leaned closer and whispered to him.

"As always you were wonderful, sweetheart." He leaned over and placed a kiss on her lips.

It was a loving gesture that was captured on camera by a photographer who thought the snapshot would be picture-perfect, just like the couple.

REQUEST YOUR FREE BOOKS!

2 FREE NOVELS
PLUS 2 FREE GIFTS!

KIMANI™
ROMANCE

Love's ultimate destination!

KROM08R

Essence bestselling author

DONNA HILL

TEMPTATION AND LIES

Book #3 of T.L.C.

Nia Turner's double life as business executive
and undercover operative for covert crime-fighting
organization Tender Loving Care is getting even
more complicated. Steven Long, the man she's seeing,
suspects she's stepping out on him, and Nia's caught
in a web of lies that threatens her relationship. Will
any explanation make up for not telling the truth?

*Available the first week of February 2009
wherever books are sold.*

KIMANI™
ROMANCE

www.kimanipress.com
www.myspace.com/kimanipress

**A mistake from the past
ignites a fiery future....**

NEW YORK TIMES BESTSELLING AUTHOR

BRENDA
JACKSON

FIRE AND DESIRE

A Madaris Family Novel

When Corinthians Avery snuck into a hotel room to seduce
Dex Madaris, it was Trevor Grant who emerged from the
shower to find her wearing next to nothing, and informed
her Dex was at home, happily married.

Two years later, traveling with Trevor on business,
Corinthians tries to avoid him, but his sexy smile sets her
on fire. And when a dangerous situation arises, they find
fear turning to feverish desire, never realizing that one
passionate night will change their lives forever....

*Available the first week of January 2009
wherever books are sold.*

ARABESQUE®

www.kimanipress.com
www.myspace.com/kimanipress

KPBJ0540109